WITHOUT MERCY

JACK HIGGINS

WITHOUT MERCY

HarperCollins*Publishers*

HarperCollins*Publishers*
77–85 Fulham Palace Road,
Hammersmith, London w6 8jb

www.harpercollins.co.uk

Published by HarperCollins*Publishers* 2005
1

First published in the USA by
G.P. Putnam's Sons 2005

A catalogue record for this book
is available from the British Library

ISBN 0 00 719944 9 (hardback)
ISBN 0 00 720640 2 (trade paperback)

Typeset in Postscript Linotype Aldus by
Palimpsest Book Production Limited, Polmont, Stirlingshire

Printed and bound in Great Britain by
Clays Ltd, St Ives plc

To Ed Victor, the mentor in my life, with grateful thanks

The Gate of Fear

Ibiza

Balearic Islands

*The Plaza de Toros in Ibiza is a typical small-town bullring,
a concrete circle, benches ringed around, average bulls,
toreros desperate to make their bones. It was unbearably
hot even on the shady side at four o'clock in the afternoon
as Dillon waited at the* barrera. *As the President led the
procession on, the band started to play the 'Virgin of
Macarena', that most poignant of Paso Dobles, that promised only death down there in the ring; death in the afternoon, Hemingway had called it. The toreros tossed off their
capes, works of art in themselves, to friends in the crowd
who draped them over the* barrera, *then the* toreros *were
handed the plain fighting capes and made a few practice
swings, the horses of the* picadors *stirring uneasily. There*

was a long moment, a signal from the President, and as a bugle sounded the red door on the far side, the Gate of Fear, burst open. The bull came through from the darkness, a runaway train that skidded to a halt as the crowd roared. Peons moved out to try him, capes ready, the scene looking like the most dangerous thing on earth, but Dillon knew no fear. He vaulted over the barrera down into the arena. The crowd roared as he ran forward and flung himself on his knees in front of the bull and bared his chest. 'Hey, Toro. Just for me; the Pass of Death,' because he knew that was all it would take and he deserved it. She was dead and it was his fault and the bull charged, the crowd screamed and he cried out and came awake, sitting up in bed, soaked in sweat and more afraid than he had ever been.

WASHINGTON

1

It was Washington, early evening, bad March weather, but General Charles Ferguson, comforted by the luxury of the Hay-Adams Hotel, stood at a window of the bar and enjoyed a scotch and soda. Newly arrived from London, he was curiously exhilarated by the rain pounding against the window and his proximity to the White House.

On the other hand, he also just liked the hotel for its own sake. In its sheer luxury it was everything a hotel should be, and anybody who was anybody stayed there, the great and the good and the powerbrokers. Whatever else he was, he was certainly that, the man responsible for running a special intelligence unit out of the Ministry of Defence in London, responsible only to the Prime Minister of the day, irrespective of politics.

The man for whom he waited, Blake Johnson, was head of a unit at the White House called the Basement. It had been in existence since the Cold War days, an intelligence unit answerable only to the current President, totally separate from the CIA, FBI and the Secret Service. They had achieved great things together.

Ferguson could see the main entrance of the hotel, where now a limousine drew up, two men got out and hurried up the steps. Blake Johnson was a tall, handsome man in his mid-fifties. The man with him was very big and very black: Clancy Smith, once the youngest sergeant-major in the Marine Corps and now the President's favourite Secret Service man. Ferguson greeted them warmly.

'Great to see you both.'

'No Dillon this trip?' Johnson asked.

He was referring to Sean Dillon, in the past a feared IRA enforcer, now Ferguson's strong right hand.

'There didn't seem any need, and he's concerned about Hannah Bernstein. She's really in a very bad way thanks to that Russian bastard, Ashimov.'

'President Cazalet will want to hear all about that. Let's go.'

They drove along Constitution Avenue towards the White House, where as usual these days and in spite of the weather there were demonstrators. Their driver tried the East Entrance, where they were greeted warmly by a Secret Service agent on duty, who escorted them to the President's secretary, a pleasant and cheerful lady who admitted them to the Oval Office. There they found Jake Cazalet in shirt-sleeves at his desk, as usual, working his way through a pile of documents.

'So you made it. I heard the weather wasn't too good.' Cazalet came round the desk and shook Ferguson warmly by the hand. 'Good to see you, General, as always. I think whisky is in order, considering this damn rain. Clancy, if you'd be kind enough to do the honours.' He turned to the other two and said to Ferguson, 'You took a bullet in the shoulder, I understand?'

'I was lucky, Mr President. A bad crease, thanks to the IRA mercenaries employed by Belov's people, but that's all.'

Josef Belov, the billionaire head of Belov International, had once been a colonel in charge of the KGB's old Department 3. His intentions now were as they had been then – disruption of the Western world as much as possible, encouragement and financial support for terrorism of all kinds. He had very nearly succeeded in assassinating President Cazalet and, thwarted in that, he *had* been successful in injuring Ferguson and putting one of his best operatives, Superintendent Hannah Bernstein of Special Branch, in hospital. Belov had been killed in a shoot-out in Ireland, along with his agents Yuri Ashimov and Major Greta Novikova of the GRU, as well as assorted IRA guns-for-hire. But the pain they had caused lingered on, in both the body and the soul.

'Belov was backed by the Russian government?'

'At the highest level.'

Clancy handed out the drinks, and then stood against the wall behind them, arms folded.

'Right, tell me the worst,' Cazalet said.

'I'd say that's Hannah Bernstein,' Blake told him.

Cazalet was immediately concerned. 'Just how bad is she?'

'Very,' Ferguson told him. 'Ashimov ran her down in the street deliberately. She's undergoing treatment at a specialized neurological unit right now.'

'Anything we can do, General, just ask – that goes without saying.'

'She's in good hands, Sir. She's in the care of George Dawson, one of the best brain surgeons in the business. But there's a limit to what the human body can stand, Mr President. This could be the end of her career.'

'She won't like that.'

There was silence, for there was nothing to say. After a while, Ferguson carried on.

'Thanks to the efforts of Major Roper, our computer expert, we established that Major Ashimov had fled to Belov's house in County Louth, in company with Novikova. He also established that Belov himself was there – but about to leave for Moscow.'

'And knowing Dillon, he decided to stop him.'

Ferguson nodded. 'By a beach drop, backed up by young Billy Salter.'

'Our young gangster friend? He does get around. Must have been difficult, though.'

'Mr President, that is a particularly IRA area. There isn't a policeman for miles, and strangers stick out like a sore thumb. Any kind of trouble, people keep their heads down and stay indoors. They don't want to know. It was a very tricky drop.'

'So, what was the body count?'

'Three IRA in the house, plus Ashimov. Novikova, Belov and an IRA man named Tod Murphy made it out to sea in a boat, but Dillon had rigged it with a little Semtex and detonated it by remote control.'

'By God, he's a ruthless bastard,' Cazalet said. 'After that, I think I could do with another one. Clancy?'

Clancy obliged and recharged their glasses. It was Blake who said, 'The curious thing is – this all took place three weeks ago and there hasn't been a word about it anywhere. You'd think that Belov's death would have caused ripples at least.'

The President turned to Ferguson. 'What does your Major Roper have to say?'

'That the IRA link with Belov International would explain the good people of Drumore keeping their mouths shut, but as regards the deaths of Belov and the other six . . .' He shrugged. 'They have to be accounted for one way or another.'

Blake said, 'It's as if it never happened.'

'Not quite,' Ferguson said. 'Which, in part, explains my visit. Roper picked up an item yesterday, put out by Belov International. It concerns their huge development site at Station Gorky in Eastern Siberia.'

'Which is about as far as you can get from the known world,' Cazalet said.

'They announced the arrival of their great leader, one Josef Belov, for an extended visit. A photo was included.'

'Are you sure it was him?'

'Could have been an old photo,' Blake put in.

Ferguson shrugged. 'Sure looked like him. Which brings me to another interesting thing Roper uncovered. The other year when oil concessions were up for grabs in Venezuela, Belov was in Paris putting himself about on the social scene. Except we know something else as well: he was also in Venezuela pulling a fast one on the opposition and sewing up those oil concessions.'

'Why is it I feel like applauding?' Cazalet said. 'Go on, tell me. Who was the Belov in Paris? Did you have it checked?'

'Indeed we did. A French Intelligence source tells us it was one Max Zubin, an actor of sorts, cabaret, that sort of thing, big in Jewish theatre in Moscow. Apparently it's not the first time he's impersonated Belov.'

'So where is he now? Station Gorky?'

'Wherever his masters need him,' Blake said.

Cazalet nodded. 'Sean Dillon has always been extremely thorough, so I see no reason to doubt that what's left of the real Josef Belov is at the bottom of the Irish Sea off Drumore Point. So what are they playing at?'

'I've no idea,' Ferguson said.

'We can't have that.' Cazalet finished his drink. 'Blake, if General Ferguson agrees, I'd like you to grab a lift in his Gulfstream, go back to London with him and help resolve this puzzle.'

'That's fine by me, Mr President,' Ferguson told him.

'Excellent. I want this matter resolved. Now, let's enjoy a nice dinner and you can bring me up to date on the European situation.'

LONDON

2

Ferguson hadn't bothered with a steward on the trip over, just his usual two pilots, Squadron Leader Lacey and Flight Lieutenant Parry. They passed the coast at 30,000 feet and started out over the Atlantic. After a while, Parry appeared.

'Our American cousins have been more than generous, sir,' he told Ferguson. 'Plenty of intriguing grub in the kitchen area, champagne in the fridge.'

'What's our estimated time of arrival?'

'We should hit Farley Field spot on four o'clock, General.'

He returned to the cockpit. Ferguson said, 'I'm going to make some calls. Excuse me.'

He called London on his Codex Four, first Bellamy, the doctor in charge of Rosedene, the special medical unit maintained for Secret Security Service personnel, mainly the victims of some black operation or other. He found Bellamy in his office.

'It's me. How's Hannah?'

'Well, the head tests are fine so they're transferring her back here for continuing care. The thing is, the traumas she's had the last two years have really dragged her down. Her heart isn't good – not good at all.'

'Is she receiving visitors?'

'Her grandfather and father. They're being sensible, not overdoing it. It's Dillon I've had to have words with.'

Ferguson frowned. 'Why?'

'He'd be round every five minutes if I'd let him. In a funny kind of way, he seems to blame himself for Hannah being in this situation.'

'Nonsense. If there's a woman who knows her own mind, it's Hannah Bernstein. She's always done the job because she wants to do the job. It's everything to her. I'll look in this evening.'

He thought about it for a while, then called Roper at Regency Square. Roper was permanently confined to a wheelchair as the result of an IRA bomb several years ago, and his ground-floor apartment was designed to enable a severely handicapped person to fend for himself. Everything was state of the art, from kitchen to bathroom facilities. His computer equipment was state of the art as well, some of it highly secret and obtained by Ferguson's liberal use of muscle. Roper was at his computer bank when the General called.

'So how did it go?'

Ferguson told him of his talk with Cazalet. 'I've got Blake with me. He's going to stay at my place for a day or two while we see if we can make any sense out of all this.'

'Blake's got a point when he said it's as if it never happened.'

'And that's what Belov International is confirming by announcing Belov's visit to Station Gorky.'

'Well, one thing's certain. You know this goes to the highest level in Moscow, and that would include Putin himself. The worldwide economics involved are simply too important. Whatever has happened, there's bound to be a Kremlin connection.'

'Then can't you find out what? Dammit, man, there must be traffic somewhere out there in cyberspace that has something to do with it.'

'Not that I've seen. Have we got anyone who could nose around at Drumore, do an undercover job? Pretend to be a tourist or something?'

'Hmmm, that's an idea. If you see Dillon, mention it to him, would you? I'll see you later.'

Ferguson sat there for a moment, frowning, then went to the small bar and helped himself to a Scotch. Blake said, 'Problem?'

'Bellamy at Rosedene says Dillon's going through some sort of guilt feeling over Hannah. It's as if he feels himself responsible for her condition.'

'They've always had a strange relationship, those two.'

Ferguson nodded. 'She could never forgive him all those

years with the IRA, all those deaths. She could never accept that his slate could be wiped clean.'

'And Dillon?'

'Always saw it as a great game. He's a walking contradiction – warm and humorous, and yet he kills at the drop of a hat. There's nothing I could ask him to do that he would find too outrageous.'

'Everything a challenge,' Blake said. 'Nothing too dangerous.'

'And on so many occasions she's been dragged along with him.'

'And you think that's what makes him feel guilty now?'

'Something like that.'

'And where would that leave you? After all, you give the orders, Charles.'

'Don't you think I know that?' Ferguson swallowed his Scotch down and looked at the empty glass bleakly. 'You know, I think I'll have the other half.'

'Why not?' Blake said, 'And I'll join you. You look as if you could do with the company.'

Dillon arrived at Rosedene in the middle of the afternoon, parked his Mini Cooper outside and went in. As he approached the desk, Professor Henry Bellamy came out of his office.

'Now, look, Sean, she's just been moved, you know that. Give her a chance to settle in.'

'How is she?' Dillon's face was very pale.

'What do you expect me to say? As well as can be expected?'

At that moment, Rabbi Julian Bernstein, Hannah's grand-father, came out of the hospitality room. He put both hands on Dillon's shoulders.

'Sean, you look terrible.'

Bellamy eased himself away. Dillon said, 'This life of Hannah's, Rabbi, I've said it before, you must hate it. You must hate us all.'

'My dear boy, it's the life she chose. I'm a practical man. Jews have to be. I accept that there are people who elect to take on the kind of work that ordinary members of society don't want to, well, soil their hands with.'

'You've seen her?'

'Yes. She's very tired, but I think you may say hello, show your face and then go. Room Ten.'

He patted Dillon on the shoulder, turned away and Dillon passed through the doors to the rear corridor.

When he went in, the room was in half darkness, the matron, Maggie Duncan, drawing the curtains. She turned and came forward. Her voice had a tinge of the Scottish Highlands about it.

'Here you are again, Sean. What am I going to do with you?' She patted his face. 'God knows, I've patched you up enough times over the years.'

'You can't patch me up this time, Maggie. How is she?'

They both turned and looked at Hannah Bernstein,

festooned in a seemingly endless web of tubes and drips, oxygen equipment and electronic screens. Her eyes were closed, the lids almost translucent.

Maggie said, 'She's very weak. It's a huge load for her heart to bear.'

'It would be. We expected too much from her, all of us. Especially me,' Dillon said.

'When she was in last year, when that Party of God terrorist shot her, we used to talk a lot and mainly about you. She's very fond of you, Sean. Oh, she might not approve, but she's very fond.'

'I'd like to believe that,' Dillon said. 'But let's say I don't deserve it.'

Hannah's eyelids flickered open. She said softly, 'What's wrong, Sean? Feeling sorry for yourself, the hard man of the IRA?'

'Damn sorry,' he told her, 'and you putting the fear of God in me.'

'Oh, dear, I'm in the wrong again.'

Maggie Duncan said, 'Two minutes, Sean, and I'll be back.'

She went out, the door closed softly and Dillon stood at the end of the bed. 'Mea culpa,' he said.

'There you go, blaming yourself again. It's a kind of self-justification, no, worse, an over-indulgence. Is that some kind of Irish thing?'

'Damn you!' he said.

'No, damn you, though that's been taken care of.' She frowned. 'What a terrible thing to say. How could I?' She reached out the thin left hand which he took and she gripped it with surprising strength. 'You're a good man, Sean, a good man in spite of yourself. I've always known that.'

The grip slackened, and Dillon, almost choking with emotion, let her hand go gently. The eyes closed and when she spoke again her voice was barely more than a whisper.

'Night bless, Sean.'

Dillon made it out to the corridor, where he leaned against the wall, breathing deeply. A young nurse pushing a trolley approached and paused at the door, glancing at him with a frown. She was pretty enough, high cheekbones, dark eyes.

'Are you all right?'

Her accent was Dublin Irish. He nodded. 'I'm fine. What are you doing?'

'Seeing to the Superintendent's medication.'

'I think she's gone to sleep again.'

'Ah, then it can wait.'

She pushed the trolley away. He paused, watching her go, then made for reception, ignoring Maggie Duncan's call from behind, went down the entrance steps to the car park and headed for the Mini Cooper.

Roper, having fruitlessly tried some obvious routes through the computer, sat back frustrated. Of course the real problem was that he didn't really know what he was looking for, but one thing was certain. There was something wrong here. What was it Blake had said? It was as if it had never happened. But it had.

'Time to get back to basics,' he said softly and called Dillon on his Codex Four. 'Where are you?'

'I was with Hannah at Rosedene. I've just parked outside St Paul's.'

'Visiting the Holy Mother again, are we? How was Hannah?'

'Hanging in there.'

'Good. I've had a call from Ferguson. Cazalet wants answers on the whole Belov thing. He's sent Blake Johnson over to help, but it's up to us, and Ferguson wants an explanation. I'm going round to see the Salters at the Dark Man, so meet me there.'

'As soon as I can.'

Dillon had parked outside St Paul's Church, around the corner from Harley Street, for a reason. The priest in charge was a professor of psychiatry at London University, and was much used by people operating for Ferguson who experienced mental problems. This had applied to Dillon on occasion.

He went up the steps to the entrance and entered through the small Judas gate. There was a smell of incense, candles flaring beside a statue of the Virgin and Child, a feeling of being apart, separate from everyday life, the sound of traffic outside very remote. It reminded Dillon of the church of his childhood, in County Down, which was hardly surprising, for St Paul's Church was Anglo-Catholic, the oldest branch of the Church of England. However, it moved with the times enough to allow priests to marry and to allow a woman priest, and there she was now, a pleasant, calm woman in cassock and clerical collar who had just opened the door of the vestry and was ushering a young woman inside.

She turned and there was immediate concern on her face. 'Sean?' she said, then turned to the young woman. 'Go in for me, Mary. Put the kettle on.' She closed the door and said anxiously, 'Is it Hannah? She's not . . .'

'No.' Dillon put a hand up in a strangely defensive gesture. 'Very poorly, but not that. The brain's been cleared so she's been returned to Rosedene, but she's not good. Bellamy's worried about the cumulative effect of all her injuries in the past few years. It seems her heart's not as it should be, but then you'd expect that.'

She embraced him, holding him tight for a moment. 'My dearest Sean. You want to see me?'

'As a psychiatrist or as a priest? God knows. Isn't it what the truly wicked of this world do? Try and cover their backs?' His smile was cold and bleak. 'Anyway, you're busy. Perhaps another time.'

He walked to the great door and opened the small Judas gate. 'It's appropriate, don't you think, especially for someone like me? Judas was a political terrorist called a Zealot, and my branch of the great game was the IRA.'

She shook her head gravely. 'Such talk is pointless, Sean.'

He said tonelessly, 'Ashimov ran her down like a dog, quite deliberately. As I got to her, she was trying to haul herself up by the railings and I told her: You're all right, just hold on to me, but there was blood on her face and I was afraid. It was different. Special in the wrong way. When I was driving back to Rosedene with her in the seat beside me, I swore I'd kill Ashimov if it was the last thing I did on top of the earth.'

'I thought it was Dilly who killed Ashimov.'

'Yes, but I got all those others. Belov, Tod Murphy, even Greta Novikova. I'm very even-handed, you've got to agree.'

'God bless you, Sean,' she said calmly.

For some reason it reminded him of Hannah's last words to him at Rosedene. He recoiled, God knows why, stepped out through the Judas gate, stumbled down the steps to the Mini Cooper and drove away.

Being a gangster was fine, flashy and showy and menacing, but Harry Salter had learned, at the right stage in his life, that the same talents employed in the business world could make you a fortune without it costing you thirty years inside.

The Dark Man at Wapping on Cable Wharf by the Thames was the first property he'd ever owned. It was like a mascot in spite of everything else he had now – the warehouse developments, the clubs, the casinos, the millions he'd made after giving up his career as one of the top guvnors in the London underworld. It was a second home, and it was there that Dillon found him.

The bar was very Victorian: mirrors, a long mahogany bar topped with marble, porcelain beer pumps, Dora the barmaid reading the newspaper. Trade at that time of the afternoon was light. Salter sat in the corner booth with his nephew, Billy, and his minders, Joe Baxter and Sam Hall, enjoying a beer at the bar.

Roper in his state of the art wheelchair wore a reefer coat, his hair down to his shoulders, his face a mass of scar tissue. Once a highly decorated bomb disposal expert, his career had been terminated by one IRA bomb too many in Belfast. Soon a new career had beckoned, and in the world of cyberspace he was already a legend.

'So there you are,' Roper said.

'And twice as handsome,' Harry Salter put in.

Dillon went to the bar and said to Dora, 'The usual.' She poured a large Bushmills, which he took down in a single swallow. He put the glass down and she refilled it.

Roper said to the others, 'Ferguson's on his way back from Washington after seeing Cazalet about Belov International. The President wants answers, so he's sent Blake with him to help out.'

Dillon took down his second drink. 'Have you shared the news about Belov's miraculous rebirth; his appearance in Siberia at Station Gorky?'

'I have.'

'Rebirth, my arse,' Billy said. 'Come off it, Dillon, all this talk of some double is rubbish. The photo on the website could have been taken any time.'

'I'm not so sure about that,' Harry said. 'Look at the Second World War. Doubles all over the place. Hitler, Churchill, even Rommel.'

'I'd say the double story is genuine,' Roper said. 'That time in Venezuela and Paris, he couldn't have been in two places at once.'

'Yes, but the important question isn't whether they have

a fake Belov out there,' Harry said. 'The question is why. But never mind that for now. I hear you've been to see the Superintendent, Dillon. How was that?'

'Not good.'

'I never was very fond of coppers, but Bernstein is special,' Harry Salter said.

Billy nodded. 'A lovely lady. If it hadn't been for her, we'd never have got together with you, Dillon.'

Roper said, 'How was that?'

'Really? You never heard that story?' Billy carried on, 'Well, Prime Minister John Major was hosting a function for President Clinton at the House of Commons. There was a question of security. Dillon said it was crap and that he could make it onto the terrace dressed as a waiter.'

'He what?' Roper was incredulous.

'But it could only be done from the river, see? He conned Bernstein into finding him the biggest expert on the River Thames, only it wasn't anyone in Customs or the River Police.'

'It was me,' Harry said. He smiled. 'God bless her, she never forgave Dillon.'

'And why would that be?'

'We'd a little bit of business. Diamonds on a boat from Amsterdam coming upriver. There was an informer at work. Bernstein knew we were going to be nicked that night here on the wharf. We'd have gone down the steps for ten years each, only Dillon here decided to be a naughty boy again, which meant the police didn't catch us with the loot.'

Roper turned to Dillon, 'You dog.'

Dillon reached for the third Bushmills Dora had poured. 'It's been said before.'

'The Superintendent wasn't pleased at all. Since she works for Ferguson, she's covered by the Official Secrets Act, which meant she couldn't open her mouth.' Salter shook his head. 'So, as I said, I don't think she ever forgave Dillon for that, especially as, with our assistance, he did indeed make it to the terrace at the House of Commons dressed as a waiter, and served canapés to President Clinton, the Prime Minister, Ferguson . . .'

'And let me guess,' Roper said, 'Superintendent Hannah Bernstein.'

'To be accurate, Chief Inspector, as she was then,' Billy said.

His uncle nodded. 'And still a lovely girl.' He shook his head. 'However, if we were capable of getting Dillon onto the terrace at the House of Commons to serve canapés to the President of the United States, we ought to be able to come up with an answer to this present puzzle.'

'And that's what it is,' Roper said. 'We all know what happened at Drumore. So what's all this business with Belov International?'

'The thing is,' Dillon said, 'we know, but for obvious reasons we can't advertise the fact. Belov International could be banking on that.'

'But for what purpose?' Roper demanded. 'Life goes on, even where big business is concerned.'

'*Especially* where big business is concerned,' Dillon said. 'Especially international companies worth six or seven billion with powerful government forces behind them.'

'And the bleeding Cold War starting all over again,' Harry said. 'Or so I was reading in *The Times* last week.' There was a slightly stunned silence as they all looked at him, and he shrugged. 'So I read *The Times* now and again. That's where you learn about these things.'

'So what you're saying is that the new President of Belov International might just be Putin himself.'

'Well, it would be nice to think so, because at least you can pronounce it,' Harry replied. 'Not like most Russian names. Anyway, it's clear that they're staying stum about this. And obviously, Ferguson can't say publicly that he's got a few wild men going round knocking off the opposition on behalf of the Prime Minister.'

'So it's a stalemate,' Roper said. 'A kind of you-know-that-we-know-and-we-know-that-you-know situation. I still wish I knew why.'

'To hell with it,' Billy said. 'This is what I *do* know. Dillon and I went up to Drumore Place and took them on. I personally shot Ashimov in the shoulder, turned him round and gave it him in the back. Murphy, Novikova and Belov fled out to sea, but then Dillon pointed his Howler, pressed the button and blew them to hell. I saw it with my own eyes. Now can we all have a drink on it, before Dillon works his way through the bar stock?'

At Rosedene in the late afternoon, Rabbi Bernstein had left and Professor Bellamy had given him a lift. It was quiet in the corridor as the young nurse Dillon had spoken to earlier pushed her trolley along. Her name was Mary Killane. And he'd been right. Her accent was Dublin although she'd been born in Londonderry in the North of Ireland in 1980. She'd been taken to Dublin at an early age because her father, an IRA activist, had been condemned to the Maze Prison on five life sentences for murder and had died there of cancer, something for which she had never forgiven the British Government. At the earliest opportunity she had joined the Provisional IRA, and in spite of a respectable professional life had remained a sleeper, available when required.

The call to her present assignment had been out of the blue. It had come from Liam Bell, once Chief of Staff of the Provisional IRA, now retired to Dublin to lecture in English at the University, and write a book or two, for after all, things were different with the Peace Process – except that nothing had really changed. That was the fault of the bloody Brits, and people like Liam Bell were still needed to carry on the fight, just in a different way.

She was instructed to book with a nursing agency in London, where a friend to the organization would see that she was allocated to the Rosedene in St John's Wood. There she would await orders.

But she didn't have to wait long. Returning to her small flat in Kilburn one night, she'd unlocked the door, walked in and to her astonishment found Liam Bell himself sitting, smoking a cigarette, and a hard young man in a black bomber jacket, dark hair curling down to his neck, lounging by the window. He was a dangerous-looking man, with the air of a medieval bravo about him. The shock she experienced was sexual in its intensity.

'No need to worry, dear girl,' Dell reassured her. 'There's work to be done of great importance to the Movement, and I know you can be relied on to do it. No one has a greater right than you to strike back.'

She was filled with emotion. 'Anything, Mr Bell. I'd give my life.'

'No need of that. I'm back to Dublin in the morning, but Dermot here, Dermot Fitzgerald, will look out for you. He's a scholar and a gentleman.'

'A pleasure,' Fitzgerald said.

'The thing is,' Bell told her, 'there's a patient at the Rosedene dangerous to our cause. She's a Special Branch Superintendent and responsible for the death or imprisonment of many of your comrades. You can take my word for it.'

'Oh, I do.'

'She's been at the Cromwell. We've friends there and I understand she'll be transferred back to the Rosedene tomorrow.' He took a small envelope from an inner pocket and offered it to her. 'This is something to help her on her way. Put her out of her suffering, if you like. It's called Dazone. A special drug from the States. If the heart's bad, it helps. That's one pill, but three,' he shrugged, 'it's Goodnight Vienna. Are you up to this? You've powerful memories concerning your father, but say the word . . .'

She took the envelope. 'Of course I will. It's a wonderful chance to serve.'

'Good girl.' He patted her hand and got up. 'I'll be on my way. Look after her, Dermot.'

'I will, Mr Bell.'

'And at the hospital, you watch out for a man called Sean Dillon. A damned traitor to us all.'

He left, and walked along the street to a Mercedes, where a man in a dark trench-coat sat behind the wheel. His name was Igor Levin and he was a Commercial Attaché at the Russian Embassy, or claimed to be.

'Taken care of?'

'Oh, yes,' Bell said. 'You got a good look at her, Mary Killane?'

'Naturally.'

'Keep a close eye, just in case anything goes wrong.'

'The man, Fitzgerald. Do you want anything to happen to him afterwards?'

'Jesus, no. He's too valuable. He'll be away out of it. Probably Ibiza. It'll be a big payday for him.'

Levin said, 'Well, we'll get you back to Ballykelly then. You won't have trouble at the airfield? You've served your time in the Maze Prison, surely?'

'I have a false passport. There are people in this town who'd love to know what I'm up to.'

'Always the old fox.'

'It's what's kept me ahead of the game all these years.'

'So what happens now?' Mary Killane had asked after Bell had gone.

Dermot had kissed her boldly, which had thrilled her to her toes. She'd *known* there was something between them, she'd *felt* it. 'We could start with that,' he said, 'or we could go around the corner and have a drink and a bit to eat first. What's your pleasure, lass?'

They ended up having the drink first, and then Dermot had bedded her, and the whole thing felt like the most special time in her life.

Now, pushing the trolley up the corridor to Hannah's room, the moment of truth had arrived. She felt surprisingly calm, remembering what had been done to her father and to so many others, and that this woman, this Police Superintendent, had been responsible for so much of it. She opened the door and pushed the trolley in.

She'd checked up on Dazone. It took half an hour to kick in, which was why she'd left it to the end of her shift. The curtains were drawn, the small bed light the only illumination. Hannah Bernstein looked pale, almost skeletal, eyes closed. Mary Killane had the pills ready in a small plastic cup, a little water in another one.

Hannah's eyes flickered open. She said, drowsily, 'What is it?'

'Your medication,' the woman said. Surprising how easy it was. 'There you go. I'll help you drink.' And then it was over. 'You'll sleep now.'

'Thank you,' came the murmur and Mary Killane pushed the trolley out.

In the staff room, she didn't change out of her uniform, simply pulled on a raincoat, got her handbag from her locker and went out. As she reached the entrance foyer, Maggie Duncan emerged from her office.

'Another shift over, Mary.'

'That's right, Matron.'

'Have you given any thought to what I said? We'd like to have you with us full time. Agency work is no way to live.'

'I'm thinking about it.'

'You do that. Is the Superintendent all right?'

'I've seen to her.'

'Good. I'll see you tomorrow then.'

Mary Killane hurried across the car park, speaking into her mobile at the same time. 'It's done.'

'Good girl,' Dermot Fitzgerald replied. 'I'll be with you as arranged.'

She hurried on, excited now, turned a corner and moved along a dark road, a small bridge at the end crossing a canal. There was only a single old-fashioned gas lamp giving any light, but she felt no fear. There was a footfall behind her, and she turned to see him emerging out of the shadows, a smile on his face.

'Jesus, Dermot, we'll have to move it if we're to get to the airport in time for the Dublin plane.'

He kissed her on the cheek lightly. 'Don't fret. Everything's fine. You're sure you gave her the pills?'

'Absolutely. They kick in in half an hour, but it will be quite a while before anyone twigs there's something wrong. It's her heart they've been worried about anyway.'

'Excellent. You've done an amazing job. Pity it has to end this way.'

'What are you talking about?' she said, bewildered.

His right hand came out of the pocket of his reefer coat clutching a silenced Colt .38 pistol. He rammed it into her, fired twice and pushed with his left hand so that she went backwards over the rail into the canal below.

He walked to the end of the street and the lights of a Mercedes switched on. He got into the passenger seat and Igor Levin said, 'That's it then?'

'Mission accomplished.'

'Your bag is in the back. I'll drop you at Heathrow.'

'Ibiza next stop.' Fitzgerald lit a cigarette. 'I can't wait to get in the water.'

At Rosedene, Hannah Bernstein sighed gently and stopped breathing. The alarm sounded, a jarring, ugly sound. A young probationer nurse was nearest and got to her first followed by Maggie Duncan, then Bellamy. Within seconds the entire crash team was swinging into action, not that it did any kind of good. They finally switched off. Maggie was crying, Bellamy's face was bleak.

'Time of death, five thirty-five. Agreed, Matron?'

'Yes, Professor.'

'Strange the turns of life,' he said. 'So many people loved her, yet at the end not one of them was here.' He shook his head. 'I'd better make some phone calls. I'm not looking forward to that.'

'Especially Dillon.'

'All of them, really.'

The Gulfstream was an hour late due to bad headwinds. It was just descending into the lights of Farley Field when Ferguson got the call. He listened, his face grave.

'I'm desperately sorry. Have you spoken to everybody?'

'Yes.'

'How awful for her father and grandfather. And Dillon? How was he?'

'I don't think he could take it in. He was at the Dark Man with Roper and the others. He passed the phone to Roper and apparently rushed out. Roper said he and the Salters would go after him. He's probably gone to Rosedene.'

'You know her religion will have an impact here. I'm not sure they'll allow an autopsy. Find out, would you? Thank you, Doctor, and we'll talk again.'

Ferguson sat there, face grave, as the Gulfstream rolled to a halt, then told Blake the bad news.

Blake was shocked. 'How terrible.' He raised the inevitable question. 'You mentioned an autopsy?'

'That's not certain. Generally, they're not allowed. The Jewish body is considered sacred, and the corpse must be buried within twenty-four hours. However, if it can be argued that an autopsy could save another life, for instance, by helping to apprehend a killer and prevent him killing again, then there are exceptions. You'd need an expert rabbi to determine that.'

'Sounds complicated.'

'Particularly as she worked for me under the Official Secrets Act.'

They disembarked, and as they walked towards the small terminal Ferguson's Daimler drew up and Dillon got out from behind the wheel. He stood there, leaning against the Daimler, and lit a Marlboro. His face was curiously expressionless.

'Blake – Charles. Good flight? Thought I'd come myself.'

Ferguson said, 'I'm damn sorry, Sean, damn sorry.'

'You'll be sorry yourself when you hear my news. Get in and we'll move out.'

They did, sitting in the rear while Dillon drove. 'What have you got for me then?' Ferguson asked.

'The last person to see Hannah alive was a Dublin girl, an agency nurse named Mary Killane. Maggie Duncan spoke to her when she finished her shift. Half an hour later the alarm went off in Hannah's room and she died in spite of the crash team.'

'What's your point, Sean?' Ferguson was gentle.

'An hour and a half ago a man walking his dog by the canal some ten minutes from Rosedene found a dead woman half-in, half-out of the water. Her handbag was still caught around one wrist. It was Mary Killane.'

'My God,' Blake said. 'That's a strange coincidence. And you know I don't believe in coincidences.'

'Especially with two bullets in her,' Dillon told him. 'George Langley's going to do the autopsy tonight. He's at the scene of the crime now.'

They travelled in silence for a while and it was Blake who said, 'It smells to high heaven. Hannah dies, and then someone wastes the last nurse to deal with her.'

'And somehow a dead Belov is walking around in Siberia,' Ferguson said. 'I've got an uneasy feeling they're all related.'

'But like Billy said earlier,' Dillon told him, 'if there's one certainty in the matter, it's that Belov is dead.'

'And what if he isn't?' Blake put in.

'I know what I did.'

'Maybe something else happened, something you weren't aware of.'

'In your dreams,' Dillon told him.

'Maybe. But I'll tell you what I think. I was with the FBI for a long time, and any good cop will tell you that experience tells you to go with your instincts. And my instincts tell me that everything is linked to what happened at Drumore Place. That's where we've got to begin.'

And he was right, of course.

DRUMORE PLACE

DUBLIN

MOSCOW

3

Three weeks earlier, Sean Dillon and Billy Salter were at Drumore Place, that great house that was Josef Belov's pride and joy, engaged in a desperate firefight while the villagers kept their heads down inside their cottages.

At the Royal George Patrick Ryan had the shutters up while his mother, who was the cook at Drumore Place, and old Hamilton, the butler, cowered in the kitchen where Ryan joined them.

'Mother Mary, it's just like the old days,' she moaned.

'Sure, and they never went away,' he told her, which was true, for this was still Provisional IRA country to the core. He splashed whiskey into three glasses. 'Get that down you and shut up. It's none of our affair. The nearest police are twenty miles up the coast. One sergeant and three men, and they'd drive the other way if they knew. God save the good work.' He swallowed his whiskey down and crossed himself as sporadic shooting continued.

There was silence for a while and then they heard a boat engine come to life down in the harbour. It increased in power, and Ryan hurried through the bar, opened the door and peered out. It had left the tiny harbour and moved beyond the point, when the explosion took place. There was a momentary ball of fire, and as it cleared he saw the boat half under the water, the stern raised, and it looked as if someone was scrambling over, but he could not be certain for a cloud passed over the moon.

Hamilton appeared beside him and the old lady. 'What is it?'

'Some sort of explosion on the *Kathleen*. I can't be sure, but I think I saw someone. I'm going to check.'

'You'll need some help. Get some of the men.'

'Don't be daft. They'll all stay close to home this night.'

He hurried out to his old Land Rover, got behind the wheel and drove away, down through the village, following the narrow road towards the point, no more than five minutes away, got out and ran towards the top of the steps leading down to the small beach below. It was very dark down there, only the waves dashing in, and then the cloud moved away and the moon shone through and he saw something, head and shoulders perhaps, and started down.

*   *   *

Greta Novikova had been standing in the stern of the *Kathleen*, Belov and Tod Murphy in the wheelhouse, when the explosion took place in the engine room. The two men didn't stand a chance, but the force of the blast, a great wind, drove her across the stern rail as the shattered boat lifted, and then dove down to its last resting place. She plunged head first into the water, lucky enough to slide to one side and miss the propellers. She went under, and surfaced, turning as the sea swallowed the *Kathleen*. An undertow sucked at her as if greedy to take her with it, and that frightened her and, dazed, she screamed and kicked out towards the cliffs of the point.

There was a trench in the seabed at that place, fully fifty fathoms deep, so that as the *Kathleen* descended rapidly there was a turbulence on the surface, waves driving towards the small beach, increasing in force and taking her with them.

In the moonlight, she saw Ryan plunging knee-deep in the water to reach for her. She cried out, he grabbed, waist deep in water, pulling her close.

'I've got you.' He waded onto the beach, pulling her behind him. He held her close as she gasped for air. 'Who was with you?'

'Belov – Tod Murphy.'

'And Kelly and the others?'

'There was a shootout at Drumore Place. I don't know. You must take me there.'

'Jesus, woman, you're in no fit state to go anywhere. There's blood on your face. You must have taken a hell of a battering.'

'I must find out what's happened to Major Ashimov. I must.'

And it was Kelly he was worried about. After all, if Kelly was still around, there was the IRA to consider.

He patted her shoulder. 'I've got the Land Rover at the top of the steps. I'll take you now.'

Yuri Ashimov knew none of this for he was unconscious, face down at Drumore Place, not dead, in spite of the two bullets Billy Salter had pumped into him, thanks to the nylon-and-titanium vest he'd been wearing beneath his shirt. An invention of the Wilkinson Sword Company, it was efficient enough to block even a .44 bullet. On the other hand, the shock to the cardiovascular system usually caused unconsciousness for a while.

Lying there, he stirred and groaned, moved a little and pulled himself up. He shook his head to clear it, remembering firing his pistol at Dillon, knocking the AK from his hands, thinking he'd got the bastard, and then the shot catching his shoulder, spinning him round, and his last memory, Billy Salter's face as he'd fired the heart shot. There was a chair near by; he reached for it, pulled himself up and sat down. He heard a footfall and one of Kelly's men, Toby McGuire, appeared in the archway.

'What happened to you?' Ashimov asked harshly.

'I was waiting in the summerhouse. Somebody jumped me. Knocked me out with a rifle stock.'

'Where is everybody?'

'Kelly's dead and O'Neill. I was up and around when Dillon

and the other guy came out on the terrace. I kept out of the way, but I heard what they were saying.'

'And what was that?'

Toby McGuire took a deep, shuddering breath and told him about the *Kathleen* and what had happened.

Ashimov sat there thinking about it. 'So that's what he said about Major Novikova? If she wasn't willing to take the risks, she shouldn't have joined?'

'That was it. Then he said to this guy, Billy, I expect our day will come.'

'Oh, it will,' Ashimov nodded. 'You can count on it. So they went?'

'He said he had all the keys to the cars in the courtyard. Two hours to Belfast and then home, that's what he said.'

'Right.' Ashimov rose, picked his pistol from the floor and put it in his waistband.

McGuire said, 'What happens now? A right mess.'

'Yes, it is. But we made some contingency plans, we'll be all right. The main thing is that you're still on board. Is that understood?'

McGuire looked baffled. 'Right, Major.'

'It isn't so much what I say, it's what the man in Dublin says. The Provisional IRA will take care of the clean-up here, there'll be a new team to take over from Kelly and you'll be a part of it.'

'If you say so, Major.'

'I do. Now go to the kitchen and see if you can find some spare keys for the cars.'

'On my way.'

McGuire went out and Ashimov went along to Belov's study and sat behind the desk with the satellite phone and rang a Moscow number. It was astonishing the clarity of these things, he thought, and also thought of Greta, surprised at how angry he felt.

A voice said in Russian, 'Volkov. Who's this?'

'Ashimov at Drumore. We have a problem.'

'Explain.'

When he was finished, Volkov said, 'That's certainly inconvenient, but our back-up plans are in place. You'll need to come to Moscow for a meeting at once.'

'Of course. Send a jet for me.'

'You'll make the new arrangements with the IRA?'

'No need – everything's still set.'

'Excellent. The death of Belov would be very inconvenient to our business plans.'

'Of course.'

'Another performance from Max Zubin would be in order, I think.'

'I agree.'

'On the other hand, the fewer people who know the better. The locals should not be told that Belov is dead.'

'You mean I should withhold the information from the IRA?'

'That would seem sensible.'

'All right.'

'Good. I'll arrange the plane. See you soon.'

Ashimov switched off the phone, put it down, and that's when he received the shock of his life. He looked up to find Greta Novikova standing in the doorway, Patrick Ryan's arm around her, and he was amazed at the feeling of joy that flooded through him. He had never been a man to feel much emotion for anyone and surprised himself by rushing round the desk and embracing her.

'Greta, I can't believe it. I heard what happened.' He kissed her, then held her at arm's length. 'My God, what happened to you?'

'I can't believe I'm here,' she said. 'What about you?'

'Salter thought he'd killed me, but I was wearing body armour. Belov, Murphy?'

'Gone,' she said. 'It's a miracle I'm here,' and she explained about the blast.

There was blood on the left side of her head and he examined it. 'It's not too bad, but it might need a couple of stitches. We'll get that fixed by the good sisters at St Mary's near Ballykelly.'

'The Sisters?' She was bewildered.

'They're a nursing order. Belov does a lot for them.'

Ryan had gone away and now returned with the kitchen first aid box. He rummaged in it and produced a large bandage and Ashimov patched her up. McGuire was hovering in the background. Greta staggered a little and Ashimov caught her.

'Take it easy. I'll take you upstairs to your room so you can change.'

'What for?'

'We're going to Moscow. A plane is coming to pick us up.' As he led her out, he said to the other two, 'Wait for me.'

*   *   *

In Dublin, Liam Bell sat in the sitting room of his apartment in a warehouse development. He was reading the evening paper, his spectacles giving him the look of a school-teacher, which, in his youth, he'd been. Many years of dedicated service to the IRA had taken him as far as Chief of Staff. He'd resigned a year earlier to nurse his wife through terminal cancer, and another had taken his place in the command structure. Now he was bored out of his mind and thirsting for action – any kind of action – and his phone rang and presented him with some.

Ashimov said, 'Mr Bell? Yuri Ashimov. Several years ago you made a promise that we could call you if needed.'

'You still can.'

'Do you know a man called Sean Dillon?'

'Indeed I do. If that bastard's on your back you've got trouble.'

'Listen to me. Would you be prepared to move in here with, say, half a dozen IRA men? I'd make it worth your while.'

'I thought you had Dermot Kelly and his boys?'

'Not any longer.'

'What happened?'

Ashimov gave him a version of events which excluded any participation by Belov. 'Anyway, a general clean-up is in order. You can rely on Patrick Ryan. He's a good man.'

'I was two years in the Maze Prison with him. He's one of our own.' Bell laughed harshly. 'What a bastard Dillon is. I've had my brushes with him. Anyway, I've phone calls to make, recruiting to do. You can leave it with me.'

'And the disposal of the corpses?'

'I'm an expert in that department.'

'I'll keep in touch.'

Ashimov walked through to the terrace and found Ryan and McGuire standing by the body of Kelly.

'Poor ould Kelly,' McGuire said. 'He never knew what hit him.'

'And that's a fact.' Ashimov took a silenced pistol from his left-hand pocket and shot him in the side of the head. He went down like a stone and Patrick Ryan jumped back, hands raised, fear on his face.

'No, for God's sake.'

'Not you, you fool.'

'But why?'

'Because he knew Josef Belov is dead and that doesn't suit me or those involved with me in Moscow. Listen here. You know Liam Bell, an old friend, I think.'

Ryan was astonished. 'Of course, Liam, I was in the same cell at the Maze Prison with him.'

'I've spoken to him in Dublin. He'll be here within hours with a crew. He'll take over everything Kelly was responsible for and he'll take care of this lot.' He stirred McGuire with his foot. 'They'll do a satisfactory disposal job.'

'I see.'

'He'll expect you to . . . fit in, you know.'

'I could do that,' Ryan said slowly.

'I want you to be my eyes and ears. I'll make your fortune,

Patrick, put the Royal George in your name. Would you like that?'

Ryan's face lit up. 'That would be grand.'

'One thing. Nobody, not even Liam Bell must know that Belov went down on that boat. It was just Tod Murphy as far as Bell knows.'

Ryan took a deep breath. 'Right, I'm your man.'

'Good. McGuire should have some keys in his pocket. Get them, would you?'

Ryan fished them out.

'Excellent.' They walked through to the hall and Greta came down the great stairs in a fawn coat and black trouser suit, a travelling bag slung over one shoulder. 'You look better, a lot better. Let's get moving. I'll be in touch, Patrick.'

They went out and Ryan waited. He heard one of the cars start up outside and then move off.

It was very quiet, too quiet, but he'd taken a step on the kind of journey from which there was no going back.

The convent looked more like a country house than anything else, but inside it was a very different story. The nuns were a nursing order, the Little Sisters of Pity. Belov had put a great deal of money into the place, a couple of operating theatres, all sorts of medical facilities. The result was a facility that was of great benefit to the local farming community, and further enhancement of the Belov name.

The Mother Superior, Sister Teresa, was a general surgeon. She saw Greta at once in reception, gave her a cursory check and frowned. 'You have been in the wars. What happened?'

Ashimov said quietly, 'She was in an accident.'

Greta, improvising, said, 'It was so stupid. I was on a fishing boat moored in the harbour, slipped stepping over the stern and fell.'

'Several feet. That's not good.'

'I fell into water. Such a fool.'

'Well, your head's going to need a stitch or two and I think we'll give you a quick scan.'

'Do we have time for all that?' Greta asked Ashimov.

'You can come and watch through the surgery window, but not if you smoke,' Sister Teresa said and led Greta out.

Ashimov went outside to think things over, and he did smoke. In fact, he smoked several, going back over events. He should have been dead, but he wasn't, thanks to Belov's gift of the titanium vest. Ferguson would have been behind it, because of what happened to Bernstein, the Salters and Dillon, always Dillon. Now Belov was dead. He thought of their years together in Afghanistan, Iraq, Chechnya, and this was what it had come to. Well, they would all pay, he'd see to that.

His coded mobile rang and he answered. It was Volkov. 'The plane should be with you in about thirty minutes. Has anything else happened?'

Ashimov told him of Greta's astonishing escape.

'That's good news. She could be of great use.'

'Liam Bell is organizing things in Dublin as we speak. I've taken steps to ensure that he isn't aware of what really happened. To Belov, I mean. There's only one man left who knows, besides myself.'

'And who would that be?' Ashimov told him. 'Let's hope your judgement proves sound. I'll see you soon.'

Ashimov lit another cigarette. Volkov was one of the few men who impressed him. A man of mystery way beyond the reach of any Russian government organization. He smiled slightly. He was like Ferguson, in a way. Yes, a Russian Ferguson responsible only to the President.

He threw the cigarette away as a plane roared overhead, obviously coming in to land at the runway Belov had ordered to be laid at the development there. As he went back into reception, Mother Teresa returned with Greta.

'Five stitches, I'm afraid, but I'm good at embroidery. No fracture, but considerable bruising. You must take care, my dear.'

'My thanks,' Ashimov told her. 'But we must go. That was our plane landing.'

'Glad to have been of help. Give my regards to Mr Belov.'

'I certainly will.'

He took Greta's elbow and led her to the estate car. 'Are you all right?' he said as he helped her in.

The patch on the side of her forehead was neat enough, and she touched it. 'I had a local anaesthetic. I feel tired more than anything else.'

He got behind the wheel. 'You can sleep on the plane. Moscow next stop.'

*   *   *

March in Moscow was much as to be expected. The snow had seemed to be on the verge of clearing, but was back again when they landed, a light powdering only, but crisp and cold. A limousine was waiting, a Mercedes, and they drove away instantly to the Belov International townhouse, a place of some splendour, but they had barely settled in when Volkov called.

'I need to see you at once. Bring the Major with you.'

'Where, exactly?'

'The Kremlin, of course.'

Ashimov switched off and turned to Greta. 'How are you feeling?' She'd slept like a log on the plane. 'Any better?'

'It was worse in Chechnya. Not too good in Iraq, either, come to think of it.' She smiled. 'I'll be fine, Yuri.'

'So you feel up to a visit to the Kremlin?'

Her eyes sparkled. 'My, but we are moving in dangerous waters. How exciting.'

'Then let's go.'

Snow was falling lightly as they drove through the streets, past the massive entrance to the Kremlin, moving through side streets, until they emerged at an obscure entrance at the back. They were passed through a series of checkpoints manned by uniformed guards, but never once questioned, simply waved through at each one until they reached a small courtyard behind high railings and halted at steps leading up to an archway. They went up, the door opened and a hard young man in an excellent suit appeared.

'A pleasure to see you again, Major Ashimov.' He inclined his head to Greta. 'Major.'

'We've met before?' Ashimov asked.

'Chechnya, some years ago, but I was a very junior officer. You wouldn't remember. My name is Igor Levin. This way, if you please. General Volkov is waiting.'

He led the way through gloomy corridors and backstairs, finally opening a door leading to a much larger and more ornate corridor. There were gilt mirrors, portraits from another age, fine carpeting.

'I must say, this is beautiful.'

'I imagine that Tsar Nicholas thought so, too,' Levin said.

They came to an ornate door, where a burly individual, again in an excellent suit, was seated in a high chair. A machine pistol was on a small table beside him. He didn't stand and didn't speak.

'We like to be prepared for any eventuality,' Levin said.

'Even in here?' Greta said.

'Especially in here.' He opened a door and ushered them in without announcement and stood at the back of the room, which was quite stunning, very French. Its panelled walls were beautifully painted with formal scenes of the seventeenth century, and there were portraits of the same period, a magnificent fireplace with a real fire, or so it appeared, an exquisite mirror above it. Chairs and a settee decorated the room, but the really striking thing was the huge desk in the centre of the room and the man who sat behind it. He had looked up as they had entered, and was nothing like Greta had expected. He was perhaps sixty, hair decidedly thinning, wearing wire spectacles of an old-fashioned type, a neat suit in navy blue, a dark tie. He could have been the manager of an insurance office, this man who, according to what Ashimov had told her, wielded such power. When he spoke, his voice was not much more than a whisper.

'My dear Ashimov, so you made it in one piece again?'

'My luck is good, Comrade.'

'I'm never too sure whether you should call me that any longer.'

'Old habits die hard.'

Volkov stood up, came round the desk and shook hands with Greta. 'Your luck is also good, Major.'

'Yes, Comrade.'

There was a power to him, she realized that now, and as he continued to hold her hand it flowed through her. 'More than luck, I think. I believe in God, you see, like my blessed mother before me. Everything is for a purpose.' He patted her hand. 'But I am a poor host, and for a beautiful and brave young Russian woman who has gone through the ordeal you have there is only one remedy. The finest vodka we have.' He said to Levin, 'Igor, if you wouldn't mind?'

'Of course not, Comrade General.'

'Igor,' Volkov told him gently, 'I have told you never to use my title publicly.'

'I am suitably chastened, Comrade General.'

'Hopeless. Come, we sit by the fire and talk. Igor always seems to see the lighter side of life despite having served in Afghanistan with the KGB at nineteen, then the paratroopers in Chechnya. He was in the GRU when he fell into my hands, and now he's one of my security guards. Took a bullet for me once.'

'There's nothing like KGB training,' said Ashimov.

'Yes. Now let's sit by the fire. I've things to say.'

Levin opened a cupboard and produced an ice bucket containing a bottle of vodka and frosted glasses.

'You will join us, Igor. Just one, though. You must remember your trigger finger.'

The vodka was sublime and burned its way down. 'Excellent,' Volkov told them. 'Damn Ferguson and damn the Prime Minister. Another, Igor, and then we'll get down to business.'

They sat by the fire and Volkov began. 'This is the situation. Since the end of the Iraq war, Belov International has continued to prosper. Since the vote for democracy in Iraq, the prospect is very real of the oil industry there returning to full flow, indeed to achieve a level of production beyond all expectations, and we are in the middle of it. We're talking a company worth fifteen billion and rising.'

'That would be staggering,' Greta said.

'And nothing must be allowed to put such success at risk. In other words, Belov can't die. Igor will take you to see Max Zubin tonight. We'll ship him off to Station Gorky to settle him in, let the world know where he is, and slip him back when necessary.'

'Which will totally confuse Ferguson and company in London,' Ashimov said, 'Dillon having reported back on a successful mission.'

'And we mustn't forget President Cazalet and that Blake Johnson man of his. They always exchange information with their British cousins,' Volkov pointed out.

Greta said, 'But after Dillon's report, they'll know the Belov in Siberia is false.'

'Yes, but Ferguson can't afford to disclose it – admit that his agents, acting on behalf of the Prime Minister, conducted a slaughter in the Republic of Ireland, a sovereign state. Where a highly important Russian citizen happened to be at the same time.'

'So it's a stand-off,' Ashimov said. 'There's nothing the Brits can do about it, and we keep the financial markets happy.'

'There's more to it than that. This organization that Ferguson runs, the so-called Prime Minister's Private Army. Such typical British hypocrisy. They've been committing murders for years and getting away with it. Dillon's record speaks for itself. Well, the President thinks we should lance the boil, as it were.'

'Are you suggesting what I think you are?'

'Yes. Total elimination of Ferguson's team once and for all. The General himself, his personal assistant, this Superintendent Bernstein, Dillon of course, and these Salter people, the London gangsters who've been helping him out during the last few years. While you're at it, perhaps Cazalet's man, too, Blake Johnson. Another thorough nuisance.'

'I'll see what I can do,' Ashimov said.

'It's a tall order, I know, but already started in a way. That woman Bernstein you ran down in London. She's in a medical facility Ferguson runs in St John's Wood. It would be a good start to things if you could find some means of easing her on.'

'As you say, Comrade.' Ashimov wasn't in the slightest troubled by the thought.

'Good,' Volkov said. 'I leave it all in your capable hands. I've left you, Major Novikova, on the books of the London Embassy as a Commercial Attaché. It will bring you diplomatic immunity, although I'm certain Ferguson won't make a move against you. At the worst, they could only ask you to leave. Captain Levin will have a similar situation at the Embassy to act as back-up. The appropriate documentation is in the file on my desk.' He turned to Ashimov. 'I would think it prudent for you not to return to London, if only because Dillon would attempt retribution.'

'As you say, Comrade.'

'Igor will take you to see Max Zubin to make certain he knows what is expected of him. Spend the night, then return to Ireland. Igor will go with you. I envy you your inevitable success. I don't think there's anything more.'

But there was, for at that very moment a secret door in the wall swung open and President Putin walked in.

They all leapt to their feet, for it was an astonishing moment. Putin wore a track suit, a towel around his neck.

'You must excuse me, Comrades. Affairs of state got in the way of my hour in the gym this morning, so I've been making up for it. Good to see you again, Major Ashimov. You must be feeling like a cat at the moment, a tomcat, naturally.'

'Very much so, Comrade President.'

Putin turned to Greta. 'Major Novikova.' He offered his hand. 'I hear good things about you, even if you are GRU.'

It was his little joke, a reference to the intense rivalry between the KGB, to which he had once belonged, and GRU Military Intelligence.

Greta said, 'It would have been an honour to have served under you.'

'Yes, well, in Afghanistan this one did.' He tapped Ashimov on the shoulder, 'And Captain Levin, the boy wonder.' He swivelled to look at Volkov. 'All of us served, in good times and in bad – served Russia and each other. I expect nothing less from you in this present matter.'

There was a moment's silence. Ashimov said, 'It would be our honour.'

Putin nodded, turned to Volkov and handed him an envelope. 'There is what you asked for. Read it.' Volkov opened the envelope and took out a document, which he unfolded. 'Aloud, please.'

'From the Office of the President of the Russian Federation at the Kremlin. The bearer of this letter acts with my full authority. All personnel, civil or military, will assist in any way demanded. Signed, Vladimir Putin.'

'It may help, it may not. It's in your hands now.' Putin stepped behind the secret door and it swung noiselessly back into place. It was as if he had never been.

Volkov replaced the letter in the envelope and gave it to Ashimov. 'Such power. You must guard it well. Now on your way.'

He turned, opened the secret door and disappeared as completely as had his master.

'So there we are,' Ashimov said. 'What happens now?'

'I'm taking you out,' Igor said. 'There's a very acceptable nightclub called the Green Parrot. It's owned by the Mafia, but they know me.'

'There is a purpose to this, I presume?'

'You want to see Max Zubin perform, don't you?'

On the way to the club, it was Greta who said, 'We're being followed.'

'Good for you, but it's all right. They're my people. They'll arrange Zubin's onward transportation to Station Gorky.'

'I don't understand,' Greta said. 'If Zubin is so important, why is he allowed to have so free a life? To perform in public and so on?'

'Because of his mother,' Ashimov told her. 'Bella Zubin.'

Greta was astounded. 'The actress?'

'The great actress,' Ashimov said, 'one of Russia's finest. Unfortunately, she dabbled too much in politics and was sent to the Gulag.'

'I thought she was dead.'

'No, very much alive at eighty-five and living in a comfortable condominium by the river. Her son would not wish to see her returned to a more uncomfortable situation. That's why we could trust him not to make a run for it when he was playing Belov in Paris the other year.'

Greta shook her head. 'I remember seeing her playing the Queen in *Hamlet* when I was a little girl. She was wonderful.'

'It's a hard life, Greta,' Ashimov said, 'but some things are more important.'

The Green Parrot was up a side street in an old brownstone house, a neon sign advertising the fact over an arched doorway. Levin parked outside and the doorman stepped out.

'You can't park there. Clear off.'

The other limousine pulled in behind them and three men in black leather coats got out. The doorman took one look and hurriedly backed off.

'Sorry, Comrades.' He opened the door behind him, the three men went in first and Levin, Ashimov and Greta followed.

The club was small, curiously old-fashioned, a little like some joint in one of those *cinema noir*, black-and-white thrillers from the Hollywood of the forties. The headwaiter even wore a white tuxedo as if doing an impersonation of Rick in *Casablanca*. He turned, saw Levin and his party, and his face fell.

The tables were crowded, but one of Levin's men brushed past the headwaiter as he came forward, ignored the bearded man at the microphone who seemed to have the audience in stitches with his humour, and leaned down to a table of five people in the front, three women, two men. Whatever he said was enough. They vacated the table at once and moved away.

The man at the microphone said, 'I know I can be bad, but this is ridiculous.'

Levin called, 'Max, you're looking good. How about the piano? "A Foggy Day in London Town". You know how I love all those old numbers. Let's all cheer for Fred Astaire. The Yanks are our friends now.'

He sat down with Ashimov and Greta, while the three minders stood against the wall.

Max Zubin shook his head, and waving at the audience said, 'The GRU, my friends, what do you expect? My master calls and I obey.'

He went to the piano at the back of the stage, a baby grand. A drummer and a double bass player were already there, and Zubin sat down and started a driving, complex version of 'Foggy Day' that wouldn't have been out of place in any great piano bar in London or New York.

Levin called the headwaiter over. 'Vodka, on the house, and don't forget the boys behind me.'

'It is my pleasure, Captain.'

'And a little Beluga on toast, the way I like it.'

'Of course.'

There was a roar of applause as Zubin finished and Levin stood up, clapping. 'Marvellous,' he called, 'More.'

Zubin moved into 'Night and Day', and waiters appeared hurriedly with glasses of vodka on a tray, each glass in a larger glass with crushed ice, one waiter handing them out to the security guards, the other to the party at the table, the third distributing the Beluga caviare.

Ashimov said as they started on the feast, 'You live well, my friend.'

'I could be dead tomorrow, that's what I learned in

Afghanistan and Chechnya.' He crunched toast and savoured the Beluga.

'Wonderful, isn't it?' Greta said, as she followed suit.

'It was in the Chechen capital I got a taste for it. We took the Grand Hotel in a firefight – a very bloody firefight. Found the Beluga in the icebox behind the bar in the main kitchen. A few of us survived that fight. Not many. The Twenty-First Independent Parachute Company, made up of anyone they could reach out and grab. We were wolfing that caviare down when we heard the piano start to play in the anteroom. We went out to see what was going on and there he was, an infantry captain named Max Zubin.'

'And what was he playing?' Greta asked.

'"As Time Goes By". I swear to God, just like in *Casablanca*. You know the old movie? I've seen it in American and I've seen it dubbed with Bogart speaking Russian and it's just as fantastic.' He stood up, applauded, and called, 'Max, let's do the Grand in Chechnya, in memory of the Twenty-First and all those guys we left. Let's do "As Time Goes By".'

He sat down, snapped his fingers for another vodka and ate some more toast and caviare, somehow managing to hum the tune at the same time.

'An enthusiast,' Ashimov told Greta.

'The crowd seems to like it.'

And indeed they did, large sections singing along, some in English, others in Russian. Zubin finished on a high. People cheered, stood up and clapped. He waved to everyone, nodded to the double bass player, who put his instrument down and took over the piano, then came down from the stage, shaking hands on the way, and sat down at the spare seat at the table.

Levin smiled. 'You haven't lost your touch.' He handed him a vodka, which Zubin swallowed in one gulp, then reached for another. 'Why are you being so nice to me, Igor?'

Levin said, 'Let's put it this way. The beard suits you, but it's time to take it off again.'

'Christ, no,' Max Zubin groaned. 'Not that.'

'I'm afraid so. Surely you remember Major Ashimov from Paris? I'll let him explain.'

The Zubins' apartment was a time capsule from another age. Even the maid was ageing and could have been out of a Chekhov play. The interior was more thirties than anything else, with a grand piano covered by photos of the great and the good in silver frames.

Levin, Ashimov and Greta were admitted by the maid, who viewed them all suspiciously.

'Is my mother at home, Sonia?' Zubin asked.

'Where else would she be? She is preparing to go to bed.'

'I'd like a word.'

'What a ridiculous time to call. I'll tell her you're here.'

She went out and he lit a cigarette. 'You must excuse Sonia. She is a failed actress who became my mother's dresser.'

Greta moved to the piano and examined the photos. Zubin sat at it and started to play 'Falling in Love Again'.

'Marlene Dietrich's national anthem,' Greta told him.

'You'll find her and my mother among the photos there.'

Greta was working her way through and picked one up. 'My God, this is her with Laurence Olivier.'

'In London, where we did *The Three Sisters*,' a voice interrupted. 'I made the mistake of coming back.'

And there she was in the flesh, wearing a silk robe, her hair tied back, powerful and thrilling in spite of her age.

Ashimov stepped forward. 'You look like some great warrior queen.'

'Don't try flattery, Major. I remember you well from that affair in Paris. So, you need my son again?'

'I'm afraid so.'

She turned to Greta. 'And who's this one?'

'Major Greta Novikova of GRU.'

'Typecasting, but good bone structure.'

Greta couldn't think of a thing to say. Bella did a surprising thing. As Sonia came in with the ritual glasses of vodka on a tray, the old actress patted Igor Levin on the cheek.

'He looks in on me from time to time, this one. A nice boy in spite of himself.'

Levin took her hand and kissed it. 'No man could have a greater compliment.'

They all took their vodka. 'So, this is State business?'

'Direct from Putin himself.'

'Well, to hell with him and to hell with the lot of you. Where are you taking him?'

'Station Gorky in Siberia,' Levin said.

'For a while only. You'll see him again soon,' Ashimov said.

'And I'm supposed to believe that?' She turned to Zubin. 'You'll have to get rid of the beard. A pity. It suits you.' She turned to Levin. 'Can I have him for tonight?'

'Where would he go?' Levin smiled. 'His escort will be downstairs.'

'I thought so. All right, the rest of you can get out. I'd like some time with my son.'

Which they did, there was not much else to say. She turned to Zubin who was still playing, and raised her glass to Sonia, who came over with the vodka bottle.

'If it wasn't for me you could make a run for it.'

'Things are as they are, Mama, so running is out of the question.'

'You're a good son, Max, always were. So it's the same old? Paris all over again?'

'No, I think this is rather more important. They've shown me a warrant from Putin.'

'Then God help us.' She swallowed her vodka down and tossed the glass into the fireplace.

Onwards from Moscow, the Falcon rose to 40,000 feet and moved on into the night, while Levin slept and Greta and Ashimov talked in low voices.

'What's the story on the Boy Wonder there?' she asked.

'His father was an infantry colonel, a military attaché at the London Embassy, his mother was English. Igor spent a couple of years at a posh public school in Westminster, London. He should have gone to university, but he's a strange one, marches to his own drummer. He went home on holiday and just decided to join the army without even consulting his father, who couldn't do anything about it because it would have looked bad.'

'Some KGB time was mentioned, the paratroopers and now GRU,' she said.

'Yes. He became a war hero, decorated twice. The thing that singled him out for a commission was when he took out a Chechnyan general.'

'As a sniper?'

'It was more complicated than that. He's something of an actor, and he made a very convincing Chechnyan. Worked himself close in, slit the man's throat, and walked off laughing.'

'My God.'

'That's the thing. He really doesn't care. Not about anything. His father was involved with Belov in the old days, so when the money started pouring in he got his share. Ten million sterling, that kind of money. He was killed in a car crash with his wife the other year, which left Igor very well fixed and all nicely stashed away in London.'

'So Levin could be on the Riviera. Champagne, girls, a yacht. Why not?'

'He reminds me of Sean Dillon, in a way,' Ashimov said. 'Dillon is also well fixed in the money department. You could ask why he continues to live the life he does.'

He poured Greta a glass of champagne while she thought about it. 'A kind of madness?' she asked. 'A need to live on the dangerous edge?'

'You could have a point.'

'Well, if that means comparing him with Dillon, he must be mad. When I was involved with Dillon in Iraq, he seemed to be enjoying the whole business.'

Igor Levin stirred and said, 'It's very simple. Life can be so boring.' He tilted up his seat. 'If you've finished talking about me, I'd like a glass of the old bubbles there.'

Ashimov said, 'Ah, you're awake, are you? Well, first things first. I'm going to need you, Igor, so I have something for you. When Billy Salter shot me at Drumore my life was saved by a personal gift from Belov, a nylon and titanium vest. Even stops a .45. Fits nicely under your shirt.' He took a package from his briefcase. 'My gift to you.'

Levin put it on the seat beside him. 'Frightfully good of you, old boy, but I'd still appreciate some champagne.'

He spoke in an impeccable English public school accent.

Greta poured him a glass. 'They'll love you at the Reform Club.'

'I should damn well hope so.' He sipped some of the champagne. 'I must say Dillon sounds rather like the twin I never had. I can't wait to meet him.'

'You won't have to wait long,' Ashimov said. 'After stopping at Drumore, we're off to London for you to take up your new duties.'

'Where I may be received with less than enthusiasm.'

'Not when the Ambassador sees your warrant from Putin.'

'Oh, good, I'm to have that, am I?'

He still spoke in that English upper-class accent. Ashimov opened a briefcase, took out a file and passed it across.

'Here's everything you need to know on Dillon, Ferguson, Roper and the Salters. These people are bad news, my friend, as bad as you've ever known.'

Levin flicked the file and it opened by chance at a print-out about Bernstein. He went through it quickly. 'What a woman. This is an incredible record.'

'Well, don't fall in love with her. She's the first one to go.'

'A nice Jewish girl, and you forget – my father was Jewish.'

'Your mother was Christian,' Ashimov said. 'You can only be a Jew through your mother.'

'An academic argument. All those wonderful genes. They never go away. If I was religious, I'd say it was a blessing from God. Personally, I'm rather proud of it.'

'Good for you. Now read the file and see what you're getting into. I'll fill you in on the IRA side of things later.'

'As you say.'

Levin settled back with the file, while Ashimov poured Greta another champagne and used his satellite phone to contact Liam Bell. He found him at Drumore Place.

'It's me,' he said. 'How are you?'

'Fine. We've moved in, got things arranged. No trouble from the villagers. Life, shall we say, is back to normal. What about you?'

'Well, I've a target for you, during the coming weeks.'

'And what would that be?'

'Sean Dillon, Ferguson and company.'

'Jesus! A tall order.'

'We'll discuss it in detail when I'm there. However, I'm

going to need someone from your side of the coin. A hit man who'll do the job, no questions asked, no argument, no sentimentality.'

'What you mean is you're looking for the original cold-blooded bastard.'

'No, that's you,' Ashimov told him. 'What I'm looking for is a reasonable facsimile. I know the Peace Process is supposed to have brought an end to the glorious cause of Irish unity, but I believe you do have sleepers in London. Young men and women in good suits who work in the Stock Exchange . . .'

'And hanker after the romance of the struggle,' Bell said. 'You might be surprised by how many of those there are. What would you be offering?'

'Oh, to you, a big payday. Funds for the Organization, of course, not for the personal bank account in Spain. What you pay for him or, indeed, her to eradicate someone for me is your business.'

'Would you be involved?'

'Not personally. I'll be staying there for a while with Major Novikova. I'm bringing a young colleague from Moscow who'll handle the London end. He'll work out of the London Embassy. The target is legitimate from your point of view. A high-ranking Special Branch officer who's put more of your friends inside the last few years than she's had hot dinners.'

'It'll be a pleasure,' Bell said. 'I've got ideas right away. Leave it with me.'

'We'll see you soon.'

Levin looked up. 'Dillon really is quite something. Now I'm really looking forward to meeting him.'

'Make sure it isn't your last meeting,' Ashimov told him, and poured another glass of champagne.

LONDON

4

When Igor Levin flew from Ireland to London, it was in a Belov International jet, and Liam Bell flew with him under a false identity. Levin didn't approach the Embassy, not then. He stayed in an indifferent hotel in Kensington next door to Bell, waited patiently while the man from Dublin made his arrangements with Mary Killane and Dermot Fitzgerald, and then, after the outcome, delivered Fitzgerald to Heathrow for the flight to Ibiza.

He wasn't impressed. In his opinion the whole business had been badly handled. The Killane girl, for example. Anyone with half a brain would find it too much of a coincidence that she, the last person to treat the Bernstein woman, had been murdered so soon afterwards, and so close to the hospital.

Perhaps things were done differently in Belfast. Maybe the IRA had employed such fear, such power, that they thought they could get away with anything. Or maybe they were just used to getting away with anything.

'Never mind, Igor,' he mused, after delivering Bell to the airfield for his return flight. 'You're just the hired help.'

He'd already rented a Mercedes, but now, taking advantage of his wealth, he moved into a suite at the Dorchester Hotel overlooking Hyde Park.

'Only the best, Igor,' he said and drove down to the Embassy of the Russian Federation situated in Kensington Palace Gardens. There was a snag at first, when he discovered the Ambassador was in Paris, but a further inquiry revealed that the Senior Commercial Attaché, Colonel Boris Luhzkov, in reality Head of Station for the GRU, was lunching in the pub across the High Street. Levin went out of the main gates, waited for a break in the traffic, then crossed the road.

Luhzkov was in a window seat on his own devouring shepherd's pie, a half-empty glass of red wine before him. Levin got two more and went across. He put one of the glasses on the table.

'You always like two.'

Luhzkov looked astonished. 'My God, Igor, it is you. I had a message from Moscow this morning. It said you were joining my staff.'

'Not quite true, old son. In a way, it's *you* who are joining *my* staff.'

'What on earth do you mean?'

Levin took the envelope from his inside pocket, extracted the Putin warrant and passed it over. 'Read that.'

He sat down and lit a cigarette. When Luhzkov handed it back, his hand shook. 'For God's sake, you'd better not lose it. But what does it mean, Igor?'

'That I'm on a special assignment for the President himself. I need a front, so I'm to be a commercial attaché. Any quarrel with that?'

'Of course not.'

'For the moment, I need an office and all that goes with it. I won't need an Embassy car, I've hired a Mercedes, and I don't need housing – I'm staying at the Dorchester. It's nice to be back, isn't it, Boris, and what better place for a Russian intelligence officer to stay than the best hotel in London?'

Luhzkov had totally capitulated. 'Anything you say, Igor.'

'Good. The shepherd's pie looks delicious. I think I'll have some,' and Levin turned and waved to a waitress.

Later, when the necessary office had been provided, he worked his way through GRU's computer records, cross-referencing them with the file Ashimov had provided him. Ferguson, Dillon, the Salters. Names, computer print-outs, addresses. He even checked on Bell's past and that of his men whom he'd met at Drumore. An unsavoury bunch, no finesse. On the other hand Bell must have had something going for him to have become Chief of Staff of one of the most notorious organizations in the world.

Dillon was a totally different article; his exploits spoke for themselves. The thing that impressed Levin the most was that in all those years with the IRA, the police and Secret Intelligence sources hadn't touched him once. Levin was lost in admiration.

Even the Salters surprised him. They were far from the usual run of gangsters. Harry Salter's ageing face spoke for itself, and Billy's deeds were remarkable. Men who didn't give a damn, the Salters and Dillon.

'Just like me,' Levin said softly.

Hannah Bernstein filled him with a strange kind of regret when he read her file again and looked at her photo. She'd been a remarkable woman – you had to be to make Superintendent rank in Special Branch. An Oxford psychologist, and yet she'd killed more than once. And the Jewish background. It made him feel uncomfortable, and he knew why that was.

Her death, of course, had had nothing to do with him. She'd been close to death anyway, thanks to Ashimov. The drug the nurse had used might not even have been necessary. Ashimov had killed her, really.

'Trying to comfort yourself, Igor?' he murmured. 'Levin, the honourable man? Well, not after what you've done, boyo.'

He tapped into the police security facility, and all the details of the Mary Killane killing were there: the murder scene, the names of those at Scotland Yard handling the case, the fact that there was a press black-out.

The forensic pathologist in charge of the autopsy was a Professor George Langley. Levin checked him out on the computer. Langley normally worked out of Church Street Mortuary off Kensington High Street. Quite convenient for the Russian Embassy.

However, there was nothing on the police incident screen referring to Hannah Bernstein, and Levin sat back, lit a cigarette and went to the small icebox in the corner, opened it, found the vodka and poured a large one. It calmed him down, helped him think.

So, it would seem reasonable that an autopsy on Hannah Bernstein would be performed by the same eminent pathologist who was performing it on Mary Killane. A strong chance, surely. He had another shot of vodka, returned the bottle. There was just one more thing to do. Luhzkov's remark in the pub that he'd better not lose the Putin warrant had stuck in his mind, so he took the letter out and put it through the office copier. He made three copies, put two in the office safe, one in his briefcase in an envelope and returned the original to his inside pocket.

He phoned Ashimov on his coded mobile and found him at the Royal George with Greta. 'Just reporting in. Bell got back without incident?'

'Yes. What's happening there?'

Levin brought him up to date. 'I'm just about to go out and start sniffing around.'

'Yes, do that,' Ashimov told him.

'Frankly, I've not been impressed with the way things went here. It may have suited Bell, but if that's the best the IRA can do, they're a bunch of clodhoppers. The way Fitzgerald disposed of that girl was ridiculous and unnecessary.'

'We're in the death business, Igor. There's no time for finesse.'

He switched off and Greta Novikova said, 'Trouble?'

'Just Igor sounding off. He isn't impressed with the IRA.'

'Well, that's all right,' Greta told him. 'Neither am I.'

In his office at the Ministry of Defence sat Ferguson with Rabbi Julian Bernstein and Blake Johnson. Dillon sat on the windowsill. There was a knock at the door and Hannah's father, Arnold Bernstein, came in.

'Sorry I'm late. I had an operation.'

'That's all right,' Ferguson said. 'Carry on, Rabbi.'

'Well, as you know, a Jewish body should not be desecrated by an autopsy, and should be buried within the twenty-four-hour window. But an expert rabbi may determine otherwise in exceptional circumstances. I have made a judgement, and in view of the murder of the young nurse and the circumstances surrounding Hannah's death I believe it is necessary to establish what happened. With the blessing of my son I give my permission for the autopsy.'

'I know how difficult this must be for you, but I'm most grateful. I'll phone Professor Langley now.'

It was raining hard, so Levin wore a raincoat and trilby hat and carried a black umbrella. The Church Street Mortuary was surprisingly busy, with quite a number of cars outside. It was an ageing building, probably Victorian like many in that part of London, with the look of being a rather shabby school of the old-fashioned sort.

Inside it was well decorated and surprisingly pleasant, with two girls behind the reception desk and a number of people milling around, apparently reporters.

'Come on, Gail,' a young man said to one of the receptionists. 'So was the Killane woman murdered or wasn't she? What's all the mystery?'

'I can't tell you that,' the girl named Gail said. 'All I know is that Professor Langley's on another case.'

'Is there a link?'

'That's not for me to say.'

She moved away, leaving the other girl in charge as Ferguson, Dillon, the Bernsteins and Blake came in. Levin recognized all of them from their files.

Ferguson announced himself.

'Oh, this way, gentlemen.'

She led them through to the back corridor and they disappeared through a door. The young reporter said disconsolately, 'Nobody ever tells you a thing. I'll get hell at the office.'

He took out a cigarette and Levin gave him a light. 'Who are you with?'

'*Northern Echo*. What about you?'

'*Evening Standard*. We'll just have to see, won't we?'

They found Langley in a room lined with white tiles, fluorescent lights making everything look harsh and unreal. There were steel operating tables, and Hannah Bernstein lay on top of one of them. She looked calm, eyes closed, a hood on her head, blood seeping through a little. In turn, both the Bernsteins leaned over and kissed her forehead. Ferguson said, 'Forgive me, Professor, but will you confirm what you told me on the telephone?'

'Yes. In my opinion, Hannah Bernstein was murdered. Her heart was in a poor state anyway, but I've found traces of the drug Dazone in her system, a drug which had not been part of her medication at Rosedene: I've checked on that. Recently introduced into her system and in overdose quantity.'

There was a dreadful silence, then Ferguson said, 'You will appreciate the significance of this to the Mary Killane case.'

'I'm afraid so. I've never had much faith in coincidence. I've been told the time Killane gave Hannah her medication. The Dazone kicks in in half an hour at the most, which fits into the time scale of Killane's murder.'

'Well, it saves one trial in the matter,' Ferguson said. 'Now we have to find out who shot Killane. She has an IRA connection.'

'What happens now?' Dillon demanded.

'I invoke the Official Secrets Act and put the matter before a Special Crown Coroner. He'll give what's called a closed court order. No jury necessary. A burial order will also be issued, and you, Rabbi, may bury your granddaughter. All that will take place quickly. You may alert your undertaker. I can't say how sorry we all are.'

'May she rest in peace.'

The response from Dillon was uncontrollable. 'Well, I'm

damned if I will.' He turned and brushed past the young receptionist, Gail, who had been standing at the door, and went out.

He went through the crowd, angry beyond belief, pushing against Levin, who said, 'Hey, watch it, old man.'

Dillon shook his head. 'Sorry.' He pushed on and went out into the rain.

Levin waited and the young reporter said, 'Something's going on.'

Ferguson and the others emerged, pushed through the crowd and went out, and the receptionist appeared.

'What was all that about, Gail?' the young reporter asked.

'Don't be daft. We have our ethics here. Anyway, it's more than my job's worth to talk to you.'

'Useless bitch.'

'Thanks very much,' she said, as she pulled her coat on.

Levin said to the young reporter loud enough for her to hear, 'You shouldn't speak to a lady like that. It's not on.'

She flashed him a smile of gratitude, said to the other receptionist, 'I'm going for my break,' and went out.

Levin followed. She hesitated on the step, faced by the pouring rain, and he put up his umbrella. It took a Russian, schooled at one of London's greatest public schools, to sound so charming, and it had just the right rough edge to it.

'Some people just have no manners, but to speak to a lady like that . . .' He shook his head. 'I should have punched him in the mouth.'

'Oh, he's just stupid, but thanks for being so nice.'

'I don't know where you're going, but you'll get soaked without my umbrella. Where *are* you going, by the way?'

'Oh, the Grenadier pub. I'm on a half shift until nine tonight so I have sandwiches and a coffee there.'

'What a coincidence – I was going to call in there myself. Shall we go together?'

He shielded her from the heavy rain, an arm slightly around her waist. 'Are you a reporter too?' she asked.

'So they tell me.' They reached the pub. 'Come on, in we go.' It was still early and there was plenty of room. He helped her off with her coat. 'May I join you? I could do with a sandwich, too.'

She was obviously attracted. 'Why not? Prawn on salad, and tea.'

'Oh, we can do better than that.' He went to the bar, gave the waitress an order and came back with two glasses of champagne. 'There you go.'

'I say, this is nice.' She was sparkling with pleasure.

'You deserve it. You're in the death business. Not many people could do what you do.'

'Oh, I don't know.' She drank the champagne and ate her sandwiches, and he bought her another glass and got to work. 'The things you have to put up with in your work. I mean, look at what happened earlier.'

She was a little tipsy and very flushed. 'Well, I must admit, it was very unusual.'

'You were there?'

'Well, I showed them all in to the professor, so I was standing by the door when he told them his findings.'

'Just a moment.' Levin got up, went to the bar and returned with two more. 'What were you saying? It must have been awful.'

'Well, I shouldn't really say anything,' but she leaned forward.

The whole story came out, naturally, and then she checked her watch and gasped, 'Oh, I'm late already.' She jumped up and he helped her into her coat.

'I'll walk you back.' It was still raining. He said, 'A pity you're on shift tonight. We could have had dinner.'

'Oh, my boyfriend wouldn't like that.'

Levin managed to stop himself laughing out loud. He took her to the mortuary entrance through the rain.

'Take care,' he said and walked away.

And then, as he went to the entrance and paused to look back, he noticed a black hearse. Something made him pause. Rabbi Julian Bernstein emerged. Behind him, pallbearers came out with a coffin.

He watched it being put into the hearse, and the rear door closed. As Rabbi Bernstein got into the front of the hearse behind the driver and the pallbearers got into another limousine, Levin cut back. There was the name and telephone number of the undertaker in gold leaf under the rear door. He memorized it and walked on to the Embassy. Once in his office, he phoned Ashimov.

'Things have moved.'

'Tell me.'

Levin did. 'I told you they'd been clumsy, your IRA chums. It won't take a man like Dillon long to see which way things have gone. You'd better see that Fitzgerald keeps his head down in Ibiza. Do you want me to go out there and take care of him?'

'Don't be stupid, Igor, I need these people. Stay there, check out the funeral and keep an eye out for Ferguson and company.'

'So you don't want me to knock off Dillon for you?'

'Not now. Just obey orders, Igor.'

Levin sat back and thought about it, then rang the undertakers. 'I'm hoping to send flowers as a token of respect for Miss Hannah Bernstein. I'm not sure whether the body will be there or at home.'

'Oh, here overnight.'

'And the funeral?'

'Ten o'clock in the morning at Golders Green.'

'So kind.'

He thought about things for a while, then decided to go for a drive, which took him to Wapping and Cable Wharf and the Dark Man. It was almost night, lights on the river, and he parked, one of many cars, so things were busy. He went and stood on the edge of the wharf and lit a cigarette. He'd always liked rivers, the smell of them, the boats, but now he felt curiously empty. It was Bernstein. He kept thinking of her photo, the look on her face. Dammit, her death was not really his affair, there was an inevitability to it. So why did he feel as he did? The Jewish link? But that was nonsense. It had always meant little to him, and death had been a way of life for years.

'Pull yourself together, Igor,' he murmured and flicked his

cigarette into the Thames. He took a small leather pouch from his pocket, extracted a minuscule earpiece, another device developed by the GRU, and pushed it into his right ear. The chip it contained enhanced sound considerably. Then he crossed the Wharf and entered the Dark Man.

Ferguson, Dillon and the Salters were all there, including Roper in his wheelchair. They had the corner booth, but the bar itself was busy. Levin got a large vodka and helped himself to an *Evening Standard* someone had left. He had luck then, for a man and a woman in a small two-person booth next to his quarry got up to go, and Levin moved fast to take their place. He was protected from view by the wooden wall between the booths, but when he gave his earpiece a quarter turn he could hear what was going on perfectly. He started to work his way through the newspaper and listened attentively.

Billy Salter was talking. 'What's going on? This bird, this Mary Killane. What's the connection?'

It was Roper who intervened. 'An IRA connection from childhood. Her father was a Provo hard man. He died of cancer years ago in the Maze Prison. The mother took the girl to Dublin when she was very young.'

'You've checked out what happened to her thoroughly?'

'Charles, I could tell you the schools she went to, where she trained as a nurse. All that.'

'Have you checked whether she was a member of the IRA herself?'

'As well as I could, and she wasn't.'

'Was she a member of any political groups, anything like that?'

'As far as I can tell, which is considerable, she's not a member of any group connected to Sinn Fein, I can guarantee that.'

It was Dillon who cut in. 'She wouldn't be. Her worth would be her being in the Republic and uninvolved. Going by her age, she'd be a sleeper.'

'What in the hell is a bleeding sleeper?' Harry asked.

'The new wave, Harry. Nice, decent, professional people who work in hospitals or offices or universities, a lot of them London Irish. Born here, English accents. A perfect cover – until they're activated.'

'In a way that applies to you, Sean,' Ferguson said. 'Your father brought you here as a little boy. Your education was English.'

'True. You don't need an Irish accent to be Irish. The IRA discovered that with me a long time ago, and these days it's even more important. If you think they've given up, you're sadly mistaken.'

'So Mary Killane's task was to give Hannah Bernstein an overdose,' Ferguson said. 'But why?' There was silence. Roper said, 'As a Special Branch Officer, Hannah not only put members of the IRA away, she killed them.'

'So what are you saying?' Blake said. 'Somebody in the hierarchy waits until she's almost dying anyway before deciding to have her put down?'

'Like a dog,' Dillon's voice was almost toneless, without feeling.

Billy went to the bar and ordered more drinks. They were still sitting in silence when he returned. 'Revenge is the only thing that makes sense. Whoever it was wanted their own back. Because of the IRA connection, we're assuming it's the IRA. But could she have been doing it for somebody else?'

One of the waitresses brought the drinks. Dillon looked at his Bushmills and swallowed it down. 'Whoa, Billy. A girl like her, her whole background smacks of decency. I bet she went to Mass twice a week. And she's a nurse, she chose a caring profession. A girl like that wouldn't kill a fly normally. She would need strong persuasion to do what she did. When I was a boy, the Jesuits at school right here in London taught me an important thing. "By the small things shalt thou know them."'

It was Billy, in many ways Dillon's other self, who said, 'And the small thing here is the fact that her father was an IRA activist.'

'Who died in a British prison,' Roper said.

'A girl like her would need to believe fervently,' Dillon said. 'She'd have to believe it was the right thing to do. A girl who goes to Mass. So what would make her do such a thing? She would need to believe it was acceptable, if you like.'

'A political act, in a way?' Roper said.

Ferguson shook his head. 'An act of war.'

'Which explains why the IRA connection is so important,' Harry Salter said. 'But who would it be? Who put her up to it?'

Roper said, 'And then was reckless enough to knock her off afterwards?'

Ferguson said, 'well, the Murder Squad is working the case.'

'They'll get nowhere,' Dillon said bleakly. 'You leave this with me. I'll find the truth here, if it's the last thing I do.'

'Nothing stupid, Dillon?'

'Oh, he's always that,' Billy said.

Ferguson nodded. 'Which leads us to a bit of business. The terrible thing that's happened has left me short-handed in my department. I could ask for someone from Special Branch to replace Hannah, but I've decided not to. Billy, you've impressed me, more than you know, in the past few years. You know what it entails, you've helped out enough, killed on many occasions.'

'Now you're being nice to me. What is this?'

Ferguson took an envelope from his pocket. 'In there you will find a warrant card making you an agent of the Secret Intelligence Service in my employ, filling the gap left by Superintendent Hannah Bernstein. The photo was easy. Blame Major Roper for obtaining the more complicated information.'

Harry Salter turned to Roper. 'You conniving bastard.'

Billy said, 'Shut up.' He took out the warrant card and opened it. He turned to Dillon, then back to Ferguson. 'What is it the Yanks say? Proud to serve.'

'Excellent. Do remember one thing. When you present yourself at the Ministry of Defence, do wear one of your better suits. Dillon, of course, has his own standards. You don't need to report at nine o'clock in the morning. I intend to be present at Golders Green at ten o'clock at

Superintendent Bernstein's interment. I'm sure I'll see you there.'

Harry Salter said, 'I think you'll see us all there.' He turned to Roper. 'Don't worry about your wheelchair, old son. We've got a People Carrier thing. Takes eight. We'll go together. What about you, Dillon?'

Dillon was very pale, his eyes dark holes. 'I'll see you there. I'll make my own way.'

He went to the bar, got another drink and came back. Blake Johnson said, 'I'd join you, but I've got a plane standing by. As I said before, my instincts tell me that some of the answers to the Belov affair might be found at Drumore Place. I was thinking of dropping in at Belfast Airport on my way back, hiring a car and driving down there, an American tourist on the way through to Dublin. How does that sound?'

'Jesus,' Billy said. 'Are you sure?'

Dillon said, 'Your plane is official, booked out by the Embassy?'

'Of course.'

'Right. We took out Kelly and his boys, but that is still IRA country. I'd take a Walther PPK for your armpit and a Colt .25 with hollow-point cartridges in an ankle holster. If they find the Walther, there's a chance they'll miss the Colt.'

'That bad?'

'I've said. It's IRA country. Kelly's gone, someone comes in to fill the vacuum.'

'Shall I go with him?' Billy asked.

'Don't be silly. You'd spoil his American tourist image.

We've got things to do here anyway. I'm leaving. I'll see you in the morning.'

He turned and left, and Levin, glancing up, caught his eye. Levin went back to his newspaper. Dillon, on his way out, frowned. There was something there, but he was tired and his brain wasn't functioning as well as normal. There was a terrible pressure on him, his one thought Hannah and what had happened to her. All the violence, everything he'd done for Ferguson, the killings, the mayhem, and she had been thrown into it, and Dillon, as he walked to the Mini Cooper, was left with the inescapable feeling that it had somehow been his fault.

Behind, as the rest of the group stirred, Levin got up and left. He went back to his Mercedes, got in and phoned Ashimov.

'Have I got news for you.'

Ashimov was sitting after dinner beside the open fire in the Great Hall of Drumore Place with Greta and Liam Bell. 'Tell me,' he said, and listened. After a while, he said, 'Excellent. You stay on in London and keep a close eye on Dillon. Leave Blake Johnson to me.'

He switched off, turned to Bell and Greta and said, 'We're going to have an interesting visitor. One of President Jake Cazalet's most trusted associates.'

'What's he coming for?' Greta asked.

'To find out what's happened here since Kelly and the rest of us faded from the scene.'

He told her what Levin had heard. 'He's good – damn good, but so is Blake Johnson. I'll pull his photo out of the computer for you,' he told Bell. 'A war hero in Vietnam, then the FBI, now the President's most trusted security man.'

'We'll give him a warm welcome,' Bell said.

Greta put in, 'If he sniffs around and finds nothing, wouldn't that be better?'

'Possibly.' But Ashimov's eyes were glittering. 'All right, we've seen off Bernstein, but what a coup to get Johnson. That would really hurt Cazalet, hurt all of them.' He turned to Bell. 'We'll make a decision when he turns up tomorrow.'

'I'm your man,' Bell said, and finished his drink.

IRELAND

LONDON

5

For Blake, it started early the following morning. His first stop was the American Embassy in Grosvenor Square to call on the Ambassador, as a matter of protocol.

The Ambassador was all cordiality. 'I appreciate we haven't been able to do much for you this time, Blake. It's a matter of security, I understand.'

'Absolutely,' Blake told him. 'A matter under Presidential warrant.'

'With you, that usually means dealings with Charles Ferguson. I notice your Gulfstream is using Farley Field, that small RAF base Ferguson uses for his special operations.'

'That's right.'

'Enough said. My transport people tell me you have a stop-over in Belfast.'

'A visit to make. I'll only be on the ground a few hours.'

'Blake, we first knew each other in Saigon thirty-five years ago. I know what kind of visit you make.' He came round the desk and embraced Blake warmly. 'God bless, my friend, and take care. My regards to the President.'

An Embassy Mercedes and a chauffeur took him from there to the chapel in a very short space of time. It stood on the edge of the cemetery and there were a number of limousines parked outside, drivers in uniform standing around. A large notice at the door said 'Private Bereavement'. Blake went in and found a modest company assembled. Rabbi Bernstein was being helped by another rabbi who was wearing black ribbons and handing them out to people who were obviously family members up at the front, who pinned them to their clothes. The coffin was very plain, in accordance with Jewish custom, and closed.

Ferguson, the Salters and Roper stood at the back of the pews, Dillon slightly apart, though Billy Salter stood close to him. They both wore black suits and ties and crisp white shirts, and looked like the Devil's henchmen. In a strange way it was as if they were brothers, faces bone white, skin stretching taut over cheekbones.

A eulogy was made. The other rabbi whispered to Bernstein, who made a hand motion. He said to the assembly, 'My grief speaks for itself that my beloved granddaughter is taken too early. There is one person who knows her worth more than most.' Billy turned to look at Dillon, but Bernstein carried on, 'Major General Charles Ferguson, for whom she worked, on secondment from Special Branch, for a number of years.'

Ferguson walked down the aisle and joined the two rabbis. 'What can I say about this truly remarkable and gifted human being? A scholar of Oxford University who chose the life of a police officer, who placed her life at risk, who was wounded more than once, who rose to the rank of Detective Superintendent in Special Branch – these are extraordinary achievements.'

Dillon took a step back, Blake was aware of that. Ferguson turned to Bernstein and said, 'Rabbi, excuse me if I pre-empt your role, but I must quote, with your permission, from Proverbs.'

'With my permission and my blessing,' Julian Bernstein told him.

In a strong voice, Ferguson said, 'A woman of worth, who can find? For her price is far above rubies.'

Dillon took a huge, choking breath, stepped even further back, turned and went out, and Billy went after him.

Dillon was standing by the Mini Cooper. It had started to rain. He took a trench-coat out and pulled it on. Billy waved to Joe Baxter and Sam Hall, who were standing by the People Carrier, and Hall produced a large black umbrella and hurried over, opening it. Dillon lit a cigarette, hands shaking.

Billy held the umbrella over him and said to Baxter, 'Get the flask out.' Baxter did and Billy said, 'Bushmills. Get it down.' Dillon stared at him vacantly. 'She'd expect you to.'

Dillon swallowed. He paused, then had another swallow. He shook his head, face flushed. 'Tell me, Billy, why does it always rain at funerals?'

'I'd say it's because the script demands it. It's life imitating art. You want another one?'

'Maybe just one.'

At that moment, Igor Levin arrived late. He parked and went forward to the entrance, glanced briefly at Dillon, then went on. There was something more, Dillon was aware of that, but his emotion was too great. He drank a little more Bushmills and returned the flask to Joe Baxter, and a moment later people emerged from the chapel.

There was a family plot, the open grave ready. People huddled round, a festoon of umbrellas against the rain. Dillon and Billy stood at the rear, Ferguson and company on the other side, Levin hidden among a group of friends, the umbrellas concealing everything.

As the coffin was lowered, the other rabbi put an arm around Julian Bernstein and said in a loud voice, 'May she come to her place in peace.'

Dillon turned to Billy. 'I'm out of it. The rest is for family. The Kaddish, the prayer for the dead, I've no business with it. I'm not sure if I was even a friend.'

'Come off it, Dillon. She thought the world of you.'

'Not really, Billy. I brought her too much grief. I can't get that out of my head. I dragged her into one lousy job after another.'

'No place she did not willingly go, Dillon.'

'So why do I feel so bloody guilty?' He got in the Mini Cooper. 'I'll be in touch, Billy.'

Blake Johnson hurried over and leaned down, 'Sean, are you okay?'

'See you, Blake. Take care in bandit country.'

He drove away. Blake said, 'What do you think?'

'A volcano waiting to explode.'

'I thought so. Anyway, I have to go now.'

'Take care in Ireland.'

'I will.'

Blake went to his limousine and was driven away. Levin, standing near by, anonymous in the umbrella-ed crowd, had heard the exchange between Blake and Billy. Now he returned to his Mercedes and phoned Ashimov, telling him of events at the funeral.

'So he's on his way?' Ashimov asked.

'So it seems.'

'Well, we've passed a computer print-out of his photo to the lads. I think he's assured of a warm welcome.'

'You're in charge,' Levin said.

Actually, the smart thing, he thought, would be to allow Blake Johnson to nose around a little, accept his pose as an American tourist and then send him on his way. On the other hand, he'd already learned not to expect the smart thing from the IRA, and Ashimov was beginning to worry him. He was proving far too emotional. But then that wasn't his business, he just took orders, and he drove away.

*   *   *

At Farley Field, Blake found his Gulfstream waiting, two American Air Force pilots standing by in flying overalls.

'Any problems?' Blake asked.

'None, sir. Good weather for Belfast.'

'Not raining?'

'Hell, it always rains in Belfast, sir.'

'I don't know how long I'll be. We'll see. You must excuse me for a minute. I have to go see someone.'

By arrangement with Ferguson, he had an appointment in the operations room with the Quartermaster, an ex-Guards sergeant-major. The man had the weaponry waiting as Dillon had suggested, a Walther in a shoulder holster and a .25 Colt, a snub nose with a silencer.

'Like you asked, sir, hollow point and the ankle holster you ordered. Will you be all right with this lot in Belfast, sir?'

'Diplomatic immunity, Sergeant-Major.'

'I was wondering about the shoulder holster, sir. Is that wise?'

'Yes, if things go that way with the people I'm dealing with, they'll think they've disarmed me, only I'll still have the ankle holster.'

'If your luck is good, sir.'

'Oh, it always is, Sergeant-Major.'

He went out to the Gulfstream, where he found a stewardess, a young sergeant named Mary, who was there to cater to his needs onwards to Washington. They took off and climbed to 30,000 feet and she came and offered him refreshment.

All he had was a brandy and ginger ale. Funny, as he sipped it he remembered the British Navy Commander who'd introduced him to it in Saigon back in good old Vietnam all those years ago. Of course the Brits weren't supposed to be there, but their Navy, with Borneo experience, had offered considerable expertise for American swift boats in the Mekong Delta. To the Royal Navy, this drink had been a Horse's Neck since time immemorial, and Blake, especially when confronted with stress, loved that mixture of brandy, ice and ginger ale beyond most things. It was the kind of thing that made life worth living. He savoured every drop and thought of the present situation, which inevitably brought him back to his dear friend Sean Dillon. So many things they'd accomplished together. In various ways, Dillon had been part of saving two American Presidents from an untimely end, and in the affair with President Clinton and Prime Minister Major he'd taken wounds that had come close to ending his life.

But he was still here. It was Hannah Bernstein who had gone, and Blake, surprised at his own emotion, waved to Mary and ordered another brandy and ginger ale. It was one too many, but this was Ireland after all.

So what awaited him in Ballykelly and Drumore? To his surprise he found that he didn't really care. He'd survived Vietnam, the curse of most of his generation, and had medals to prove it. He'd survived the worst the FBI could offer, had taken a bullet to save his President's life, had survived even worse things since.

'What can these IRA clowns do to me?' He finished his

Horse's Neck, opened his briefcase and took out a small miracle of modern technology which clipped low down behind the belt. A back up if his mobile phone went which it well might.

'To hell with the IRA. Time to move on,' he said. 'What will be, will be.'

The Gulfstream descended, landed and taxied all the way round to the Special Affairs arrivals. Mary opened the door and he got up.

'Okay, son, let's get it done,' he breathed.

It was what his old unit commander used to say in Vietnam. It was amazing how everything that ever touched you in your life stayed with you until the end.

'See you later, Mary,' he said, and went down the Airstair door.

His Air Force pilots were right. It was raining as he drove out of the airport in a BMW. He'd already tasted the difference in the way people spoke. He'd certainly experienced an Irish accent on many occasions, but the Northern Irish one was totally different. He switched on his routefinder and punched in his destination. The details of where to go and how flowed through, and he followed them.

And what a wonderful and beautiful place it was, he thought, as he drove through the mountains and then crossed the border into the Irish Republic and followed the coast road into County Louth towards Drumore.

An hour and a half later he came to Ballykelly, rain driving in, came to the development and airstrip with a huge sign saying 'Belov International'. He paused by the main entrance, got out and looked. A man in a security uniform came out of the gate hut and walked across.

'Can I help you?'

Blake said, 'No, I'm driving down to Dublin from Belfast. I was surprised to see "Belov International". I didn't know they were in Ireland. Back home in Texas they're huge. Is Drumore down the road?'

'It is, sir. Eight or ten minutes.'

Blake nodded and drove away. The security guard went back to his hut and phoned Liam Bell.

'The American's just been here. He's on his way to Drumore now.'

'Good man.' Bell switched off his mobile and turned to Ashimov and Greta as they stood outside Drumore Place. 'He's here. What do you want to do?'

Ashimov glanced at Greta. He was very worked up. 'All right, let's see how he behaves.'

Greta said, 'Yuri, let him nose around and then go. There's no you, no me, and Josef Belov is supposedly a couple of thousand miles away. He'll find nothing and do no harm.'

'You don't see it, Greta. This is one of our prime targets, the American President's right-hand man.'

'If he dies here, it will send a message,' she said.

Ashimov appeared to struggle with himself. 'All right.' He turned to Bell. 'We'll just go and observe him. Greta and I will stay out of the way, see what happens. But if he says or does anything suspicious, take care of it.'

'Good man yourself,' Bell said. 'Leave it to me.'

Blake came down in the BMW and there was Drumore Place up on the hill and the village below, the small port, no more than half a dozen fishing boats, perhaps thirty cottages and houses, the pub, the Royal George, a fine view out to sea and a strong coastline. Blake took the car down, went through the main street, and ended up in the car park in front of the Royal George.

He got out of his BMW and went towards the low wall and looked down at the harbour. Behind, up on the hillside in the copse, Ashimov and Greta were watching. He passed her the glasses.

'It's him.' She looked and Bell came forward. 'So, what do you want?'

'Let's see what he does.'

Below, Blake went towards the Royal George. There was a strangeness to the village, he'd noticed that, a lack of people, which said a great deal. He opened the door and went in.

Patrick Ryan was behind the bar, and over by the window two of Bell's men, Casey and Magee, sat in a window table enjoying Irish stew. Blake went to the bar and Ryan said, 'And what can I do for you, sir?'

'I'm passing through on my way to Dublin.' Blake accentuated his American accent. 'Lovely harbour. Thought I could have some lunch.'

'Indeed you can, sir.'

Blake turned and glanced at Casey and Magee. 'Maybe I'll have what those guys are having, and a beer to go with it.'

Ryan gave him that, returned from the kitchen and said, 'It's on its way, sir.'

Blake said, 'You know, I'm from Texas and one of our biggest firms is Belov International. I was amazed, when I passed through Ballykelly, up the road, to see they have a branch there.'

A girl came through with his stew and put it on a nearby table. Blake said down and Ryan said, 'A grand man, Mr Belov, done wonders for the community, the village.'

Blake said brightly, 'Oh, he comes here, does he?'

'Owns the big house, Drumore Place. We see him now and then, but he goes around the world, if you see what I mean. Was here recently, but I believe he's in Russia at the moment.'

Blake was already working his way through the Irish stew. He was aware of the two men by the window, lighting up cigarettes, sitting there, staring at him. It occurred to him that he could be in trouble here. He wolfed down the stew, finished his beer and went to the bar.

'What do I owe you?'

Ryan said, 'Have it on the house, sir. We don't get many tourists this time of the year. You're our first.'

'Well, that's damn nice of you,' Blake said and went out.

When he went to the BMW and got into it, however, his keys were missing. When he got out, Casey and Magee were standing there.

Up on the hill, Ashimov and Greta each watched through binoculars and Bell stood by.

Casey said to Blake, 'What a pity, but that's life.' He moved behind him and Magee took a Browning out of his waistband.

'You've made a mistake, my friend.'

Casey reached inside Blake's jacket and removed the Walther. 'Well, would you look at that? I'm amazed a tourist would get through security with that.' He put it in his pocket.

'Oh, it happens,' Blake said.

'Yes, well, you just come with us and we'll show you the grand place Drumore is. Mr Bell's orders.'

Casey pushed him along and Blake went, Magee in the rear, all the way down to the tiny harbour and those few fishing boats, and not a soul in the place.

They went along the wharf and pushed Blake down to the deck of a fishing boat. Casey followed him, Magee cast off, went in the wheelhouse and turned the engine on and moved through the harbour, turning at the end of the point. Casey presented the Browning and Blake sat down in the stern, took the .25 Colt from the ankle holster and shot Casey between the eyes. He went backwards, the Browning flying from one hand and over the rail into the water.

The boat swerved, Magee killed the engine and came to the entrance of the wheelhouse. Blake shot him in the right thigh, knocking him over.

He leaned down. 'I've been good to you. I could have killed you. Instead I've crippled you. I'm sure your IRA chums will see to you when I've gone.' He reached in Magee's jacket and found an old Smith & Wesson .38. 'I'll see you in hell, son.'

The boat had bounced back against the wharf. He went over the rail and up to the pub, a gun in each hand, and high on the hill Greta said, 'You got it wrong, Yuri, and you, Liam.'

At the Royal George Blake burst in the front door and discovered Ryan turning from the bar. 'Hold it right there. My keys. I'd say you're the most likely to have them.'

He held up the weapons like a gunfighter, and Ryan was terrified. 'All right, I've got them.'

He handed them over and Blake said, 'So, Belov's in Russia and you've got a new boss since Mr Kelly passed on, a Mr Bell.' He smiled, on a high. 'I've got a friend named Sean Dillon. He says he has an excellent remedy for people like you.' He rammed the Colt .25 against Ryan's left ear and fired. Ryan cried out and went down.

'You're lucky, you bastard,' Blake said. 'You're still alive.'

He left Ryan writhing on the floor, went out, got in the BMW and drove off.

On the hill, Greta lowered her binoculars. 'Well, I don't know what we're going to find inside the Royal George, but I'd say the whole thing has been a monumental cock-up.'

On his way back over the Atlantic, Blake called Ferguson and went over the experience.

'My God, you've been in the wars,' Ferguson told him. 'You say one of the men mentioned someone called Bell as being in charge?'

'That's it. See if that strikes a chord with Dillon, and I'd give it to Roper as well. He usually comes up with someone.'

'I'll see to it. Safe journey, Blake. Regards to the President.'

Blake switched off and leaned back. He felt great. Mary said, 'Can I get you anything, sir?'

'Actually, you can, Mary.' He smiled. 'You can get me a Horse's Neck.'

The carnage in the village was immediately apparent. Greta, Ashimov and Bell stood on the wharf while two of his men assisted Magee over the rail of the boat and into a Land Rover.

'Shall we pick up Pat Ryan at the pub as well? He's lost half an ear, Mr Bell.'

'What else would you do with him? Take them to the convent at Ballykelly. They're in safe hands with Sister Teresa.'

The men drove away. Beyond, by the harbour entrance, the body of Jack Casey floated up and was swept out to sea.

'What happens to him?' Greta said.

'This is my patch,' Bell said. 'Everybody keeps their head down, nobody sees a thing. None of this happened. As for Casey, just on the other side of the jetty where the body's drifting now there's a ten knot bore running because the tide's turning. It'll take Casey out into the Irish Sea fast, food for fishes.'

'Really? How interesting.'

She left him talking to Ashimov and walked back to the pub and onwards to Drumore Place. She went into the Great

Hall, got herself a vodka, went and stood by the fire thinking about it, then phoned Levin who was in the Piano Bar at the Dorchester, having a late lunch.

'Why, Greta, darling girl.'

'None of that nonsense. Blake Johnson arrived at Drumore, posing as an American tourist. Igor, he's so old he was in Vietnam. He's fifty-five at least. He should have been in his box by now.'

'You know my mother was English, but her mother was Irish. And whenever there was bad news, that old Irish lady would say to me, it was as certain as the coffin lid closing.'

'Well the coffin lid's closed tight.'

'Really?' He was laughing. 'Tell me the worst.'

When she was finished, he said, 'So he sends one corpse drifting out to sea, cripples another and disposes of half the ear of Ryan, the publican at the Royal George?'

'There's more to it than that. Ryan said that when threatening him Blake Johnson mentioned Bell having taken over from Kelly. He also mentioned his friend, Sean Dillon.'

'Oh dear. What's happening to the walking wounded?'

'Taken to the convent hospital at Ballykelly. The Little Sisters of Pity. They'll keep quiet enough.'

'I should hope so.'

'Ashimov should have let Johnson nose around, have lunch and move on.'

'Well, he didn't. He's on a holy crusade to get the lot of them, and the chance of stiffing Blake Johnson was too good to miss.'

'What happens now?'

'I should imagine Blake has already phoned Ferguson, who will ask Dillon and the good Major Roper if the name Bell means anything to them in connection with the IRA.'

'It's a mess,' she said.

'It's a can of worms, my love. However, I'll handle it. I'll phone Volkov in Moscow, give him the bad news and cover your back as well as my own. But that's only because I like you.'

She thought about it only for a second. He had something about him, this young man, she recognized that and took it on board.

'Right, we'll see how it goes.'

'As far as Yuri's concerned, if anyone gets blamed for it all coming out, it's me not you, so keep your mouth shut.'

'Fine,' she said. 'I'll leave it to you.'

She switched off, went and got another vodka, and Ashimov stamped in. 'What a mess!'

'It was certainly that, Yuri.'

He went and poured himself a drink. 'I had him in my hand, Blake Johnson, the President's man, the ultimate coup.'

'It would have been a greater coup to allow him to pass through empty-handed,' she said. 'I told you. But you just had to give Bell the wink, didn't you? Sometimes, Yuri – I just don't know,' and she walked out.

In London, at the Ministry of Defence, Ferguson listened to Blake, then called Dillon and Billy into his office. He gave them an account of what Blake had told him.

'Bloody marvellous,' Billy said. 'That's put the bastards in their place. What do you think, Dillon?'

'So there's a new bunch in power from the Provisional IRA. And some guy told Blake that Mr Belov was in Russia. Where does that get us?'

'Maybe if we traced that Bell person they mentioned. Does the name mean anything to you?'

Ferguson shook his head. 'I'll give it to Roper. He might find something.'

'What about the murder inquiry?' asked Dillon.

'Still proceeding, Sean.'

'Then maybe I should have a look myself.'

'I'd really rather you didn't.'

Dillon shrugged. 'I'll get on then.'

Outside, he paused at his desk, only for a moment. Billy said, 'What are you going to do?'

'What do you think? I'll see you later,' and he went out.

'Wait for me, Dillon,' Billy called and went after him.

On the phone to Volkov, Levin explained everything that had happened. He waited while Volkov considered the matter. Finally, he said, 'I agree with you, Igor. Major Ashimov has been foolish in this matter. Dillon is far from being an idiot. He's probably already made the link between the nurse and the IRA. Now this thing at Drumore. With Roper's assistance, Dillon may hunt down the Bell connection sooner than you think.'

'What should I do?' Levin asked.

'Watch them all carefully, Igor. One day soon we'll need to make hard decisions, and we'll need to know what – and who – our liabilities are.

Levin went back to the Dorchester, but instead of going up to his suite he went into the Piano Bar. It was half busy, cheerful and sophisticated as usual. He sat on one of the banquettes, ordered a glass of champagne and glanced at the newspaper. At that moment, Dillon and Billy walked in.

The bar manager, Guiliano, approached. 'Mr Dillon, a pleasure. What can I do for you?'

'I'll have the usual, and the boy here orange juice. And if you don't mind it, I'll give you a tune on Liberace's grand piano there, before your usual pianist comes in.'

'It'd be a pleasure,' Guiliano said.

Levin slipped on his earpiece. He could hear them perfectly. 'So what's new?'

'I'm leaving it to Roper for the time being. Let's see if this Bell thing hangs together. If anybody can find the answer, it's Roper.'

'Oh, dear,' Igor murmured, as Dillon walked down to the piano, opened it and started to play. 'We can't have that.'

As he got up, Dillon seemed to look across at him. Levin smiled and called, in his finest public school voice, '"As Time Goes By" old man. Never fails.'

He walked out and went upstairs. Billy went to the piano. 'Who was that?'

'God knows,' Dillon said. 'I think I've seen him somewhere before, but for the life of me I can't remember where. Good idea on the music though,' and he started to play the tune.

Upstairs in his suite, Igor opened the file he'd received in Moscow, found a number and rang it. When there was an answer, he said, 'George Moon?'

'That's right.'

'The midnight bell is ringing.'

Moon said, 'That's fine by me.' Silly buggers, all this code stuff, he thought.

'I'll see you in half an hour at the Harvest Moon pub in Trenchard Street. I'll recognize you. Be alone.'

'Fine by me. Side entrance. There's a light like a moon over the door. A moon for Moon – fitting, right?'

6

He checked his briefcase, the Walther with the silencer. In the room safe in the wardrobe of the suite he had £5,000 in mad money. He took out £2,000 in fifties, stowed them in the briefcase, put on his trench-coat and left.

He took his Mercedes, drove in the general direction of Soho, and beyond Brewer Street he finally came to the pub in Trenchard Street, an old Victorian sort of place. He parked some distance away and walked through the rain, not bothering with the umbrella.

The light over the door in the side alley had the shape of a half moon on it, sure enough. Levin glanced up, then pressed the bell. After a moment the door opened and a rather tarty young woman appeared.

'I've an appointment with Mr Moon.'

'So what's your name?'

'Mr Nobody to you, sweetheart. Just lead the way.'

'All right, keep your shirt on.' She was quite attractive in her own way, a cotton skirt tightening over her buttocks, high-heeled ankle boots on her feet.

She turned at the top of the stairs and paused to open a door. 'Had a good look, did you?'

'Definitely. Not to be missed.'

'Cheeky bastard.'

'Most men are.'

She smiled in spite of herself. 'You like having the last word, don't you? In here.'

She opened a door and ushered him into a room lined with books like a small library. There was a large desk with a lamp, the light low, and the man seated there was small, balding, wearing steel spectacles. He nodded to Levin, and held out a limp hand without getting up. Behind him a man leaned against the wall, hard, brutal, with the flattened nose of an ex-boxer, and arms folded.

'I'm George Moon. No need to say who you are. I know your principals and that's sufficient. Cup of tea for me, Ruby, although considering this gentlemen's antecedents I expect he'd prefer a large vodka.'

'Yes, oh great one.'

She went out. Levin said, 'A lot of character there.'

'A lot of everything. A very naughty girl. Harold?'

The man behind him moved close enough to smell, and it was not good. Ruby opened the door and said, 'Tea's brewing, George.' She had a bar tray, a bottle of vodka on it and a glass.

Harold said, 'All right, china, arms wide.' His hands went for a body search. Levin said, 'Now who's being naughty? I don't like that, Harold.' His right hand came out of his pocket clutching the Walther and he rammed it under Harold's chin. 'Now go back to propping up the wall like a good boy, or I'll castrate you.'

Harold, in shock, eased away. 'Do as the gentleman says, Harold.' That was Moon.

Igor turned to Ruby, who was smiling. She said, 'My God, a right hard bastard. Who'd have thought it? Ready for your vodka then?'

'Why not?' She poured a large one and he drank it down. 'Fabulous. I'll have another.'

He held the glass out and placed the Walther on the desk as if daring Harold, who glowered at him.

'So what can we do for you?'

Levin opened his briefcase and took out the money it contained in two packets.

'It's simple enough. A man lives in Regency Square, in a wheelchair most of the time, a Major Roper. I want him seen to.'

'Permanently?'

'That would be the best solution. After all, anything could happen to somebody like that. He could end up dead in his wheelchair, the victim of an opportunistic burglar. There's two thousand here, if you accept the assignment, and another two on completion. Just one thing.'

'And what would that be?'

'You do it now – tonight.'

There was silence for a moment. Harold said, 'Regency Square's only twenty minutes away.'

'That's true,' Moon nodded. 'As I know your principals,' he said to Levin, 'I presume this is a political matter?'

'None of your affair.'

Moon nodded and turned to Ruby. 'You'll keep an eye on those bastards behind the bar. You never know what they'll get up to.' He handed her the £2,000. 'Look after that, love.'

'You're going yourself, George?'

'Why not? I'll keep an eye on Harold. Find a raincoat for me and an umbrella.'

'Yes, George.'

Levin took a computer print-out from his briefcase, with a photo of Roper on it and his address. Moon picked it up and checked it, then handed it to Harold, who looked and shrugged.

'Piece of cake.'

Moon said to Levin, 'You coming, or are you just watching from afar?'

'I'll see you after your successful completion, or let's hope I do.'

'That will be entirely satisfactory.'

'So you trust me not to vanish into the night?'

'Oh, absolutely. I've dealt with your people on many occasions. Whey would they let me down? There's always a next time. I'm well aware how powerful they are.'

'I'll see you later then.' Levin turned to Ruby. 'And you.'

'God, but you're a cold-blooded bastard.'

'It's been said before.' He grinned, brushed past her, went down the stairs and back to his Mercedes, got in and drove away. He made it to Regency Square. There was plenty of parking space at that time of the evening. He found one very close to Roper's place, pulled in, switched on the radio and sat there listening to it and waiting.

Roper, busy at his computers, had had enough, and his stomach told him as much. There was an Italian on the corner of the square by the main road. They always did well by him and his wheelchair. He pulled on his reefer coat and a cap in the hall and went out into the rain.

Levin saw him at once, and so did Moon and Harold, who'd just arrived and parked at the side of the square.

'How convenient,' Moon said.

'How do we do it?' Harold asked.

Moon nodded down to the main road. 'I always prefer to keep it simple. It looks nice and busy down there. We push him along the pavement and simply let go. He's bound to run in front of a truck or something.'

They got out of their car, Moon put up his umbrella and they crossed the road as Levin watched. He had an insane desire to laugh. Did those cretins really think it was going to be that easy?

'Dear God almighty,' he murmured.

Harold had a hand on one side of Roper's wheelchair now, Moon on the other. 'Be a nice gentleman now,' Moon said, 'and you'll come to no harm.'

'Come to no good, you mean,' Roper said. He eyed the two of them. 'I've been here before. Last time it was the Mafia. What's your religion?'

'I wouldn't dream of telling you, love.'

'Ah. Well, then we can't do business, I'm afraid,' Roper said. Then he took a silenced Walther from the right-hand pocket of his wheelchair and shot Harold through the side of his knee.

He went down with a curse and Moon said, 'Oh, my God.'

Roper grabbed him by the coat. 'What's your name? Come on, quick, or I'll give it to you too.'

Moon was in such a panic, he told him. 'Moon – George Moon.'

'Who sent you?'

'I don't know. I hadn't seen him before in my life.'

He pulled away, turned to run, and Roper shot him in the right thigh. He hit the pavement, writhing. Roper said, 'Remember this – somebody tried to mug you and it went wrong. That would be a good line if you wanted to stay out of court when the police come.'

'Yes,' Moon babbled. 'Yes.'

Roper went down the square, taking out his mobile and dialling 999. 'Ambulance needed in Regency Square. Two men down. Looks like a shooting.' The operator asked for his name, he switched off and called Dillon.

'Sean, I've had a spot of bother.' He explained what had happened. 'I'll wait for you in the Italian restaurant at the end of the square.'

'I'll call Billy and we'll be with you soon, and I'll notify

Ferguson. I don't like the sound of this. First Hannah, now you. I think you'd be better off in the Holland Park safe-house.'

Ruby was upstairs at the Harvest Moon when the bell sounded at the alley door. She went down, opened it and Levin smiled at her.

'We need to talk.' He moved in and followed her upstairs.

She led the way into Moon's office and turned, 'What is this?'

'Moon and Harold made a big mistake. You'll be hearing from them quite soon. They are, as we speak, seeking treatment in the accident and emergency department of some third-rate National Health hospital.'

'I've just heard. Had a phone call from the hospital. It said they'd been mugged by a black street gang. Is it bad?'

'Gunshot wounds to the legs, and so richly deserved, just like the IRA. I've never seen such incompetents. The story about being mugged does two things. It keeps them out of court and it doesn't involve the people I work for. If it did, George and Harold would be dead in the near future, one way or the other.'

'So what do you want here?'

'Two thousand, Ruby?'

'You've got a cheek.'

'It's the principle of the thing. I'll do you a favour. Give me a thousand and you can tell Moon I came back and took it all. A thousand for you.'

She thought about it, then went and unlocked a cabinet at the end of a bookcase, took out a packet of banknotes and tossed it to him.

'He's my husband, you know.'

'Then I'm sorry for you.'

'It's not as bad as you think. He swings the other way.' She smiled. 'I'd get out of here if I were you. I'll be getting callers.'

He turned to the door, turned again and tossed the thousand pounds on the desk. 'Oh, what the hell. Tell him I took the lot,' and he went downstairs and moved back along the alley to his limousine.

Dillon and Billy arrived with a People Carrier, loaded Roper inside and a number of personal effects he needed, and took him to the Holland Park safehouse. This had happened before in times of stress. Because of this, Ferguson had had all the right computers and technical equipment installed to suit Roper's special needs.

So Roper was settled in and the Military Police sergeant on duty, Doyle, said, 'General Ferguson will be along soon, Mr Dillon. There's a message from Special Branch. It seems George Moon and Harold Parker insist they were mugged by two men at pistol point and they can't identify them because it was dark, it was raining and they were black.'

'Black, my arse,' Billy said. 'I've known Moon for years. He's a slimy toad. There's more to this, Dillon.'

'So let's go and find out what it is. We'll be back later,' he said to Roper and went out.

At St Michael's, Dillon and Billy found Moon and Harold under sedation and awaiting surgery. Billy flashed his new warrant card from Ferguson and forced his way in. It was amazing how powerful it made him feel. Moon and Harold were waiting in a side ward, both sedated.

'It's me, George, Billy Salter.'

'What in the hell do you want?'

'Mr Dillon here and I are working for the Intelligence Service.'

'Fuck off, Billy. They wouldn't employ a thief like you.'

'Now you're upsetting me, George. No big black's shooting you and Harold.'

'Well, the police are happy. That takes care of it.'

'Unfortunately, the guy who stiffed you, George, the guy you were trying to do away with, is a very good friend of ours, so we know what you were up to. Who put you up to it?'

'I'll say one thing for old times' sake, Billy. They could snuff you out like a match, swallow you whole. Now, Harold and me was mugged by two big black men. They had Cockney accents so they must have been born here.' He raised his voice. 'Nurse, I feel terrible.'

Billy said, 'You deserve to, you toad. I'll pay you back.' He nodded to Dillon. 'Let's go.'

*   *   *

Of course, it was another failure he had to report, whichever way you looked at it. In the GRU files there was quite a list of IRA people like Moon available for employment. It occurred to Levin that reliability was not their strongest feature. The whole affair had been farcical, but it would still look like a failure to Ashimov, never mind Volkov.

The truth was, you could never rely on anybody but your-self, so he drove to Hangman's Wharf and parked close to the Dark Man, but not for any particular reason. Just thinking about it. There was the Bentley parked there, Harry Salter's pride and joy, according to his file, and as Levin watched, Joe Baxter came out of the pub, unlocked the door, rummaged around then went back into the Dark Man. The thing was, he didn't bother to re-lock the door.

It was a wild card, crazy, but he might get away with it. He opened the glove compartment, found the mini tool kit, opened it and selected a pair of wire cutters. He moved fast, darting along the pavement, opening the door, reaching inside, releasing the catch to the bonnet. It sprang open, he went round, raised it and went to work, slicing at cables, brake fluid already spurting out. The bonnet went down with a thump, he turned and went back to his Mercedes. There was no point in waiting, it could take forever, but then, as he reached for the key, Harry Salter appeared with Joe Baxter and got into the Bentley. Baxter was driving and switched on. The engine roared. He moved away, tried to turn the Bentley. It glided back and bumped against another car. There was the sound of the engine revving again as it moved away and he obviously tried to brake. The Bentley proceeded at speed towards the edge of the wharf, ready to go straight into the Thames. At the last moment it skidded, bounced off a bollard and ended up with the front wheels over the edge of the wharf.

Baxter and Salter managed to extricate themselves, there was much shouting, people poured out of the pub, and Levin drove away laughing. Salter and Baxter should have been choking to death, drowning at the bottom of the Thames. It was unbelievable what had happened. Life was just a farce after all, a comedy, a dark one, but still a comedy.

At the Harvest Moon Ruby answered the bell at the side door and found Billy Salter, Dillon behind him.

'What do you want, you sod?'

'And I always thought you liked me, Ruby. Just a word. Me and my friend, Mr Dillon, would appreciate that. You see, we've been to St Michael's, and George and Harold have told the police they were mugged, a racial attack in reverse. They've got nothing else to say.'

'So what's the problem?'

'Well, you see we know who shot them, a friend of ours who was actually attacked by George and Harold in his wheel-chair. The thing is, he was armed, Ruby, he's that kind of man.'

'So?' She still stood there, holding the door.

'George is a hit man, that's what he's done for a living for years.'

'So what we'd like to know is who paid him,' Dillon told her.

'I don't have any idea who he was,' and she flinched, aware that she'd been caught out.

'Come on, Ruby, I've got a warrant here. We could take you in.'

'Okay, a guy came, spoke to George. No names, no pack drill, George said. He knew the man's principals and they were frightening people. I mean, he'd obviously worked for them before.'

'But he didn't know the man?' Dillon asked.

'No. There was one funny thing, though.'

'What was that?'

'When I was told to get him a drink, George said that considering the gentleman's antecedents he'd probably prefer a vodka.'

'So he was Russian?' Dillon said.

'No, a real gent. Drop-dead good looking, public school voice. He was back here a little while ago. Told me what had happened, but I'd already had the police on.'

'Why did he come back?'

'His money. Two grand. Took the lot,' she lied.

They were still standing in the hallway. Billy glanced up and saw a security camera. 'That appears to be on.'

'It is.'

He reached up, switched it off and removed the tape. 'Upstairs, Ruby. We'll have a quick look on your TV.'

Levin was there, of course, his one mistake, his face quite clear. 'We'll keep this,' Billy told Ruby. 'You say quiet and we'll stay quiet, okay?'

'Men.' She shook her head. 'Piss off, Billy.'

Driving away, Dillon said, 'There's something about our man. It's as if I know him.'

'Not me,' Billy said. 'But the Russian link is cool.'

Dillon's mobile rang, he answered it, then switched off and turned. 'That was Ferguson. He's at the Holland Park safehouse with Roper, and now your uncle.'

'Harry? What in Christ for?'

'Somebody cut the brakes on the Bentley. He and Joe Baxter ended up hanging over the edge of the wharf. It's a miracle they survived.'

'This is beginning to stink, big time,' Billy said.

'You don't have to tell me. Just get us there.'

At the safehouse they were all assembled. It was a bad business all round. They'd just run the tape through and found Levin entering the Harvest Moon. They established that he didn't mean a thing to anyone.

'So where are we?' Dillon asked.

'This is a serious situation,' Ferguson said. 'The death of Superintendent Bernstein, followed by what happened to Blake in Drumore and now the attacks on Major Roper and Harry Salter.' He shook his head. 'Billy could have been with you, Harry. It could have been both of you.'

'Just wait till I get my hands on them,' Salter said. 'Just wait.'

There was silence. Dillon lit a cigarette. 'Well, I'd say it's more than a coincidence that four members of the Prime

Minister's private army have been targeted, Charles. That only leaves you and me. Blake was extra.'

'Exactly, so the sooner we discover the identity of the gentleman on the security tape, the better.'

Dillon said, 'Show me a picture of him on your computer.'

'Happy to oblige. There is one thing I wanted to run by you. The name, Bell. I've come across one. A Liam Bell, once Chief of Staff to the PIRA, in the Maze Prison for some years. Retired some time ago. Lives in Dublin.'

'The schoolteacher?' Dillon said. 'That's what they used to call him. He was retired years ago. I thought he was dead.'

Dillon thought about it some more and said to Ferguson, 'If Roper can give Billy the details on Bell, you could send him over in the plane from Farley Field tomorrow. See if he's around. Is that OK with you, Billy?'

'Sure, but what about you?'

'Things I'd like to check out here. Is that all right, Charles?'

'I'll make the arrangements.'

Miles away in Siberia, in his suite in a hotel on the Station Gorky development, surrounded by snow, Max Zubin spoke to his mother, Bella, in Moscow. She was as vivacious as usual, slightly loud.

'What are they doing to you?'

'Not much. Shaved my beard.'

'I bet you look ten years younger.'

'What about you?'

'They treat me well. I have a big black car with a driver.

He hangs around downstairs. I can go anywhere. The supermarket, the theatre, the Bolshoi.'

'Well, you couldn't exactly run away. They've got me.'

'And they've got me, too, so you can't run away. What's going to happen, Max?'

'I don't know. Volkov spoke to me yesterday. He said I might have to turn up in Moscow again and play my part.'

'Well, whatever else you are, you're a fine actor, my son.'

'From you, that's the ultimate compliment. I love you, Mama.'

'And I love you, my son. God bless.'

Ferguson spoke to Blake and brought him up to speed. 'There's something going on here and we don't know what it is.'

Blake said, 'The name Bell, I've got that right, no question.'

'Well, we're all on the case now.'

'I'm not sure what I can do, but I'll speak to the President.'

When Blake went into the Oval Office a few minutes later, Cazalet was by the fire, smoking a cigarette, Murchison, his flatcoat retriever, at his feet. The dog was the most intelligent Blake had ever known. He'd often suspected it of talking to the President. On a famous occasion it had hurled itself at a waiting assassin and saved Cazalet's life. Clancy, as usual, hovered.

'Well, I've said it before, Blake, but you're a remarkable man. Three members of the Provisional IRA, one dead and two down? Amazing!'

'They were going to give me the deep six off a fishing boat, Mr President. I decided otherwise.'

Cazalet said, 'Clancy, Scotch and soda. Can you believe this?'

'Absolutely, Mr President. If you can get a Navy Cross in Vietnam at twenty-one, that means you can handle yourself.'

'Hell, you did the same thing in ninety-one in Iraq,' Blake said. 'Mind you, Iraq was pussy.'

'Excuse me, sir, but I might just spill your drink.'

'Oh, you wouldn't do that to a superior officer, Sergeant-Major.'

'Stop the war games, we've all been there.' Cazalet toasted Blake. 'Ferguson is right. Superintendent Bernstein murdered, you attacked, Major Roper. There seems to be a vendetta against Ferguson's group. Do you think I should speak to the Prime Minister?'

'There's not much he can do, Mr President. I suspect that, as usual, it's all down to Dillon.'

'Well, good luck to him,' and Cazalet toasted Blake again.

Levin phoned Ashimov at Drumore Place and got Greta first. 'How are you doing?' she asked.

'Bloody awful.' He told her what had happened.

'Not so good.'

'Where's Ashimov?'

'Playing snooker with Bell. He left me the phone. Said he didn't want to be bothered.'

'Oh dear, let's hope Blake Johnson doesn't appear on the scene again.'

'I wouldn't mention that, if I were you. I'll transfer you.'

Ashimov said, 'So, what's happening?'

Levin went into detail, finding he was rather enjoying it.

Ashimov said, 'This isn't good, Captain. You disappoint me.'

'Well, the bloody IRA must have disappointed you with their botched job on Bernstein and their total incompetence in the Blake Johnson affair. The idiots I used for Roper were on your list. The Salters' Bentley was just bad luck.'

'You're making excuses,' Ashimov roared.

'Take it up with Volkov. I have. When I've something to say, I'll phone. Goodbye.' He put the phone down.

Dillon stayed on with Billy, drinking a cup of tea in the kitchen while Roper worked away at his computer. They went to check on him when he called out, 'Have I got news for you!'

They went in to find him at his computer bank, and on the screen was Igor Levin.

'So who is he?' Dillon asked. 'A Russian?'

'Oh, a strange hybrid.'

Roper went on to describe Levin in detail.

When he had finished Dillon said, 'So he's appointed as a commercial attaché at the Russian Embassy. We all know what that means.'

'What?' Billy asked.

'In the old days, KGB,' Roper said, 'but our boy is GRU, Russian Military Intelligence. Flew in two days ago. Staying at the Dorchester.'

'He's what?' Dillon said, and gasped. 'Christ, I've seen him there in the Piano Bar. He was at the mortuary. He was even at the Dark Man.'

'But the Dorchester?' Billy said. 'The Russians must be treating their agents well.'

'No, Billy,' Roper said. 'He's a rich man in his own right.' His fingers danced on the keys. 'His father was a military attaché at the London Embassy, his mother English, his grandmother Irish. Is there no end to him?'

'Apparently not,' Dillon said.

'Big war hero, languages. Christ, he went to Westminster School for a few years.'

'A man of parts,' Dillon nodded. 'Billy, would you take me round to my place at Stable Mews? I do believe I have a staff pass key for the Dorchester. We'll pay his suite a visit.'

'Not without me, you won't,' Roper said. 'A hotel as outstanding as the Dorchester doesn't give out room numbers to anyone. I, on the other hand, can penetrate most systems.' His fingers danced again. 'Six-ten,' he said.

'We'll see you later,' Dillon said, and he and Billy left.

At the hotel, they checked the Piano Bar and had a stroke of real luck. Levin was at a corner table having some sort of pasta and a glass of champagne, listening to a trio playing jazz at the end of the room.

'Move it,' Dillon said, and they hit the lift fast and went upstairs.

The corridor was long, the carpet luxurious. Dillon had the key ready in his hand, pushed it in the electronic lock when they reached six-ten. The green light came on, the door opened automatically.

'Fast,' Dillon said. 'Bedroom, check if the safe in the wardrobe's in use. I'll do the sitting room.'

He went one way, Billy the other. The sitting room was the height of luxury, but having stayed in such rooms before at the hotel Dillon knew what to expect. It was like staying in a fine English country house. There was a large TV screen on the wall, a cabinet with video, a copier, a computer link, he knew that. But there was more. A spectacular piece of luck – Levin's briefcase.

'Billy,' he called, got the briefcase open, rummaged around and found the envelope containing the Putin warrant. A Russian speaker, it made perfect sense to Dillon.

'Jesus, Billy, Vladimir Putin and his team sorted it for him.'

'The bloody Russian President,' Billy said. 'If you nick it, he'll know.'

'No need, there's a copier in the cabinet.' He ran the warrant through, folded the copy and put it in his pocket, put the other in the envelope and returned it to the brief-case. 'Out of it, fast.'

Which they did, running down the stairs at the far end instead of using the lift. In the car Billy did the driving and Dillon phoned Ferguson.

'We'll meet back at Holland Park,' Dillon said.

'What the hell for?'

'The most astonishing thing you'll have seen in years. Trust me.'

In the computer room at the Holland Park safehouse they ranged around Roper and his screens.

'So Levin is posted to London as a commercial attaché,' Roper said.

'With one hell of a warrant to back him up and signed by Putin himself,' Dillon said. 'Couldn't you do something about that, Charles? Speak to Head of Station?'

'They'd claim diplomatic immunity, and in theory, what, after all, does the letter say? It refers to the bearer, not a specific individual. No, I don't think it would wash. You can't even prove what it refers to.'

'I must say I agree,' Roper said. 'And I don't think we'll get anywhere with Moon and his chum. Sticking to their mugging story keeps them out of court because I've got to keep to my story. Keeps me out of court, too, if you take my point.'

'Right,' Ferguson said. 'At least Levin doesn't know we're on to him. I'll leave him in your hands, Sean, while you, young Salter, make for Farley Field in the morning and head for Dublin. Any questions?'

'Not really,' Dillon said. 'I just want answers.'

7

The Citation X landed at Dublin Airport mid-morning and taxied to the diplomatic arrivals section. Billy, Lacey and Parry had been through a lot together in the past on Ferguson's behalf. As they walked to the arrivals section, Lacey spoke.

'I'm usually dropping you on some beach at night in deep trouble. I sense something different.'

Billy produced his warrant card. 'The General needs a replacement for Hannah. I'm it for the moment.'

'Good God.'

'Yes, well, what you see is what you get. I shouldn't be too long.'

'What can I say? Good luck.'

Billy moved on, produced his passport at reception. There was nobody around except a man in a raincoat, maybe forty, smoking a cigarette, a scar on one cheek which to someone of Billy's expertise had been made by a broken bottle. The girl at the desk handed him back his passport.

'Ah, Mr Salter, your fame precedes you. How's Sean Dillon these days?' asked the man.

'Up and running,' Billy told him. 'Who might you be?'

'Jack Flynn, Detective Chief Inspector, Special Branch. I go back a long way with Dillon. You might say I'm an admirer. I've heard the whispers about you and him in past years, so when one of Ferguson's planes comes in with the one passenger, and it's you, I wonder.'

'You mean, what's a well-known London gangster doing here?'

'In one of Ferguson's planes is the point.'

Billy took his warrant card out. Flynn said, 'Holy Mother of God, that I should see the day.'

'We lost part of Ferguson's team, Superintendent Bernstein.'

'I've heard. She was an outstanding officer. Helped us out in the Garda, many times.'

'What you haven't heard is that her death was no accident. She was helped on her way, if you follow me.'

Flynn's face was like stone. 'You're saying someone topped that lovely woman? Who would do a thing like that?'

Billy thought about it, wondered what Dillon would have done and knew it would never be the obvious thing and in this case it would be to talk to Flynn. But there was something about Flynn, and if Billy knew about anything in this life he knew about coppers.

'I'm teetotal, but I could do with a cup of tea.'

'Well, this is Ireland, and if you can't get a decent cup of tea here, where else would you? You've got a hire car, I see. You can follow me. In the main concourse there's a decent café.'

Which Billy did, noticing that Flynn had a uniformed driver, large and burly. They parked close to the main entrance, leaving the driver in charge.

'Good man yourself, Donald,' Flynn told the constable. 'Don't let them give you a ticket.'

They got the tea, sat in a booth at the café and Flynn lit a cigarette. 'So what have we got here?'

And Billy told him: Mary Killane, the link with the IRA, Liam Bell – everything except the circumstances surrounding Belov.

Flynn said, 'Twenty years in the job, nothing surprises me, but it's a hell of a story.' He shook his head. 'But Liam Bell.'

'You wouldn't be IRA yourself?' Billy asked. 'I know what you bleeding Irish are like.'

Flynn grinned. 'No, that was my elder brother, as you're asking. You're all right with me. There was a day, but it's long gone and we should move on. I'm surprised about Bell. I thought he was long retired.'

'Well, maybe not.'

'I assume this is all hush-hush. We shouldn't even be talking.'

'Which means you shouldn't be helping,' Billy said. 'I've got his home address and a mention of one or two places he might be.'

'Pubs, you mean. That's easy. The Irish Hussar down on the quays by the river. That's where all the old hands go, and a few hangers on, trying to look big.'

'So what would you suggest?'

'Well, as I've nothing better to do and it is my patch, I'll leave first with Donald, just to show you the way, you follow on and we'll take it from there. One thing: Are you carrying?'

'Now would I do a thing like that?'

'Absolutely. Just make sure it stays in your pants.'

Billy smiled. 'This sounds like the beginning of a beautiful friendship.'

The police car led him to O'Connor Street, number fifteen, a neat bungalow, with garden and garage, nothing special at all. Flynn and Donald kept on going, Billy pulled up in his car and tried the front door of the bungalow. The bell was only an echo in an empty house, he had that feeling. He went round the back to check, returned to find a late middle-aged lady peering over the fence.

'Can I help you?' Strangely enough, her accent was English.

Billy said, 'I was hoping for Mr Bell.'

'You're English,' she said.

'So they tell me.'

'So am I. My husband was Irish, but he's been dead for twelve years. I should have gone back, really.'

Billy said, 'Like I said, I was looking for Mr Bell. An insurance claim.'

'I don't think you'll find him around. He's left his keys with me in case there are any problems.'

'Did he say when he'd be back?'

'No. I had to phone when there was a water board problem.'

'And spoke to him?'

'No – somebody else. Drumore Place, they said. I left a message.'

'You've been very kind,' Billy told her and left.

A couple of streets away he pulled up behind Flynn and Donald and conferred. Flynn said, 'Drumore, now that's in County Louth on the coast, a known fact, so you've got your link with Kelly. You did a good job there, taking that bastard out.'

'We just need confirmation that Bell really has taken over.'

Flynn said, 'It's a strong IRA area and Josef Belov's been a power in the land. Everybody's behind him, and that includes the IRA. They'll never let go in Ballykelly and Drumore.'

'Fine. I just want to confirm that Bell is running things now, so what do I do?'

'Go to the Irish Hussar for your lunch and ask questions. They'll suspect you straight away because you don't drink. Let's see what happens.'

'Great. Lead the way,' Billy said.

*   *   *

The Irish Hussar was on a cobbled street fronting the River Liffey. The police vehicle coursed by and turned into a parking bay. They drove round to the side alley and went in.

The bar was old-fashioned, rather Victorian, everything an old-fashioned pub should be: plenty of bottles crammed behind the bars, mirrors, mahogany, a fresco painting of Michael Collins holding the Irish tricolor high at Easter 1916. The modern changes were the tables crammed in, making the pub more a restaurant than anything else.

Billy chose a table by a bow window. A young waitress descended on him. 'Will you be eating?'

'Considering that the smells from the kitchen are driving me potty, yes I am.'

'So what can I get you?'

'Orange juice.'

Three young men at a nearby table appeared to find this funny. Billy smiled. 'Please. And I'll have the Irish stew, since I'm over from London for the day.'

She hesitated. 'You don't have an Irish accent.'

'Well, when you're London Irish that isn't likely. What's your name?'

'Kathleen.'

'Well, Kathleen, I'm an Irish Cockney who seeks orange juice and Irish stew.'

She smiled. 'Coming up.'

Billy tried Dillon on his mobile and found him. 'How are things?'

'Not too bad. I've been mulling over what's happening

about Killane and Hannah. Frankly, I think uniform branch at Scotland Yard are dragging their feet.'

'Be fair,' Billy said. 'Maybe there's not much coming up.'

'You could be right. What about you?' Billy went through it. Dillon said, 'I remember Flynn. Give him my best. He's good, Billy.'

Kathleen returned with an orange juice and his stew and crusty bread. 'There you go. Anything else?'

'I'm here on business,' Billy said. 'Supposed to catch up with a Liam Bell, only he seems to be away.'

She stopped smiling and Billy attacked the stew. 'This is fantastic. So, you've no idea where he is? I understand he comes here all the time.'

'I wouldn't know.' She turned and fled and the three men at the next table stopped talking and looked at Billy in silence.

The stew was so good, he actually finished it and washed it down with the orange juice. The looks from the three men said it all, and Billy checked the .25 Colt in his waistband at the rear. No point in delaying things. These bastards obviously wanted to have him, so they might as well get on with it.

He called Kathleen over and gave her a £20 note. 'Jesus, that's too much.'

'It's been a sincere sensation,' he said, and smiled. 'Don't worry, I'll be fine.'

Suddenly, she smiled. 'My God, I don't know who you are, but I think you will.'

Billy reached over, kissed her on the cheek, went out of the pub and turned into the alley at the side. The three young men from the next table erupted after him and Billy turned to meet the rush, not afraid, he never was. Years on the street had taken care of that.

'Now then, lads, what's the problem?'

One of them grabbed him by the tie. 'You've been asking after a good friend of ours, Liam Bell, you English bastard.'

'Now that's not nice,' Billy said. 'And me as Irish as all of you.' Which was perfectly untrue.

One of them said, 'You don't even have an Irish accent.'

'I didn't know you needed one.'

The man pulled his tie, the other two moved in. Billy pulled the Colt .25 from the back of his waistband and fired between their legs at the cobbles. He kept a hand on the one who clutched his tie and wiped the Colt across his mouth. The others jumped back.

'I'll only say this once, otherwise you can have it in the knee. Where's Bell?'

The youth was quaking. 'He was recruiting for a job in Drumore up in Country Louth last I heard.'

Billy released him. 'There you go. It wasn't too hard, was it?'

He replaced the Colt and one of the other two took a swing at him. There was a minor mêlée, and Flynn and big Donald came running round the corner. A few pokes from Donald's stick were enough. They went off, dejected, one with a handkerchief to a bloody face.

Flynn stuck a cigarette in his mouth. 'You don't take prisoners, do you?'

'I could never see the point.'

'Neither could I. Let me know what the outcome is. I'm fascinated.'

''That's a promise,' Billy said. 'You can rely on it. Regards from Dillon.'

He got in his car and drove back to the airport.

Dillon had showered and changed, wondering how Billy would make out in Dublin, then drove round to Holland Park. He found Roper in the computer room with Ferguson.

'Any word on Billy?' he asked.

'Not yet. You're expecting a lot, Dillon, but then you always did.'

'I just expect people to come up to expectations. Coming up with the goods is another way of looking at it, which Scotland Yard seems to be rather spectacularly failing to do in Hannah's case.' He turned to Roper. 'Any news at all from the Murder Squad?'

'It's early days, Sean. You're expecting too much.'

'It's one of their own we're talking about,' Dillon said.

'Leave it alone,' Ferguson said. 'This is a job for uniform and Special Branch, and certainly not for us. You don't interfere.'

'Sounds definite enough,' Dillon said. 'I'll give it my consideration.' And he went out.

Levin had been on his tail since leaving Dillon's cottage in Stable Mews, which could have been difficult with someone of Dillon's experience, but there was London traffic to help. Not that he was exactly inexperienced himself, and he stayed well back and followed

Dillon went to Mary Killane's place. He really was worried that the Murder Squad didn't appear to be making much progress. Where she had lived, Kilburn, was the most Irish area of London. There were pubs there that would make you think you were back in the old country. Republican, Protestant, take your pick.

Dillon was an expert on all of them, had lived there as a boy newly come from Belfast with his father, so if you were a nice Catholic girl who was going out for a drink you'd never go to a Prod pub, only a Catholic one. Mary Killane didn't have a car, so you were talking about walking unless she'd a fella who picked her up at the flat. In any case, within a reasonable walking distance to here there were a few Catholic pubs.

Most were clean enough. He showed her photo and got nowhere. There were others that had IRA connections, especially from before the Peace Process, there being little action in London these days. One such was the Green Tinker, the landlord one Mickey Docherty. A huge IRA supporter in the old days, he'd been picked up twice although nothing had ever been proven.

Dillon found him just before noon when the bar was empty except for two old men in cloth caps drinking ale at a corner table and playing dominoes. Docherty was reading the *Standard* at the bar, and the look on his face when he saw Dillon was comical.

'My God, it's you, Sean.'

'As ever was. Get me a large Bushmills.'

Docherty did as he was told, and when he turned, Dillon had a computer photo of Mary on the bar. He took his whiskey and drank it. Docherty's face said it all.

'I can see by your face you know her.'

'What's she done?'

'Got herself killed.'

Docherty crossed himself. 'Mother of God.'

'Don't start getting pious with me. Who did she come in with?'

'And how would I be knowing that?'

'Because there's an IRA connection and a possible Liam Bell connection, so tell me what you know. If you don't, I'll be back tonight to haunt you. I'll cripple you, both knees. This is important to me.'

'All right, Sean, I hear you.' He turned, poured a whiskey, hands shaking. 'Nice girl. A nurse. She was a sleeper.'

'How do you know?'

'I took letters from Dublin for her and the fella.'

'Which fella?'

'Well, he was a sleeper, too. Dermot Fitzgerald.'

'What did it say in the letters?'

'How would I know?'

'Because you steamed the envelopes open.'

Docherty was panicking. 'I only did it a couple of times. They were just notes, no signature. Things like phone a certain number at such and such a time. Fitzgerald was a handsome rogue. A real scholar. Doing an MA at London University.'

'A scholar and a gentleman thinking it was romantic to be in the IRA?'

'There was word about him.'

'What kind of word?'

'That he'd killed three or four times.'

There was silence. 'Do you have his address?'

'Only round the corner, but he's gone.'

'Gone where?'

'Ibiza. He told me a couple of days ago. Said he'd made a bit of money and was going over there for a while. Likes to dive.'

Dillon thought about it, then took another computer photo out, Levin's this time. 'Anyone you know?'

Docherty shook his head. 'Definitely not.'

Dillon put the photos away. 'I hope I don't have to come back.'

Igor Levin, following Dillon to The Green Tinker, had glanced through a window, seen him approach the bar to talk to Docherty. He moved on and discovered a door to a separate saloon bar. He moved in. There was no one there, but there was an access door into the other bar, and when he put his earpiece in he could hear what passed between them from the moment Docherty recognized Mary Killane and was told she was killed.

There was really little else Levin could do. He waited by the front door, giving Dillon time, then moved out and went along the street to his Mercedes. Once behind the wheel, he phoned Luhzkov at the Embassy, and asked him to do a trace on Dermot Fitzgerald and flights to Ibiza.

In Dublin, Flynn sat in his favourite bar and had a large whiskey. He had a problem. A fine officer, Hannah Bernstein, had gone down, and he felt that. On the other hand, there was a question of family loyalty and his brother, not ex-IRA at all, but still active. So he did the good thing, or the bad thing, and gave him a ring. Billy Salter had come calling, maybe Liam Bell needed to know. Afterwards he felt even worse and consoled himself with another whiskey.

Levin phoned Drumore Place and got Ashimov. He told him what Dillon had learned at the Green Tinker. 'The important thing is we've checked through the GRU computer and Dermot Fitzgerald left London Gatwick for Ibiza the day before yesterday.'

'So what are you saying to me?'

'That if I was Dillon and fired up like he is, I'd be on the next plane over on Fitzgerald's case. If he can find him and squeeze him, he'll know it was Liam Bell behind the execution of Mary Killane, and that's a direct lead to Drumore Place and what goes with that.'

'Do you think I don't know?'

'So what do you want me to do?'

'Get after Fitzgerald. Get rid of him.'

'Are you going to come?'

'I've other things to do.'

'Can I say something?'

'Anything you like as long as it's relevant.'

'Getting on Fitzgerald's tail is one thing, but there's another side to it. Why waste him? If Dillon comes after him, which he will, we'd get two for the price of one.'

Ashimov said, 'That's good. I like that.' He thought about it. 'I tell you what. I'll send a company Falcon from Ballykelly. It can bring Greta. She could be useful to you. It'll collect you at Archbury, then onwards to Ibiza.'

'Sounds good to me.'

'Then let's do it.'

At Holland Park, Dillon found Roper and gave him the information he'd obtained from Docherty about Fitzgerald. He had no known criminal connections, but was on the books at London University. A BA in English Literature. His thesis for his Masters degree was on the pending list.

Roper trawled through the passenger lists for Ibiza and confirmed that Fitzgerald had left. 'Anything else?'

'This diving business. Check that out if you can.'

'I can do anything, old lad.' Roper went through the PADI list, the World Association of Professional Divers, and nodded. 'There you are. A master diver. So what do you want to do?'

'I think I should go after him. I know Ibiza well. I used to go there a lot in the old days. A good friend of mine ran an outfit flying floatplanes between the islands. I flew for him. I wonder if he's still at it? Aldo Russo, Eagle Air. He's Italian. Has strong Mafia connections, or did have.'

Roper went back to his computer, which came up trumps again. 'There you go. Still up and running, but would you be? How much flying have you done lately?'

'I've kept my hand in. Mostly weekend stuff these days. I can fly anything short of a Jumbo, but who says I'm going to fly?'

'I think Ferguson will say no to you going. He wants the Hannah investigation to stay in the hands of Scotland Yard.'

'Look, Mary Killane eased Hannah's going with those pills, but the IRA contact between her and Fitzgerald is more than a coincidence and I'd take a large bet with you he killed her. It makes sense. She's the nurse with access. Afterwards she's got to be got rid of. On top of that, he clears off to Ibiza.'

'You could persuade me,' Roper said, but at that moment Ferguson came in, immaculate in black tie.

'What's going on?' he said.

Dillon told him, not that it did any good. 'I told you, I don't want you to intervene. The Yard will handle it. All right, you've done well, Sean, and so has young Salter in Dublin. It's a step forward knowing that Liam Bell is at Drumore Place, but I'm not having you running off to Ibiza. I'm at St James's Palace for a luncheon with the Prime Minister. He'll want to know how things are, so leave it alone.'

'Whatever you say.'

He went out. Roper said, 'But you're not going to leave it alone, are you?'

'Not a chance. I'm going to presume on friendship. I'm going to phone Lacey at Farley Field and tell him a priority job's come up and I need a Citation flight to Ibiza tonight. I'll say Ferguson has ordered it. That clears you.'

Roper sat back, frowning, then said, 'Give me a Marlboro and we'll call it quits.'

'My pleasure.' Dillon took one himself.

'Only one thing,' Roper said. 'I make the call. Lacey trusts me.'

'So where does that leave you with Ferguson?'

'What can he do?' Roper smiled. 'I'm handicapped. He'd end up in front of a tribunal. I'll tell Lacey you'll be there in two hours. Go on, get out of here.'

He phoned Lacey and stated his requirements, the usual schedule, the Quartermaster for weaponry, and then he phoned Billy Salter.

'Something's come up,' he said and told him. 'What do you think?'

'That he's not been the same since she died, not his old self at all. What's more, to go off on a hunt like this, on his own, in the state he's in is barmy.'

'So what are you going to do?'

'Pack a suitcase.'

'I thought you'd say that. They're expecting you at Farley, too. Stay in touch.'

IBIZA

8

The Falcon, with Greta on board, dropped in at Archbury and picked up Levin. 'You've been busy,' she said as they took off again.

'What's happening?'

'The net's closing in.' She told him about Billy Salter in Dublin.

'So now they know definitely,' Levin said. 'Thanks to a family-minded Dublin detective.'

'They know Liam Bell is in charge of Drumore, they're aware that Max Zubin is playing Belov at Station Gorky. They don't know about Ashimov or me.'

He smiled. 'Or me.'

'So let's keep it that way.'

'You've got Fitzgerald's address, details of what he's up to? He knows we're coming?'

'Oh, yes. Bell's been in touch with him.'

'That was a mistake.' Levin opened the bar cabinet and got the vodka out.

'Why?' she asked as he poured.

'He could wonder why. He could wonder whether the only present we're bringing is a bullet in the head.'

'Not with me along.'

'A good-looking woman to make him feel comfortable?'

'Why not? Tell me one thing. You really think Dillon will turn up?'

'Absolutely.'

'It should be an interesting trip then,' and they toasted each other. 'Here's to Mary Hall.'

'Who's that?'

'Me, Igor. That's what it says on my passport.'

When Billy arrived at Farley Field, he was delivered by Harry, grumbling as usual. 'I mean, what's he got you into now?'

'I'm a member of the Security Services, Harry. They yell, I jump. It's called doing your duty.'

'Only Ferguson doesn't know.'

'He will when he's finished dinner, Roper will see to that.'

They parked outside the terminal building, went in, and there was Lacey in flight overalls talking to Dillon. 'The

Quartermaster's left you the usual bag, Sean, said you'll find everything you want inside.'

Billy and Harry looked on. 'There you are, you little Irish bastard,' Harry said.

Lacey said, 'I'll go and get us started.'

Dillon frowned. 'Does Ferguson know about this?'

'He soon will. Roper's in charge.' Billy picked up the Quartermaster's bag and took his own from Harry. 'Come on, Dillon, let's get moving,' and he led the way out and walked to the Citation X.

Flying through the night at 30,000 feet, Dillon indulged himself on half a bottle of Krug champagne. 'So what's the first move?' asked Billy.

'To find Fitzgerald. Roper's going to check diving sites and the kind of hotels divers use. If that doesn't work, I'll try my old friend Aldo Russo.'

'Italian, not Spanish? How come you were involved with him?'

'Way back in the old days when I was the pride of the IRA, I was sent to Sicily to buy arms, only the Mafia knew British Intelligence was on to them, so they moved Russo, his wife and son to Ibiza, and used that as a base. There were Spanish elements who didn't like it, thought the Mafia were encroaching on their territory.'

'What happened?'

'I did him a favour one night when a bit of business came up at the last minute. I offered to drive his wife and son home. Two men who'd been given the contract ambushed us, wounded the boy and his mother.'

'Don't tell me. You took them out?'

'Something like that. God, it was thirty years ago. The son is a lawyer in Palermo now.'

'Working for the Mafia?'

'Who knows?'

'And the wife?'

'Cancer, ten years ago.'

There was silence for a while. Billy said, 'When it's time, it's time. I suppose Russo has never forgotten what you did. Italians are funny like that.'

'Honour is everything, Billy, you know that.'

'Or respect,' Billy said.

Dillon's Codex Four went and Ferguson exploded. 'What in the hell do you think you are playing at?'

'Don't blame Roper, he was trying to make it official for Lacey. As for Billy, he's only here because he's a sentimentalist. Thinks he owes me.'

'Put him on – that's an order.' Dillon handed the phone to Billy.

'Yes, boss.'

'For God's sake, watch him. The whole thing's put him on a knife edge. I don't want to lose him.'

'Do you think I do? Listen, I've got a good feeling about this, especially with Russo on board. I'll hand you back.'

'Who's Russo?' Ferguson demanded of Dillon.

'Roper will fill you in. I used to deal with him for the IRA. Ex-Mafia.'

'There's no such thing. It's like saying ex-IRA. Once in,

never out, isn't that the truth of it? Oh, for God's sake, go to hell in your own way, but keep in touch.'

'An angry man,' Billy commented.

'No, really. He cares, Billy, about what we do and what happens to us.' He finished the last drop of champagne.

Billy said, 'I've never been to Ibiza. What's it like?'

Dillon said, 'Great in the old days, more tourists now. I used to love the old city, Ibiza town, the bars, gypsies, bullfighters, the flamenco dancers.' He shook his head. 'Best-looking women you've seen in years.'

'Sounds good. You like the bulls then?'

'A lot of people wouldn't approve, but there's something about a man putting himself straight in front of a charging bull.'

'It must be awesome.'

'It is.' Dillon pushed his seat back. 'I'm going to have forty winks.'

He closed his eyes and Hannah flooded in. Why did it have to be her, and how much had he been responsible? He saw Ashimov plough her down in the street, experienced again his own shots missing and Hannah sliding down the railings and there was blood falling down her face and he was afraid and horrified.

And then the vision again, the Plaza de Toros, the bull-ring in Ibiza, the *toreros* in uniform, the *picadors* on horse-back, the band and then everything focusing on the red door on the other side, the Gate of Fear, and the bull roared out and came straight for him.

He came awake with a kind of convulsion, a cry on his lips. Billy grabbed his arm. 'You OK?'

Dillon said, 'Bad dream, that's all.' He managed a smile, and his phone went. It was Roper.

'I've tried for Fitzgerald through the Divemasters' Association and the general run of hotels they use. He was at a place called Sanders, but booked out earlier today. I've managed to come up with one useful item. A Belov International Falcon left Ballykelly first thing this morning carrying one passenger, a woman named Mary Hall.'

'Who in the hell is she?'

'God knows. The plane streaked across to Archbury, where, guess what? It picked up Igor Levin, commercial attaché at the Russian Embassy.'

'Destination?'

'Ibiza.'

'So, it gets even more interesting. Keep pushing on Fitzgerald. See what we can come up with. Everything is happening quickly. Let's keep it that way.'

'I'll try.' Roper switched off.

Levin had phoned Luhzkov at the London Embassy and the GRU computer had come up with the Sanders Hotel as the place where Fitzgerald was staying.

He said to Greta, 'I'm keeping the plane as a precaution. He might have moved on, just in case. Let's go and check his hotel, this Sanders place. I'll get a cab.'

The Sanders Hotel wasn't exactly a dead end. The man on reception was a shifty sort of individual who made the point that Fitzgerald had left in a hurry. It was Greta who instinctively knew he was holding back.

'So he was only here for a day? You know he always stays longer.'

The man replied instinctively. 'Well, yes.'

Levin took out an English £50 note. 'Don't try my patience. Where is he?'

The receptionist, of course, opened up. Fitzgerald had decided to move on to Algeria, 200 miles away. He'd taken the ferry to Khufra. He'd often gone there in the past for the diving.

'And this was when?'

'Yesterday. I wouldn't go there, *Señor*, it's a rough place.'

'Where would he stay?'

'God alone knows. There are bad people there. Perhaps the Trocadero. Doctor Tomac owns that. They're friends.'

'Is he a real doctor?'

'The only one they've got. He runs the hotel, the club, the smuggling. He's into everything.'

'Is there an airport there?'

'A dump.' The man fingered through some tourist brochures and passed one across. 'The Khufra. A terrible place.'

Greta took it. 'Are we going?'

'Of course, back to the airport.'

The senior pilot was called Scott, the other Smith. He informed them of the destination and Scott looked it up and made a face. 'We're OK for fuel, but not much else. We'll probably have to do our own maintenance if we stay long.'

'You'll probably need pistols if we stay long, but never mind. Let's get on with it. How long?'

'An hour. Not much more.'

Later, as the Falcon rose to 30,000, Greta read the brochure and discussed it with Levin.

'The Khufra Marshes. Hundreds of square kilometres of salt marsh on the Algerian coast near Cape Djuinet. Reeds twelve metres high and more. Marsh Arabs. Villages built on wood pilings. They've lived that way for centuries, mainly fishing. They also have Berber tribesmen called Husa who ride horses that over the centuries have been bred to swim in the salt marshes.'

'Sounds like the last place God made.' He smiled. 'But we'll manage. I usually do. Give me a moment, I want to speak to Volkov.'

He made the connection on the aircraft phone and put it on conference, placing a finger on his lips to Greta.

'Where on earth are you, Igor?'

Levin explained about Khufra.

'It sounds disgusting.'

'I'd imagined you would have known of my mission and Major Novikova's part in it.'

'No, actually. I'm sure Major Ashimov will get around to informing me when it suits him.' The silence was ominous. 'We must return Josef Belov to the real world soon, Igor. Station Gorky is well and good, but since Ferguson and Johnson know who he really is, let's take the wind out of their sails. Let's flaunt him in Berlin or Paris.'

'London?' Levin asked.

'My goodness, what a coup. It's so delicious because Ferguson and company wouldn't be able to do a thing about it.'

'A neat point.'

'So, take care and watch over Novikova. Such beauty must not be placed in jeopardy.'

'As you say, Comrade.'

'And wear my gift at all times. You are too valuable. I can't afford to lose you.'

'I'll take care, you may be certain.'

Greta said, 'What does he mean, wear my gift at all times?'

'Remember what saved Ashimov's life when Billy Salter shot him? A nylon and titanium bulletproof vest.'

'So?'

'These things are miraculous. The other year, two Chechnyans made an attempt on Volkov's life when we were leaving an office in Moscow. They shot his driver and a security man.'

'And Volkov?'

'I got between. Took a bullet in the left shoulder, another in my left thigh, ruining a perfectly good Brioni suit. But I shot one between the eyes and the other in the heart.'

'Christ almighty.'

'Volkov was delighted to be alive, but annoyed I hadn't kept one alive to be squeezed. So he did the same as Ashimov – presented me with a nylon and titanium vest with an order to wear it at all times.'

'When I was in Iraq with Dillon on my last assignment, he was wearing one.'

'There you are then. It's indispensable to all the best assassins. So let's have a drink and decide on our next move.'

The flight to Khufra was no big deal and the approach to the coast was particularly interesting. The Khufra marshes extended for miles, one creek after another, dangerous reefs, many Arab fishing boats battling with the coast, a few villages down there in the reeds.

There was always the desert, of course, stretching into the marsh country, and then Khufra town, the airstrip and a few old concrete buildings, the kind that looked as if they were surviving the Second World War.

The control tower was basic. Captains Scott and Smith handled the controls between them and landed, rolling to a halt beside a couple of old hangars.

They called ahead. A police captain named Omar greeted them with some enthusiasm, the magic name of Belov International weaving a spell even here on the edge of nowhere.

'It's a pleasure to meet you,' he said, his eyes roving over Greta.

She tried to ignore his sweaty armpits. Levin said, 'I believe my pilot booked us into the Trocadero?'

'And Doctor Tomac has sent the Land Rover for you.'

This was obviously intended as a compliment. Levin said to Scott and Smith, 'I'm not sure how long this will take. I'll leave you to come to town, but make sure the Falcon's secure.'

'Dr Tomac has already made arrangements. This will be taken care of.'

They walked towards the Land Rover, and Levin's phone rang. It was Luhzkov from London. 'I thought you should know. GRU contacts confirm that one of Ferguson's Citations booked out of Farley Field, destination Ibiza, passengers Dillon and his Salter friend Billy. The word is Billy's gone up in the world. He's now officially an operative of the Special Security Services. Apparently his criminal past has suddenly disappeared from all his records.'

'Ferguson really is one of a kind,' Levin said. 'The KGB would have been proud of him. Thanks for the information.'

Levin followed Greta into the Land Rover. As they drove away, he told her what had happened.

'So they're on their way? What's that mean? They'll still have to run Fitzgerald to earth. They won't know he's come over here.'

'But, Greta, we want them to know. It'd be much better if Dermot Fitzgerald ended up in that great IRA heaven in the sky, even better if Sean Dillon and young Salter accompanied him there.'

'That's asking a lot where Dillon's concerned.'

'Perhaps, but I'd say these Khufra marshes would be a perfect killing ground.' He smiled and lit a cigarette. 'Yes, I know it's all terribly unpredictable, but I like that.'

'It's just a game to you.'

'Always has been, my love,' and he smiled.

Just before landing at Ibiza, Dillon got a call from Ferguson. 'You're just about to land, I see?'

'That's right, and the average Spanish café does what they call a full English breakfast.'

'I've been thinking things over and I still don't approve. It's the Murder Squad's business. Let them get on with it.'

'Well, they have and haven't got very far. OK, we know Fitzgerald's got here, Roper has information on that, except that we know he's already moved. By the time Scotland Yard and the Home Office apply to the Spanish police and obtain the necessary warrants, God knows where he'll be.'

'At least I'm confining you to the island,' Ferguson said. 'I'm recalling the Citation.'

'We'll manage. I'm going to get him, Charles, I promise you.'

When they got out of the Citation at the airport, Lacey said, 'What's going on, Sean? Ferguson himself is recalling us at once.'

'Oh, I've been a naughty boy again. Don't worry about it. Just do as the great man says and we'll get on.'

They hailed a taxi and he told the driver to take them to Eagle Air at a small village up the coast from where Russo ran his operation.

'I'll call Roper and let him know what's happened,' he told Billy.

Roper said, 'He's not pleased, although he's not been the same since Hannah. On the other hand, it's inconvenient he's recalled the plane.'

'Why?'

'The latest word is that the Falcon has moved on to Khufra on the Algerian coast.'

'Which means that Fitzgerald is probably one step ahead
of him.'

'I'd say so.'

'We'd better get after them, then.'

The overnight ferry moved into Khufra town, nosing into
the port. There were smaller hills draped with white
Moorish houses, narrow alleys in between. The port itself
was small, fishing boats, two or three dhows, various motor
launches and, way beyond, the marshes. The wind blowing
in from the sea was warm and somehow perfumed with
spices.

Dermot Fitzgerald loved it, stood there at the rail as they
floated in. He'd been here many times, loved the women,
the food, the diving. If there was trouble, there was Tomac
to take care of things and, beyond, the marshes for refuge.
It was like coming home, and he slung his shoulder bag and
went down the gangplank, pushing his way through a forest
of outstretched arms and walked up through the cobbled
streets to the Trocadero.

Dillon brought Billy up to date as they followed a winding
road down to Tijola, a harbour with a small pier, no fishing
boats because they'd have gone out early, a scattering of
houses. The interesting thing was the two floatplanes down
there, one of them floating in the harbour, the other seated
on a concrete slipway below the sea wall.

They were Eagle Amphibians, an old plane, but sturdy and robust, originally designed for service in the Canadian far north. One useful extra was that you could drop wheels beneath the floats and taxi out of the water onto dry land.

Dillon found a mechanic working on the engine of one of the floatplanes on the concrete ramp who greeted him warmly. '*Señor* Dillon,' he said in Spanish. 'How wonderful.'

Dillon answered in the same language. 'Great to see you.' He gave him a quick embrace and broke into English. 'So where's Aldo?'

'They're running a few young bulls up at the Playa this morning. He's gone to watch. It's just for youngsters. You know how it is?'

'We'll catch up with him there. We'll leave our bags.'

'No trouble, *amigo*.'

The Plaza de Toros in Ibiza is typical of most small towns in Spain, not much more than a concrete circle, but the public were only interested in what went on inside the ring anyway, and this, early in the day, was different. No band, no embroidered capes and suits, no blaze of colour. Just a motley crowd of youngsters hoping to try their luck and perhaps look interesting to someone important. There were a few older men scattered round the front row, including Aldo Russo, seated on what was normally the President of the Plaza's bench.

Dillon went up behind him and clapped him on the shoulders. 'Aldo.'

Russo glanced up and his face registered astonishment. 'Holy Mother.' He jumped up and embraced Dillon. 'Why didn't you warn me?'

'My visit came up in a hurry. This is Billy Salter,' he said in Italian. 'One close to my heart. A younger brother in all but blood.'

It was a Mafia saying and meant much. Russo looked Billy over. 'A younger brother?' he said in English. 'I think he's been around the houses, this one, I think he's made his bones.' He shook Billy's hands. 'Maybe your friend has told you I'm Mafia. Fifteen years ago we had much trouble with Maltese gangs in London.'

'What kind of trouble?' Billy asked.

'They interfered. I went as *consigliere*, counsellor. They wouldn't listen. Attacked my car one night when they'd promised safe conduct.'

'What happened?'

'My face was slashed. I was on my knees when a famous London gangster, who'd heard of the plot and didn't approve, came to my rescue with half a dozen men. You see, the Maltese had offended him, too.'

'It was my Uncle Harry,' Billy said. 'I grew up on that story as a kid. Black Friday. He smashed what they called the Maltese Ring.'

'He is still well, he is still with us?'

'Ask Dillon.'

Russo embraced him, kissed him on both cheeks. 'What a blessing.'

Below, the Gate of Fear opened and a number of young,

rather scrawny bulls ran out. Young men postured and started to flutter their capes.

'Years ago, Dillon used to come and see me, and being younger and foolish I'd get up to the kind of nonsense we're seeing now.'

'A bit of fun,' Billy said.

'Most of the time, but every so often amongst the young bulls there is a special one, and I picked it one day. I tried the cape, slipped, it tossed me over its shoulder and this one,' he nodded to Dillon, 'vaulted over the *barrera* down into the arena, and when the bull turned to charge he dropped on his knees, tore open his shirt.'

'Jesus,' Billy said.

'He called, "Hey, *toro*, just for me." The bull came to a halt and two *peons* pushed me away and the bull stood there snorting and Dillon walked up to it and patted it on the muzzle.'

'What happened?'

'The crowd roared, overflowed the *barrera* into the ring, carried him round on their shoulders. It couldn't have been louder on the Playa in Madrid. In the bars here they used to call him the man who seeks death, and what he did that day is known as the Pass of Death.'

Billy turned to Dillon, who said, 'Maybe that's what I was looking for all this time. Who knows? Now can we go and get a drink? There's something I need to discuss.'

The café close to the Playa wasn't too busy at that time in the morning. Inside, the place was light and airy, the walls were whitewashed, the bar top was marble, bottles crammed against the mirror behind. Bullfighting posters were all over the walls. Four fierce-looking gypsies sat at a table drinking *grappa* and playing cards. Two young men sat in the corner with guitars and countered each other. The bartender was old and ugly, the scar from a horn in his left cheek.

'A friendly lot,' Billy said.

'If they're on your side.' Russo called to the barman. 'Whisky all round, Barbera.'

'Not me,' Billy said.

Russo turned to Dillon. 'He doesn't drink?'

'No, he just kills people.'

'But only when necessary,' Billy said.

Russo shook his head. 'I must be getting old.'

The whisky was brought, they toasted each other. '*Salut*,' Russo said. 'What's it all about then?'

Dillon told him.

Afterwards, Russo said, 'Trust you, Dillon, to take on not only the IRA, but the Russian Federation. You couldn't make it easy, could you? But I see where you're coming from. The woman, the police superintendent. That was dirty. They shouldn't have done that, and to use the young nurse, then kill her.' He shook his head.

'So what do we do?' Billy asked.

'Oh, I still have considerable influence on this island,' Russo told him. 'My name is enough. To start with, I'll call the receptionist at the Sanders Hotel.'

He took out his mobile and made the call. 'This is Russo. What can you tell me about an Irishman called Fitzgerald? Moved in, then moved out. Where did he go?'

The call lasted several minutes. He finally switched off. 'Interesting. He left on the overnight ferry for Khufra on the Algerian coast, two hundred miles away. Apparently he's a friend of Doctor Tomac, who owns the Trocadero and just about everything else in Khufra and is, on occasion, a business associate of mine.'

'Go on,' Dillon said.

Russo did, not forgetting to mention Levin and Greta.

'Well, we know who he is, and she's the mysterious Mary Hall,' Dillon said.

'So what's your connection with this Doctor Tomac?'

'Cigarette smuggling, mainly. There's more money in that than hard drugs these days, and the court sentences are infinitely smaller. I have a diving concession there. Eagle Deep. It's exceptional diving. Special clients book me to fly them over in one of my floatplanes.'

'Would we be special clients?' Dillon asked.

'Well, let's say I owe you, my friend, and anyway, as we're not into the tourist season, there isn't much trade and I'm bored and this sounds interesting.'

'Then let's do it,' Dillon said. 'I couldn't be happier.'

At Tijola, Russo gave Pedro his orders when they loaded the plane, then said to Dillon, 'You're still flying?'

'I keep my hand in.'

'Then it's all yours.'

He sat beside Dillon, Billy behind. Dillon strapped himself in, fired the engine, allowed the Eagle to slip down the runway into the harbour, let the wheels up and called the tower at Ibiza airport. He indicated his destination, there was a pause and then he got the good word. He taxied out to sea past the end of the pier, turned into the wind and boosted power. He pulled back the column at exactly the right moment and the Eagle climbed effortlessly over an azure sea and lifted.

'How's it feel?' Russo asked.

'Couldn't be better.'

Russo opened the map compartment, reached in and produced a Browning. 'I presume you two are tooled up?'

'Absolutely.'

'Good, because this is the Khufra we're going to, where anything goes.'

THE KHUFRA

9

Dr Henry Tomac was very large, sixteen or seventeen stone, wore a creased fawn linen suit and a Panama hat, even though he was sitting at a booth table at his pride and joy, the Trocadero. Awnings at the front kept it cool and dark, the great fans in the ceiling rotating relentlessly.

The barmen were Algerians, dressed in white shirts and trousers, scarlet bands at the waist, the headwaiter wearing a scarlet tarboosh. You could eat at the Trocadero as well as drink, and the company was mixed and very rough, but Tomac had a number of villainous-looking men who kept things in order because Tomac demanded order and what Tomac said went in Khufra town.

He sat at his private booth, waving the odd fly out of the

way when Dermot Fitzgerald entered, worked his way through the tables, put down his bag and stood there.

'May I join you?'

'Dear boy, of course you may. Champagne, Abdul,' he called to the headwaiter.

'You may not want to.'

'Oh, dear, have you been a bad boy again?' He savoured the champagne Abdul poured. 'All right, tell me.'

'So this Russian agent Levin and the Novikova woman, you got word that they were coming, that's it? And you've come over because you're worried they might intend to do away with you?'

'Something like that.'

'Well, they are. The receptionist at Sanders Hotel gave me a phone call earlier. Told me about a couple, a good-looking man and woman, most interested in your whereabouts. It fits in neatly with a call I've had from Captain Omar at the airstrip, about a Russian executive jet, and a good-looking man and woman, on their way here. Their pilot brought them in on behalf of Belov International. I'm impressed, Dermot.'

'What can I do?'

'Well, I'm not sure – because there's *another* strange thing. I've had a *second* call from my friend, the receptionist at the Sanders Hotel. He's had a query about your whereabouts from a man he couldn't afford to offend. A business acquaintance of mine.'

'Who?'

Tomac told him.

Fitzgerald was totally thrown. 'I don't know this person. Mafia? It doesn't make sense.'

'Yes, well, he obviously knows you. He flies floatplanes here, runs a diving centre. Maybe he's acting for certain people in London who'd like to lay hands on you. You seem to be in demand, Dermot.'

'Help me, for God's sake.'

'It will cost you.'

'How much? I can pay well.'

'Get out of sight. You can use my apartment. If necessary, I'll send you to the house at Zarza in the marshes, or one of the diving boats might be better. We'll see.'

Fitzgerald cleared off, and a few moments later Levin and Greta appeared, followed by a waiter with their bags. They paused at the top of the stairs, Greta causing quite a stir, then came down and crossed to the bar. Tomac stood up.

'Miss Hall.' He put her hand to his lips. 'No more delightful visitor has graced my poor establishment.'

'Doctor Tomac.'

'At your service.' It was like a game they were playing.

'I dislike subterfuge. For good reasons I have been travelling incognita. I am in fact Major Greta Novikova, this is Captain Igor Levin of the Russian GRU. We're here on state business, serious business.'

Tomac managed to look grave. 'Please join me. Have the bags sent to the rooms, Abdul. Have some champagne served. This is obviously a matter of the highest importance.

Have you spoken of this to Captain Omar, our chief of police?'

As the champagne arrived, Greta said, 'In Ibiza we were told that in Khufra there was only one person worth talking to, and that is you, Doctor.'

'You flatter me, Major.' He toasted them. 'To your very good health. Now in what way may I assist you?'

'We seek a young man named Dermot Fitzgerald.'

'For what reason?'

'To save him from those who mean him more than ill-will,' she said. 'His life could be in danger.'

'Two men, we suspect,' Levin said. 'One called Dillon – Irish. The other, Salter.'

'Good heavens.' Tomac managed to look shocked, and at that moment a plane roared quite low overhead.

'What would that be?' Greta asked.

Tomac glanced out. 'Oh, a floatplane from Ibiza, Eagle Air. They come in all the time and tie up by the diving centre. Look, this is all very disturbing. Why don't you settle into your rooms and we'll talk again?'

'I look forward to it.'

Greta walked towards the bottom of the stairs, followed by Levin, who paused and turned. 'By the way, you didn't say whether you knew Fitzgerald.'

'No, I didn't, did I.'

Tomac adjusted his Panama, picked up his stick and walked out.

*　　*　　*

Dillon made an excellent landing outside the harbour and Russo took over and taxied round to the other side of the pier. There were a couple of sizeable diving boats tied up to a small jetty, a flat-roofed white building with a canopy of deep blue, and a notice that said Eagle Deep Dive Centre. There was a concrete ramp, as on Ibiza, and Russo dropped his wheels to taxi up.

An Arab was tidying up on the deck of one of the boats and two heavily tanned men stripped to the waist and in jeans were drinking beer in the stern of the other. They both looked around forty, hair long, muscular, fit.

'Not Arab,' Dillon said.

'No, that one is on the other boat, Ibrahim. The others are mine, not only good Italians, but Mafia. The one with the scar on his cheek is Jack Romano. The other is Tino Cameci. They like it here. It's like a holiday. I phoned before we left. We're expected. I said you were a master diver looking for action.'

'Well, so is the Boy Wonder here. Did you mention Fitzgerald?'

'Yes. Romano says they know him. You see the other diving centre a hundred yards along? Tomac owns that.' There were three diving boats. 'Along with most things here. They tell me Fitzgerald hangs out there when he's around.'

He took the Eagle up on the ramp and switched off. Romano and Cameci came to greet them and Ibrahim came also and got their luggage. Dillon held on to a brief-case.

'We didn't expect you for a while, boss,' Romano said in Italian.

'Something came up. Dillon here is like a brother to me.'

Romano's eyes widened. 'The Dillon who saved your son, your wife, may she rest in peace?'

'My friend here doesn't speak Italian,' Dillon said.

'But a gangster of the first rank in London. His uncle, his *capo*, saved my bacon in that great city years ago, so we are all friends. Let's have a drink on it and we'll discuss why we're here.'

Sitting under a canopy in the stern of Eagle One was very pleasant. They split a bottle of Chianti, ice cold because Russo liked it that way.

Romano said. 'We know this guy Fitzgerald. He's been coming on and off for a couple of years. He's a friend of Tomac. Dives from his joint.'

'Is he any good?' Billy asked.

'He thinks he is. You and Dillon, do you both dive?'

Billy smiled. 'It's been known.'

Dillon opened his briefcase and took a computer sheet out. 'This Fitzgerald has been a student at London University. I got a friend of mine to access his file. This is his photo. You confirm it's him?'

They both examined it. 'Definitely,' Romano said. 'And you tell me he's IRA?'

'Well, I was IRA and I did many things, but to persuade a young nurse to give this woman, my sick friend, an overdose, then shoot the nurse dead when she's done her work, I don't think I ever did a thing like that.'

'It's a thing no man should do.' Jack Romano bit his thumb.

Cameci said, '*Infamita*.'

'Well, let's have another drink to a suitable death for him.' Russo reached for the bottle and Tomac came along the boardwalk.

'Tomac's come visiting.'

Tomac paused, Ibrahim on Eagle Two bobbed his head to him and there was a brief exchange.

Dillon murmured. 'Fruits of a misspent youth, but I speak Arabic. Tomac said, "I see you, Ibrahim." Ibrahim said: "I see you, *Effendi*." Tomac said: "Remember who your friends are?"'

'Is that so?' Russo said, but by that stage Tomac was at the gangway. 'Ah, my good friend Russo. Permission to come aboard.' All this was delivered with perfect bonhomie.

'Why not?'

Romano stood up and gave him a hand, and Tomac eased his great body along the gangway and made it to a chair.

'Have a glass of Chianti,' Russo told him, 'Ice cold, just the way you like it.'

'The way *you* like it?' Tomac wiped his sweating face with a large handkerchief and nodded. 'Gentlemen.'

'Allow me to introduce Mr Dillon and Mr Salter,' Russo said. 'I've just flown them from Ibiza.'

'Ah, here for the diving, gentlemen?'

Dillon said. 'I hear it's spectacular. I was urged to visit by an Irish friend, one Dermot Fitzgerald.'

'I don't think I know him.'

Dillon took the photo from the briefcase again. 'Perhaps you recognize him?'

'No, I'm afraid not. Of course I can't be expected to remember all our customers. Many people come to dive here. You will be staying long?'

'As long as it takes,' Billy said.

'Do you intend to stay at the Trocadero?'

'No, we'll spend the night here,' Russo told him.

'How agreeable, but I'd be desolated if you failed to visit my poor establishment before you leave.' He heaved himself up. 'Until later.' He negotiated the gangway and departed.

'Well, at least *we* know he's lying,' Dillon said.

There was a small coffee stall just along towards the pier. Ibrahim had walked over to it, was standing there, drinking a cup, and Tomac paused as he passed, only briefly, and moved on. Ibrahim came back to Eagle Two and Russo called him to the rail.

'What did Tomac want?'

'For me to watch what your guests do and let him know.'

'And will you?'

'I am your man, but if it pleases him to think otherwise . . .' Ibrahim shrugged.

'Good. Have you anything to say to me?'

'My cousin was down from the airport, the one who works for the police. He says the plane which landed earlier is Russian and owned by a company called Belov International.'

'Who was on it?'

'A man and a woman. They've moved to the Trocadero.'

'And the plane?'

'Still at the airport. Two pilots. They are staying at the crew's emergency quarters behind the bar.'

'That's interesting. Go along to the Trocadero and ask your cousin Ali, the porter. See what's going on. This man Fitzgerald, you will recognize. I understand he's dived here many times. I want any information on him and the man and the woman from the airport.'

Ibrahim went obediently. Russo said, 'We'll see what happens. In the meantime, let's have a swim.'

At the Trocadero, Fitzgerald listened intently while Tomac filled him in.

'So, we have these Russians from the GRU who claim their mission is to protect you from these two men, Dillon and Salter.'

'What shall I do?'

'I'll tell Abdul to take you in the Land Rover to the house at Zarza, only he won't. He'll take you to the diving centre. I'll phone Hussein and tell him to expect you. You can stay in one of the diving boats or the old dhow, the *Sultan*. Keep your head down till we sort something out. This is going to cost you ten thousand pounds, I trust you realize that.'

'No trouble, I'm good for it.' Fitzgerald picked up his bag. 'Let's get moving. I don't trust either side in this.'

Tomac's next move was partly a result of his devious nature. He was smiling to himself as he went downstairs and found

Greta and Levin in the bar by the window. He eased himself down beside them.

'This man you seek, Fitzgerald, is at a house in Zarza six miles up the coast from here in the marsh. He's waiting to be picked up in a couple of hours to be taken to Algiers. Something to do with smuggling. Nothing to do with me, but the information is sound.'

'How do we get there?' Greta asked.

'I'll have Abdul take you in the Land Rover.' He puffed out his cheeks. 'Why, I don't know, as it can't possibly profit me. You'll be armed?'

'Naturally,' Levin told him.

'A wise precaution in these parts.' He heaved himself up. 'I can only wish you luck.' He went and spoke to Abdul and shuffled away.

'What do you think?' Greta asked Levin.

'I don't see a better offer on the table.' Levin shrugged. 'Why would he double-cross us? What would be the purpose? Come on, let's go and get ready.'

Tomac phoned the Eagle Deep Dive Centre and asked for Russo.

'You know the old house at Zarza?' Tomac said.

'Yes.'

'This Fitzgerald man. I have it on good authority that he'll be there in about two hours waiting for a lift to Algiers.'

'A long drive,' Russo said.

'Well, maybe he wants to go as far away as possible. If the information is useful, use it. Pay me back another time.'

He switched off the phone and started to laugh. It was really very funny. It would have been nice to have seen it.

So that's it,' Russo said. 'I don't know what he's playing at, but it's up to you.'

It was Billy who spoke. 'We'll go for it. What else is there to do here? Come on, Dillon, let's get tooled up and go and take the sod on.'

'If he's there, Billy.'

'I'll take you myself in the Ford,' Russo said. 'Even on these roads and a run into the marsh, it's forty-five minutes at the most. What have you got to lose?' He turned to Romano and Cameci. 'You two mind the store.'

The coast road was barely surfaced. There was the occasional small farm, lots of date palms, almond trees, thin cows, ribs showing, sheep, even the odd camel.

'It's like something out of the Bible,' Greta said.

Levin smiled. 'Darling, they'd probably cut my throat. You, of course, they'd sell in the slave market.'

'Thanks very much.'

Abdul, enigmatic as he drove, turned the Land Rover into the beginnings of the harsh and pungent smell of the marsh. As they started along the dike roads, wildfowl and seabirds stirred protestingly.

The sky had darkened and Greta said, 'What's wrong?'

'Summer storm,' Abdul told her. 'A cold front from the sea. Soon we get rain.'

The sun had vanished, and the reeds, ten foot high at least, seemed to stretch to eternity. It was as wild and desolate as anything Greta had ever known, mile upon mile of the great reeds stretching into the distance, an eerie whispering as the wind moved among them and a strange mist fell. And then it started to rain.

'There are ponchos in the back locker,' Abdul said.

Levin pulled them out. They were obviously ex-military, with hoods. He passed one to Greta and pulled the other one on himself. As they progressed, there were birds everywhere, wild duck, geese. The one good thing was the flattening of the clouds of mosquitoes in the deluge.

And then, at the end of one of the dike roads, they turned onto a kind of island. An overgrown garden, all sorts of foliage, date palms, a gloomy, weather-beaten clapboard house with a terrace, a large porticoed entrance, French windows.

'I'd say this was once a plantation,' Levin said to Greta.

Abdul nodded. 'There was a French family here for many years, a century or more. They drained part of the marsh, made it prosperous, then the war came and General de Gaulle took the hard line. The French people left, local farmers took over and they were no good. Nature returned.' He shrugged. 'The door is always open. I leave you here. I'll park under the trees down the track and wait – we're too early, I think.'

They got out, hoods up in the pouring rain, and went forward, both of them with a Walther ready. Greta paused at the bottom of the steps leading to the wide terrace, the front door opened and Sean Dillon stepped out, Billy on one side, Russo on the other.

'Hold it right there,' Dillon said, and then she pulled her hood back.

'Why, Dillon, it's you. Baghdad all over again.'

The look on his face was astonishing, absolute total shock, and he dropped his hand that held the Browning with a twenty-round magazine up the butt.

'My God, Greta.'

Taking advantage, Levin pushed her away, flung himself to one side and fired, but at the angle he was, it was Russo he caught, chipping his left shoulder. He kept on rolling as he hit the ground, went into the reeds and disappeared, and Billy fired after him to no avail. Russo got up, clutching his shoulder.

'It's OK. Could be worse.'

Dillon held out his hand. 'Mine's bigger than yours,' he told Greta.

She smiled. 'Of course,' and gave him her Walther.

In the reeds, Levin watched them move in out of the rain. A lucky shot might have got one of them, but with a handgun at that range not all three, and there was always the chance of hitting Greta. There was only one place to go, really. He eased his way back through the reeds and found Abdul standing by the Land Rover in the rain, holding an umbrella and peering through the trees. Levin slipped up behind him and tapped the back of the skull lightly with his Walther.

'No sign of Fitzgerald at all. I bet you enjoyed watching.'

'It's not my fault, *Effendi*, I was following Doctor Tomac's orders.'

'Who was the man I shot? Do I know the other two?'

'Aldo Russo. He owns Eagle Air and the diving centre. He's a dangerous man. Mafia.'

'What's his connection with Tomac?'

'Cigarette smuggling to Europe. It's big business.'

'Now we come to Fitzgerald. He's here, so where is he?' Abdul hesitated and Levin rammed the muzzle of the Walther against his ear. 'I'll blow it off.'

Abdul came to heel quickly. 'Next to the Tomac Diving Centre an old dhow is moored, the *Sultan*. He's there. The boss told him to stay out of the way.'

'Excellent. I like cooperation, so you can drive me back to town and we'll see what Tomac has to say about this almighty cock-up.'

Dillon, Billy and Russo had arrived only twenty minutes before Abdul and Levin. There were old stables at the rear and Russo had suggested hiding the Ford in there and waiting in the house. That the absence of Fitzgerald and the arrival of Levin and Greta had been more than a surprise, went without saying. Billy was stunned by Greta.

'It's like Lazarus out of his coffin and walking again, only he was a fella.'

'My goodness, Billy, you actually read the Bible,' Greta said.

'Never mind the repartee. Levin hasn't hung around long, has he?' Dillon told her.

'Don't be silly,' Billy said. 'He did the smart thing.' He'd taken off Russo's flying jacket and his white flying scarf and was binding it round the wounded shoulder.

'So what happened to you back there at Drumore?' Dillon took out his cigarettes and offered her one.

She decided to let it all hang out. 'Somebody blew up the *Kathleen*. I suppose that was you, Dillon?'

'I'm afraid so.'

'I got blown over the stern by the blast. Belov and Murphy weren't so lucky.' She turned to Billy. 'Not that you did much better. A bullet in the shoulder and back for Ashimov didn't do much to a bulletproof vest.'

Dillon was cold with fury. 'So it's been Ashimov behind everything?'

'Revenge, Dillon. You killed Belov, his greatest friend, the man who was like a father to him.'

'So Max Zubin hangs around in Station Gorky, black-mailed by his mother's presence in Moscow. Liam Bell runs things for the IRA at Drumore, and you and Ashimov set about a murder campaign?'

'Revenge, Dillon, like I told you.'

'This guy Levin, he's good, only he hires bum people. Harry Salter's Bentley, Roper in his wheelchair. Even the business with Hannah was a botch-up.'

'He'd nothing to do with that.' She was surprised how defensive she felt. 'It was hardly Igor's fault if the material he was supplied with was rubbish.'

'IRA rubbish, as Blake found when he took them on at Drumore.'

'Yes, he was good, but Bernstein was Ashimov. He arranged it with Bell. It was Bell who recruited the young nurse and Fitzgerald. Once she'd done her job, Fitzgerald shot her, then left for Ibiza with his loot.'

'A good payday.'

She felt even more defensive. 'I wasn't involved. It was Ashimov and Bell. I've told you.'

'Sounds good, only here you are with your new associate, trying to knock off Fitzgerald.'

She was almost pleading. 'It was Mary Killane who murdered Bernstein, not me.'

'Mary Killane didn't murder anybody. She was a tool.' Dillon shook his head. 'I'm tired of this. Let's get back to Khufra and sort Tomac out. At least he's got one use. He can give you some medical treatment, Aldo.'

On the way to town, Levin gave the whole thing serious consideration. That Greta was in the hands of the opposition was beyond dispute, as was the fact that to get her back from Dillon, Salter and Russo would hardly be likely. In fact, the obvious thing would be to cut his losses and run. He phoned Captain Scott at the airstrip.

'Something's come up. Can you be on standby for a swift departure?'

'Of course.'

'No trouble with air traffic control?'

Scott laughed. 'What air traffic control?'

'Can you refuel here?'

'Very cheaply. Where for?'

'I'd say Ballykelly direct.'

'And Major Novikova?'

'It looks like she may have to make other arrangements. Get on with it.'

He sat there thinking about it, the entire situation. It was droll in a way, yet he was beginning to tire of failure, particularly when it was hardly his fault.

He said to Abdul, 'I'm going to the Trocadero to say goodbye to Doctor Tomac, then I'm leaving.'

'Without the lady, *Effendi*?'

'The other side has got her. Too bad. There is one thing you can do for me, though. Take me to the *Sultan* and introduce me to Fitzgerald.'

'*Effendi*, please.' Abdul was pleading.

'You'll do exactly as I say, otherwise I'll kill you.' Levin said calmly. 'Now get on with it.'

They parked outside the Tomac Diving Centre and Levin said, 'Go on, lead the way.'

'As you say, *Effendi*.'

Abdul seemed resigned now and headed up the gangway, along the deck on the starboard side, and entered a corridor with reverse cabin doors.

'Go on, call him,' Levin said.

Abdul did. 'Are you there, Mr Fitzgerald? It's me, Abdul.'

'I'm in the saloon,' a voice called.

Abdul led the way. It was large with a high ceiling, walls of mahogany, old-fashioned cane furniture and a long bar, many bottles ranged on the shelves and Fitzgerald standing behind, pouring Irish whiskey into a tall glass and then a splash of soda.

'Doctor Tomac has sent me.'

'What's he want?'

He came round the bar, and Levin pulled Abdul to one side. 'It's not what he wants, it's what I want. Dermot Fitzgerald?'

Fitzgerald seemed to freeze, the shock intense.

'Igor Levin. I've a message from Mary Killane. Rot in hell, you bastard.'

His arm swung up, the silenced Walther coughed, and he shot Fitzgerald between the eyes, hurling him back against the bar to bounce off and fall to the floor.

'Excellent,' Levin said. 'Now you can take me to the Trocadero. You'll wait for me a few minutes, then take me to the airstrip. Is that understood? Do as you're told and I won't kill you.'

Levin went straight up to his room and collected his luggage. He'd hardly bothered to unpack, so it only took a minute or two and he was downstairs in the bar. There was no sign of Tomac, and Levin went out and dumped his bag behind Abdul.

'Where would Tomac be?'

'In his apartment at the top of the stairs.'

'I'll be back.' He reached for the keys. 'A precaution.'

He went upstairs, whistling, opened Tomac's door and walked straight in. The doctor was sitting behind his desk, reading glasses on the end of his nose, the Panama still on his head. He looked up, frowned slightly, no more than that.

'My dear sir. You look like a man in a hurry.'

'I am. Bound for the airstrip where I'll be flying away out of your life for ever.'

'And Major Novikova?'

'Unfortunately, in the hands of the opposition. There was no Fitzgerald at Zarza. Only Dillon, Salter and Russo. They got the major, I shot Russo and did a runner.'

Tomac tried to brazen it out. 'No Fitzgerald? I don't understand.'

'Oh, I caught up with him in the saloon of the *Sultan*, thanks to Abdul. He's on his back there now, eyes staring at the ceiling like you usually do when you've been shot in the head.'

'This is all most unfortunate.' He took off his spectacles.

'Yes, isn't it?' Levin reached for the door handle. 'Dammit, I was forgetting something.'

He turned, the silenced Walther coughed again and Tomac went over backwards in the chair. 'Yes, that was it,' Levin said and went out.

Abdul was still at the wheel and Levin got in the Land Rover beside him. 'Right, the airstrip, and when you get back I'd check on Doctor Tomac. He didn't look too well to me.'

They were waiting at the airstrip, there was an instant take-off and they climbed up to 30,000 and headed out to sea. Levin phoned Volkov and reported in.

Volkov listened and said calmly, 'At last, a success. It's a blessing that Fitzgerald's been taken care of.'

'A pity about Novikova. What can we do about that?'

'Very little at the moment. I would imagine she'll return to London with Dillon and Salter. Ferguson will put her in the safehouse at Holland Park, which is hardly the Lubianka. She poses no threat. Ferguson knows everything she knows.'

'Shall I speak to Ashimov?'

'You'd like that, wouldn't you?'

'I like keeping him in his place.'

'Then do it.'

Volkov switched off. Levin lit a cigarette, smiled then phoned Ashimov.

On board Eagle One they sat in the saloon, got Russo's scarf off and shirt and examined the damage. Romano got the first aid box, but it was Greta who examined it.

'Let me look. I did a field nursing course years ago for Afghanistan.' She shook her head. 'I can do a patch-up job, but it needs more than stitching. The bullet's cut across the shoulder. He'll need treatment at hospital level.'

'Well, that can wait until I'm back in Ibiza,' Russo said. 'Just get on with it.'

Which she did. Romano said, 'So this whole thing was a mess?'

'You could say that,' Dillon said.

'Well, we could have told you. After you left, Cameci and I caught sight of that Fitzgerald guy on the deck of the *Sultan* down the jetty.'

Dillon glanced at Billy and stood up. 'Watch her.'

Greta said, 'Where would I go, for God's sake?'

They went up the gangway and paused at the top. It was very quiet. Dillon drew his Walther and Billy fanned out to one side and they finally came to the saloon and discovered Fitzgerald's body.

'That's it then,' Billy said.

They went out on deck and the Falcon roared overhead at five or six hundred feet and climbing.

'And there goes Levin,' Dillon said.

'You could say he did you a favour,' Billy observed.

As they went down the gangway, Dillon called Roper on his Codex Four at Holland Park. 'We've got Novikova, believe it or not. Still in the land of the living. Fitzgerald's dead, Levin just left in his Falcon, so draw your own conclusions. Try and find out where he's going.'

'Will do.' Roper laughed. 'It's better than the midnight movie on TV.'

They returned to find the others assembled in the stern of Eagle One. Ibrahim was included, and looked scared.

Romano said. 'He's been up at the Trocadero to see his cousin, Ali. They've sent for the police. It would seem Doctor Tomac's turned up shot dead in his apartment.'

Greta said, 'My goodness, Igor has been busy.'

Russo said, 'Don't be stupid, lady. You want us to stay

here and explain things to Algerian police? You'd have sex
every time you went to the shower whether you liked it or
not.' He turned to Romano. 'Did you refuel?'

'Of course.'

'Good. Then let's get out of here, back to Ibiza. You'll have
to fly the whole trip, Sean.'

They took off ten minutes later, Dillon and Russo in the
front, Billy and Greta in the rear. As they turned to climb,
Dillon glanced down and saw two Land Rovers racing along
to the jetty.

'Police,' Russo said. 'Arriving too late as usual.'

'I know,' Dillon said. 'Just can't help it,' and he set course
for Ibiza.

Things going smoothly, he went on autopilot and called
Ferguson. 'It's me,' he said.

Ferguson, at his Cavendish Place apartment, was testy. 'I
was expecting you. Roper's spoken to me.'

'We've got out of Khufra by the skin of our teeth. My friend
Aldo Russo is slightly damaged. Greta Novikova, returned from
the grave, is in our hands. I presume you'd like to see her?'

'I certainly would.'

'Especially as she tells me Boris Ashimov also survived
Drumore. Do we get the Citation?'

'Of course you do. You only have to get off the bloody
phone.'

'Everything OK?' Billy asked.

'So it would appear. You know Ferguson.'

*   *   *

Dillon was lighting a cigarette one-handed when the engine suddenly missed a beat and spluttered. It was Russo who checked.

'Oil pressure.'

Dillon said. 'Life jackets under the seats. Get them on.' He pulled on his own and turned to Russo. 'What do you think?'

'That we've been well and truly done. Maybe it was Levin, more likely one of Tomac's boys. Look at the oil gauge.' It was fluctuating alarmingly. 'I'd say somebody's put water in the oil. Over a period of time, as the engine heats up, the water builds up into a head of steam. Usually blows the filler cap off. That's why the oil gauge is going wild. I'd say the engine will stop any moment now.'

They were coming into the Ibizan coast, descending, nosing towards the bay and Tijola, and the engine did indeed splutter and die. They started to glide with a strong cross-wind bouncing them.

'If we're lucky, I can land, but notice the waves. If they tip us over, we'll go straight down. How deep, Aldo?'

'Six or seven fathoms.'

'Right, this is the way it goes,' Dillon said. 'If we land and tip over, get out fast and swim. We're close to the shore. If we tip over and go straight down, don't do a thing until we settle on the bottom. Wait while we're there and don't try to open the door until enough water's got in to equalize the pressure.'

Even Billy was alarmed. 'For Christ's sake, get this right, Dillon.'

Dillon dropped the Eagle in, but the waves were swirling sideways and the plane dipped and went straight down.

'You know what you're doing?' Russo cried.

'Believe it or not, I've been here before,' Dillon said.

The water was dark and clear, the instrument lights still glowing, and the plane lifted a little, coasted forwards and landed on the bottom of the bay. Clear sand, a rock here and there, and the water was over their heads and Dillon pushed the door open, turned and grabbed Greta and pushed her out.

He floated up holding Greta's hand, Billy to the left of him, Russo to the right. You had to be careful about coming up from depth when diving, but they didn't have much choice. They broke through to the surface, Greta gasping.

'You all right?' Dillon demanded.

'Well, I wouldn't say you know how to please a lady,' Greta said, 'but I'm sure it beats the showers at Khufra Prison.'

'Good. Let's get going,' and they turned and swam the few yards to the shore.

Later, at the airport in the VIP lounge, they sat waiting, Billy, Dillon and Greta, for the arrival of the Citation X.

'We certainly see a little bit of everything,' Billy said. 'I mean, what was that all about?'

The automatic door opened and Russo came in, his arm in a sling. 'So here you are.'

'How did you get on?' Greta asked.

'Fifteen stitches. I can't feel my arm.' He leaned down and kissed her. 'Thanks for what you did. Listen, *cara*, if you'd like an older man, I'm available. I've got a great villa in Sicily at Agrigento.'

'It's a good offer, but I'll get by.'

'With Ferguson in the safehouse?'

'You don't understand, Aldo. He can't do anything to me, can't accuse me of anything. It's not that I'm not guilty. It's because Dillon and Billy are guilty too and Ferguson can't admit that.'

'Well, as long as you know what you're doing.' He kissed her again and Lacey came in through the door.

'Ready for take-off.'

Dillon said to Russo, 'Sorry about the plane.'

'No big deal. Not too deep and near the shore. The crew will have her up easy.'

'If you say so.'

They all got up and Russo put his good arm around Dillon. 'Any time, my friend, any time.'

'You must be mad,' Dillon said, and led the way out.

LONDON

IRELAND

10

When they landed at Farley Field the Daimler was waiting, with Ferguson beside the driver. There was also a Shogun with the Military Police Sergeant-Major from Holland Park, Henderson, and a black sergeant called Doyle. They stood, waiting, watchful, in navy blue blazers and neat ties, normal except for the earpieces and that special look common to security men all over the world.

They disembarked from the Citation and walked towards the Daimler and Ferguson got out. 'Major Novikova, what a pleasure. I seldom get the opportunity to greet someone risen from the dead.' He held out his hand, which she took instinctively. 'I hope they've been looking after you?'

Which reduced her to helpless laughter. 'Come on,

General, let's get on with it. Let's see what you're going to do with me and then I'll comment. One thing is certain. I'll need a hairdresser. Prolonged immersion in sea water is not to be recommended.'

'I'm sure we can manage that. I'll have one brought in.'

'To the Holland Park safehouse?'

'Such a good address. Excellent quarters, totally secure, wonderful company. Major Roper's there. Very special man. You'll get on famously.'

'While you pick my brains.'

'Now, would I do that to you, Major?'

'Absolutely,' and she climbed into the Daimler as he held open the door for her.

At Holland Park they were joined by Roper and sat round the table in the conference centre, Henderson and Doyle standing against the wall keeping a watchful eye on things.

'You must think you've been through the wringer, Major,' Ferguson told her.

'You could say that. Life with Dillon and Billy is a bit of a roller coaster.'

'Now tell me about the Putin warrant. I can take it as definite that the President himself passed that document across?'

'Yes, I was there with Ashimov.' She shrugged. 'And Levin.'

'And?'

She smiled. 'Ah, I see you don't know everything?'

'Oh, but I do know most things. Volkov, for example? What can you tell me about him?'

'I only met him once. He appears to control Belov International for the government. The President joined us, handed over the warrant, told us he expected us to do our duty in this matter. Never mentioned Belov, just left.'

'What's the point of the exercise?'

'Two, actually. Belov International is so important to the country at the moment, they don't want the sort of movement on the world financial markets that would take place if there was news of Belov's death.'

'And what's your second point?'

'Volkov thinks you and your people are a great nuisance and better put out of the way once and for all.'

'Thanks very much,' Billy told her.

'Would you say the President agrees?'

'The President is clever. He hands out a warrant, but it gives not the slightest indication what it's for.'

'The bearer of this letter acts with my full authority. All personnel, civil or military, will assist in any way necessary,' Dillon said. 'That can mean everything or nothing, but not from Volkov's point of view.'

'And Ashimov's been happy to assist him,' Greta said.

There was a pause. Roper said, 'So an unhappy Max Zubin still sits there in Station Gorky.'

'Yes, I thought you'd know about him. Well, he's shaved the beard off. It is an extraordinary resemblance, so they tell me. He posed as Belov once before. Ashimov was there.'

'Yes, we know that.'

'And his mother in Moscow?'

'I've met her. Fantastic woman, one of our greatest

actresses. She leads an open life. I mean, where would she go with him to think of?'

'And where would he go?' Dillon said.

'Any plans for him to be moved?' Roper asked.

'I believe so. An appearance in Moscow or Paris. I suppose a sight of him would dispel any rumours about Belov, keep things looking normal.'

'Yes, I suppose they would.'

'What about Levin?' Ferguson asked. 'Where do you think he's gone?'

'He had the plane, so he'll have gone to Ballykelly. Ashimov is there.'

'Really? How interesting.' Ferguson stood up. 'I must take that on board. Enough for now. Your hairdresser, after all, he's top priority. We'll meet again later.'

At Hangman's Wharf there was a magnificent warehouse development. It was Harry's pride and joy, walking distance from the Dark Man and turned into apartments of total luxury, unique in design.

The ultimate was the penthouse, vast, spread across a huge top floor, reached by two private lifts, one in front, the other at the back. Where the original cargo gates opened, there were now terraces of hardwood jutting twenty feet out over the river, and from the penthouse it was a seventy-foot drop.

The furnishings were cedar and mahogany, a great desk for Harry Salter in the corner, sofas, sumptuous carpets everywhere, Indian, Chinese, and in the open plan design a fabulous kitchen area with graceful hoods taking the fumes away and Harry's personal chef, Selim, from the restaurant, Harry's Place. He had energetically supervised the meal, mainly Indonesian, for the Salters, Dillon, Ferguson and Roper. Even Henderson and Doyle, seated at the far end of the bar and keeping a watchful eye on things, had been well taken care of. And there was Greta, of course.

'You've been very frank, Major,' Ferguson told her. 'Why?'

'Well, to be practical, I suspect you know most of what I told you. I might have done a little filling in, but that's all. Anyway, what happens now? You can't arrest me. That would be terribly inconvenient.'

'You think so?'

'I know so. Every job you and your people do is a black operation. It never happened, never existed. Dillon and Billy would never dream of going out there under orders and killing everybody on sight, but they do, which leaves me in the clear. So what happens to me?'

'If he sends you back, love, I think old Volkov would either shoot you or send you to the Gulag.' That was Billy.

'Of course you could claim asylum,' Roper said.

'If I found myself on the pavement, the most you could do is ask Colonel Luhzkov to send me home. I have diplomatic immunity.'

'How boring,' Ferguson said.

'And what a bleeding waste,' Harry put in.

'What if I made you a proposition?' Ferguson said.

'Throw in my lot with you?'

'Oh, no, something much more subtle. What if I gave you a chance to return to the fold, your own people?'

'What, hand me over to Lubzkov? Tell him to fly me out?'

'Much, much better than that. Now listen to me. There's one thing I suggest you do first, though.'

'And what's that?'

'First, let me ask you where you think Levin might be.'

She frowned. 'Drumore Place, probably.'

He handed her his Codex Four. 'I'm sure you know his number. Give him a call. Tell him what you think of him. After all, he dumped you at Khufra.'

She sat looking at him, then shook her head. 'What would be the point?'

'I'd like to know if he is there. I'd like to know if Ashimov is still there. I want them, and don't kid yourself, I intend to have them. Dead or alive, it makes no odds to me.'

'So what does that mean?'

'If you won't join in, we'll go and find out for ourselves. Dillon, young Billy here. Come to think of it, I'll go.'

Billy said, 'Not another bleeding beach drop.'

'Any approach from a plane would alert them,' Ferguson said. 'No, we'll do what we've done before. A passage by night, Billy. Oban to the Irish coast. It will do me good, a little rough weather and sea air. Does it suit you gentlemen?'

Dillon was smiling, Billy shrugged and Harry said, 'Only if I can come, too.'

Ferguson said, 'That's it then.' He smiled at Greta. 'You, my love, will be left in limbo with Major Roper at Holland Park.'

'That's actually illegal,' she said.

'Well, I could just as easily have you deported via the Russian Amabassador, direct to Moscow. I don't think it would do your career plans much good, do you?'

'My God, you're just as bad as they are.'

'True. It's the nature of the game we all play, and in my own way I'm sure I'm just as unforgiving as General Volkov. You see, there's one unfortunate thing about this whole wretched business which won't go away.'

'And what would that be?'

'Detective Superintendent Hannah Bernstein.'

There was a moment of terrible silence, as if a chill had touched everyone there.

Dillon's face was white, skin stretched, the eyes dark holes. It was as if Death had come to meet them. Strangely, it was Billy who spoke in a gentle voice.

'She was a special lady. She deserved better.'

There was nothing Greta could say, and Ferguson sighed. 'You could have joined the team, Major. You blew it. So, we'll leave you in limbo.'

Levin sat in the Royal George as rain swept in from the sea, finished his fish pie and ordered another vodka from Patrick Ryan, who had only half a left ear: a row of surgical clips holding it together, the whole lot glistening with surgical spray.

'When did you say he'd be back?' he asked Ryan, referring to Ashimov.

'Two, maybe three hours. He and Liam Bell went down

to Dublin. I heard them talking. It was something to do with the Russian Embassy.'

There was a roaring overhead. Levin said. 'That sounds like an approach to Ballykelly.'

'It could be.'

He went off to the kitchen, and a moment later Levin's phone rang. Ashimov said, 'I'm still at the Embassy in Dublin awaiting orders, God knows why, but I've news for you.'

'And what would that be?'

'Volkov wants you in London. They're sending a Falcon.'

'I think it's just flown in.'

'You're to report to Luhzkov and await orders.'

'Have you any idea why?'

'Not in the slightest.'

'Is it safe, for God's sake?'

'Of course it is. You're a commerical attaché at the Embassy, Ferguson can't touch you. It would cause a diplomatic incident and they wouldn't like that at the moment.'

'Why?'

'Don't ask questions, just do as you're told.'

He switched off. Levin sighed, went behind the bar, found a glass and reached for the vodka. The door burst open in a gust of rain and wind, and Liam Bell swept in with one of his men, Connor.

'There you are. How was Ibiza?'

'Hardly noticed. Algeria was crap.'

'Give me one of those.'

Levin dosed it out and one for Connor. 'So you've come back alone? I've just had Ashimov on the phone from Dublin.'

'He was closeted with the Ambassador, all highly bloody secret and not for the ears of a peasant like me. Told me he wouldn't be back until tomorrow and sent me packing.'

'And me thinking you were such good friends.'

'Don't make fun of me.' Bell grabbed the vodka bottle and poured another.

'I couldn't if I tried.'

He walked round the bar, and Connor, a brawny individual, grabbed him by the jacket. 'Don't you talk to Mr Bell like that, you Russian prick.'

'Actually, my grandmother on my mother's side came from Cork.' Levin tossed the vodka in his glass into Connor's eyes and head-butted him, sending him back against the bar.

Liam Bell reached under his armpit and Levin had his Walther out and under his chin in a second.

'I wouldn't – I really wouldn't. They've sent a plane for me. I'm needed in London.' He patted Bell on the face. 'Try and be good while I'm away.'

Lacey and Parry delivered Ferguson and his party to the RAF Air Sea Rescue Base at Oban on the west coast of Scotland, where they were picked up by a couple of RAF sergeants who took them by Land Rover to Oban itself.

One of them said, 'That's the *Highlander*, two hundred yards out. The inflatable at the jetty is yours. I know it doesn't seem much, sir, but it's got twin screws, a depth sounder, radar, automatic steering. It just looks bad because it's meant to.'

'I get the point, sergeant.' Ferguson smiled. 'Actually, we're old friends.'

'Safe journey back.'

'I don't care what he says.' Harry shook his head. 'It looks like a bummer to me.'

'I agree it doesn't look like it's nosing into the marina at Monte Carlo, but I suspect it will suit our purposes adequately,' Ferguson said. 'Now let's get our gear on board.'

A great deal of Oban seemed to be enveloped in a blanket of mist, and rain swept in. In the distance, clouds swallowed the mountain tops and bay and Kerrera, and there was heavy weather as waves dashed across the Firth of Lorne.

'I've said it before,' Billy moaned. 'What a bloody place. It rains all the time, it's cold . . .'

'Nonsense.' Ferguson patted his shoulder. 'Some of the finest views in the Highlands here. Now let's stow our gear and think about food.'

Everything stowed, Ferguson went up on deck and found Dillon in the wheelhouse with Harry and Billy. He was taking weaponry from the Quartermaster's bag and passing pistols across.

'One for you, Charles.'

He gave him a Walther, then dropped a flap beside the instrument panel, disclosing some clips screwed into place. He put a Walther in one, a Browning with a twenty-round clip in the other, and pushed the flap back into place.

'Just so you all know they're there. Now, what was it you said about food?'

They crossed to the jetty in the inflatable, found a nearby

pub that offered a log fire, a variety of drinks and a venison pie, which they all sampled. Later, back on the *Highlander*, they sat under the canvas awning over the stern, rain pouring off, and except for Billy, drank whisky and smoked, and Dillon turned on the deck lights, for the early darkness of the far north was closing in on them.

'So what's the plan?' Ferguson asked.

'What would you like to happen?' Dillon asked.

'I'd like us to slip in out of the night like young Lord Nelson on a culling expedition.'

'And do what?'

'Get our hands on Ashimov and Levin or, to be honest and it was a perfect world, shoot the bastards. Do you think that's too much to expect?'

'Not if we leave at six, hit the Irish coast early in the morning under cover of darkness, drape the *Highlander* with nets to look like a fishing boat. That way we can close in shore and land.'

'We've one big advantage,' Billy said. 'Dillon and me know Drumore Place, know what we're getting into.'

There was a pause. Ferguson said, 'Is that supposed to mean something?'

'Just that you and Harry stay on the boat,' Dillon said. 'And no arguments. We need somebody on board anyway to handle it if we have to make a quick getaway.'

'He's right,' Harry said. 'I mean, we'd be just lumbering around, wouldn't we?'

'I know, Harry, I too hate getting old.' Ferguson nodded. 'The ball's in your court, Sean.'

Dillon shook his head. 'There you go, calling me by my first name again.'

They left at six, Dillon at the wheel, and Ferguson joined him. It was still dark, wind stirring. 'What's the forecast?' Ferguson asked.

'Four to five when we hit the open sea.' Dillon took out a cigarette one-handed and flicked his Zippo. 'I love this.'

'So do I. Remember I told you how I tried to make up for a lost love by sailing the Atlantic run single-handed, Portsmouth to Long Island?'

'I remember what lost you your love. The woman couldn't marry a man who'd take out five IRA men in Derry who'd tried to assassinate him.'

'An old story, my boy. Is there any chance you could let me take over?'

'Be my guest.'

Dillon went out and Ferguson checked his instruments and took the *Highlander* through the harbour entrance in a long sweeping current to the Firth.

The swell started to move beneath, the masthead light began to roll rhythmically from side to side. Through the gloom he could see the red and green navigation lights of a steamer. He steadied at twelve knots and plunged forward, feeling better than he'd done for years.

*   *   *

In London earlier in the afternoon, Levin had reported to Luhzkov at the Embassy.

'So, what's all the fuss about?'

'I've no idea. I had a Most Secret from Volkov, saying to hold you here.'

'You mean physically?'

'Of course not. Hold you available.'

'And you don't know why?'

'No.'

Levin said, 'Well, Boris, you have my number. I'm staying at the Dorchester, so you'll have no trouble finding me.'

Later, sitting in the corner of the Piano Bar, indulging in a pasta salad and champagne, he was approached by Guiliano, the manager.

'So, we could have a little excitement around here,' Guiliano said.

'What do you mean?'

'A fellow countryman of yours.'

'What on earth are you talking about?'

'Putin. He's going to attend some EU conference in Paris, but there's a whisper he'll look in here on his way back.'

'You mean visit London?'

'No, visit here, the Dorchester. He'd be in good company. We've had every President in Europe stay at this hotel.'

He went to attend another customer. Levin lit a cigarette and sat there thinking about it. Maybe that was it, maybe his presence was needed in some way. It was a crazy world where international intelligence organizations could have their secrets and yet those secrets were readily available on the Grand Hotel circuit. You had to laugh, and he waved to the waiter to pour him another glass of champagne and toasted himself.

'To you, Igor,' he murmured. 'The only sane man in a world gone mad.'

Having said that, it occurred to him that under the circumstances it might be sensible to book out of the hotel until he'd seen the way things worked out, which meant staff quarters at the Embassy for a while. How dreary, but there was no help for it.

11

Later on the *Highlander*, Dillon took over and Ferguson went and sat in the saloon with Harry Salter. There was no sign of Billy. Harry said, 'He's taken a couple of pills and gone for a lie down in the aft cabin. The old sea sickness really gets to him.'

'Join me in a large Scotch,' Ferguson said. 'Finest remedy I know for sea sickness.'

They savoured it for a while, then Harry said, 'What do you think our chances are? I mean, are we daft or just a couple of old geezers sticking two fingers up at the world?'

'Never old, Harry. Old is a state of mind. The present expedition isn't particularly crazy. We slip in under cover of darkness, Dillon and Billy visit Drumore Place, lift Ashimov and Levin, bring them down to the *Highlander* at gunpoint and away. Could go very well.'

'And it could go very badly.' Harry shook his head. 'Why are we here right now with the sea rising, as far as I can tell somewhere off the Isle of Man.'

Ferguson poured him more whisky. 'Maybe it is something to do with getting old, maybe we're trying to show we can still cut it.'

'That makes sense for you and me, but what about Billy? I mean, he's rich, got everything he wants.'

'Maybe that's not the way he sees it,' Ferguson said. 'He's got everything and he's got nothing, or that's how it seems.'

'Dillon's not too badly off when it comes to cash,' Salter said.

'From his mercenary days.' Ferguson shrugged. 'People paid highly for his services. The whispers are true, Harry. He really did arrange the mortar attack on John Major and the war cabinet in ninety-one during the first Iraq war.'

'The IRA?'

'No, an Iraqi billionaire paid him big time.'

'The bastard.'

'He's never played favourites, our Sean. In the old days he'd be working for the PLO one minute and the Israelis the next.'

'What makes him tick?'

'Ah, the game, Harry, and there's always the danger that in the end, instead of you playing the game, the game is playing you. Anyway, that's enough of that. I think I'll have a little shut-eye and then I'll take over from Dillon.'

At the Royal George in Drumore, trade was brisk. In the corner booth, Liam Bell sat with Walsh, Kelly, Magee, a walking stick beside him, a relic of Blake Johnson's bullet in the thigh.

'Walking wounded.' Kelly nudged Magee.

'Well, this one's no better,' Magee said, as Ryan appeared from the kitchen. 'Are you sure you can still hear, Patrick?'

Ryan put down the tray of ale he was carrying. 'Stuff you, Magee. Would you like to buy your own?'

'Well, you've got to admit, he was a desperate kind of a fella, that Johnson.'

'Shut up,' Bell said. 'And drink up. I want some of you at the house. Walsh, Kelly, Magee.' He turned to three young men at the next table. They were new recruits, Connor, Derry and Gibson. 'You stay down here overnight with Ryan and mind what he tells you.'

They were young, arrogant and had their AK47s on the bench beside them. 'We will that, Mr Bell.'

'And keep your mobiles on at all times. Now go to the kitchen for your supper, then Ryan will work a rota for you, taking turns checking the harbour.'

After they had gone, Ryan said, 'Are you expecting trouble, Liam?'

'Christ knows what to expect in the present situation. Ashimov's staying over in Dublin. There's something up, but I don't know what. Levin's been called to London.'

'Jesus, but he needs taking down a peg,' Ryan said.

'Don't be stupid, man. It was Connor who got taken down in two seconds flat. You avoid contact with Levin at all times.

He was a paratrooper in Chechnya, medals, the lot. Anyway, drink up and we'll move up to the house. Mrs Ryan's left us a nice supper in the kitchen.'

There was quite a sea running, and cold spray stung Ferguson's face as he moved along the heaving deck and opened the wheelhouse door. Sean Dillon was standing at the wheel, his face disembodied in the compass light.

'It'll get worse before it gets better.'

'I'll take over.' Ferguson brushed past and took over the wheel. He increased speed, racing the heavy weather that threatened from the east, and the waves grew rougher.

'Go on, get below and find something to eat. I'll be fine.'

It was dark, very dark, and yet there was a slight phosphorescence from the sea now and then. At one stage there was the gleam from a lighthouse in the distance, but as they ploughed on, except for the occasional red and green lights of a ship, they might as well have been alone in a dark world.

At Holland Park, Roper was seated at the computers eating a sandwich when there was a knock at the door and Sergeant Doyle looked in.

'I've got Major Novikova, sir. She asked to speak to you.'

'Fine, show her in, Sergeant.'

She brushed past Doyle, dressed in a padded dressing gown. 'What is it?' Roper asked.

'I'm bored, tired of being locked up with two bloodhounds

taking shifts seated outside my door. How long will this go on for?' She sat down and Doyle leaned against the wall.

'As long as Ferguson wants. He could hold you indefinitely under the Prevention of Terrorism Act.'

'What if I want to be sent home?'

'They don't know you're here.' He smiled.

She said, 'At last that frozen face of yours has cracked.' He stopped smiling. She threw up her hands. 'I can't believe I said that. It was a car bomb, wasn't it?'

'IRA, one of many.'

'And you can work with Dillon?'

'Sean was never a bomb man.' He lit a cigarette and offered her one. 'You'd be better off going back to bed.'

Her mobile was on the desk close to his hand and now, for the first time, it sounded. Roper switched it on, held it to his ear. There was a hint of breathing. He offered it to her, she shook her head.

He smiled, put it to his ear again and said 'Major Novikova's residence.'

The caller disconnected. Roper moved into the emergence pattern on his computer, knowing it would be a waste of time, and it was.

'A coded instrument, and a good one. Impossible to trace.'

'Of course.'

'I'd go back to bed and consider your options, Major. He's a very reasonable man, the General, with people who are reasonable with him.'

'As you English would say, what a load of cobblers,' and she got up and walked out, followed by Doyle.

Roper thought about calling Ferguson and telling him about it, but decided against it. He couldn't even tell the general area the call had come from, so there wasn't much to tell. He wondered how they were getting on, and went back to work.

At Station Gorky, Max Zubin sat in his room and talked to his mother. He did that a lot, and was allowed unlimited time. After all, security were listening to the conversations. Her cheerful, tough humour kept him relatively sane, but all her conversations ended in the same way.

'When am I going to see you?'

'I can't say.'

'Well, Josef Belov has ultimate power, people listen to his orders.'

'But I'm just a poor Jewish actor, Mama, and I don't even get Actor's Guild minimum. Sure, there are hints I might be making a move, that's all I can say. God bless.'

Three miles off Drumore, the *Highlander* drifted under automatic pilot while they gathered in the saloon and sorted out the weaponry. Dillon and Billy wore black Special Forces' overalls and flak jackets, balaclava helmets rolled up at the moment but ready for the right sinister effect later. A Walther each in a shoulder holster, an AK47 in the silenced mode.

Ferguson and Harry wore flak jackets and each had an AK

to hand. There was a chart open on the table showing the general approach to Drumore.

'With the nets up, we'll look like any other fishing boat,' Dillon said. 'Lay offshore beyond the point. We'll go in the dinghy, it's got silencers on the outboard. Tie up on the west side of the jetty and proceed to the house.'

'Could work like a Swiss watch,' Billy said.

'Or the kind you buy off a stall at Camden Market,' Harry grumbled.

'Well, we'll see.' Ferguson smiled. 'It's good to smell powder again. Let's get on with it. I'll tell Roper it's all systems go.'

At Holland Park, Roper listened. 'So, approximately thirty minutes?'

'I'd say so.'

'Excellent. I'll stand by.'

He lit a cigarette and sat there in the shadowed room, watching his screens, his inputs to the Russian Embassy in London, his scanning of what was happening with Belov International, Ashimov, Levin, the names of all involved parties, waiting for what might come up – anything. A dirty night for it, and he waited.

Dillon and Billy went over the rail to the dinghy, Billy pushed the starter button on the engine, and it rumbled into life, a gentle, pulsating sound, not much noise to it at all. They coasted in on the west side of the jetty, beached and moved away fast, sinister figures in the darkness.

There was a light at the bar windows of the Royal George. Dillon put a finger to his lips and he and Billy approached cautiously and peered in. Connor, Derry, Gibson and Ryan were sitting round a table by the log fire, playing cards.

The curtain was half drawn, the window two or three inches open, and Dillon eased it back and heard Ryan say, 'I'll make some bacon sandwiches and tea. Derry and Gibson, take a walk round for a quick check.'

'Ah, Jesus, Mr Ryan, do we have to?'

'That's Liam Bell's orders and that's what you'll do. Now be off with you.'

Dillon and Billy hurried away, following the winding path they remembered so well all the way up to Drumore Place. There was the luxuriant garden, summerhouses, the huge terrace, French windows, light glowing dimly here and there.

'Somebody's up early,' Billy murmured.

'Well, let's take a look,' and Dillon raised his night glasses. At that moment a French window opened and Walsh and Kelly stepped out, Liam Bell behind.

'Just check the garden,' he said and turned back.

'Come on,' Dillon said to Billy and moved forward.

At Holland Park, Roper was still at his computers. To a man so badly damaged, sleep does not come easily, and he frequently worked all night, a diet of whisky and sandwiches keeping him going. There was a sudden stirring on his screens as a tracer element analysed not photos, but staff day records at Russian embassies around the world, and there was Major Boris Ashimov, overnighting at the Dublin Embassy. It was just as interesting to find out that Captain Igor Levin was back on staff at the London Embassy and resident there. He called Ferguson at once on his Codex Four, and Ferguson, in the wheelhouse with Harry, was horrified.

'Things are in motion. They're on the job now, and too late to abort. If I ring Dillon on his Codex, it could be exactly at the wrong moment.'

'It's your call, General. No Ashimov, no Levin there, just the good old IRA.'

'God, I don't have much choice, do I?' and Ferguson called Dillon, who unfortunately was otherwise engaged.

As Dillon and Billy had started up to the terrace, Bell turned the terrace lights on from inside the library, revealing Dillon and Billy moving forward.

Walsh called out, 'Intruders, Mr Bell,' and fired his AK 47. Billy ducked behind the balustrade and knocked him down. Kelly turned, stumbled and had Dillon all over him. Dillon pulled up his hood.

Kelly said, 'Christ, it's you, Dillon.'

'So it is, and I'll kill you stone dead if you don't answer my question. Ashimov and Levin, where are they?'

'Ashimov's in Dublin, due back later today. Levin flew in to Ballykelly from Ibiza and out again to London.' He was terrified. 'I swear to God, Sean.'

'And where would Liam Bell be?'

'Getting the hell out of here, if he's got any sense.'

As he said that, there was the sound of a car starting up and driving away. 'There the bastard goes,' Billy said.

Dillon called up Ferguson, 'The whole thing's gone sour, Charles. We're on our way back. Come and get us.' He said to Kelly, 'I keep my word. Run for it.'

Which Kelly did, pausing to watch them go, then calling through to Patrick Ryan at the Royal George.

'You've got bad trouble coming your way,' he said, but Ryan already knew, for earlier Derry and Gibson, patrolling the harbour, had discovered the dinghy and the outboard still warm, on the west side of the jetty.

'Well, I don't know whose this is, but it's soon taken care of.' Derry pulled a pistol out, putting three holes in it.

Offshore, Ferguson had heard and said to Harry, 'We're going in.'

'I'm with you,' Harry said and went out on deck, his AK ready.

They went in quickly to the harbour, and Dillon and Billy coming down the hill path came under fire from Ryan and Connor. Dillon hit Connor with two shots, Ryan ducked down and caught Billy in the middle of his flak jacket with a lucky shot that knocked him over. Dillon hauled him up and they continued, running headlong down the path towards the jetty and the beach. Derry and Gibson started to fire up at them, caught on the exposed path, and the *Highlander* roared in out of the darkness. Harry fired in sustained bursts at the two men on the beach by the dinghy, as Dillon and Billy burst onto the jetty, and as the *Highlander* bounced off the jetty they scrambled over the rail.

Derry was down, and Ferguson, at the wheel, dropped the flap and pulled out the Browning with the twenty-round clip and sprayed the beach as they swerved away, knocking down Gibson as well before they were swallowed up by darkness.

Later, on automatic pilot, they sat in the saloon and drank whisky. 'Well, that was brisk,' Harry said.

'And a bleeding waste of time.' Billy shook his head. 'We couldn't even get Liam Bell.'

'At the time there was no way of knowing Ashimov was overnighting in Dublin, Levin in London. It was just bad luck, and Major Novikova wouldn't cooperate.'

'The thing that really interests me is Levin being sent to London,' Dillon said. 'I'd like to know why.' He got up. 'We'll have to give him some special attention when we get back. Anyway, I'll take the wheel. The rest of you can get some sleep.'

They sky was streaked with light, and way over on his left the Isle of Man was apparent in spite of the rain. It could have been worse, Dillon told himself. At least he and Billy had walked away from it, thanks to Harry and Ferguson. It was the enemy who'd suffered. The thing was, what happened now? He lit a cigarette. His Codex Four went. It was Roper.

'You and Billy are in one piece obviously.'

'Just about. Liam Bell did a runner at the house, his boys gave us a hard time. Ferguson and Harry were wonderful. Bell's short three, maybe four men, so we did some good.'

'You certainly did.'

'The thing is, what happens now?'

'Oh, that's easy. President Vladimir Putin visits the European Union's Paris Conference tomorrow, then he intends to divert to London, have a chat with the Prime Minister, stay at the Dorchester and fly back to Moscow in the morning.'

'What for?'

'Oh, a remarkable story of greed, corruption and politics, which has only unfolded within the past hour on my screens. I've tried Ferguson, but he isn't replying.'

'Flat on his back below. They all are.'

'Not surprising. How far to Oban?'

'I'd have said two hours, but there's quite a sea running. It's going to get worse. You could do me a favour and alert Lacey and Parry.'

'Will do. I'll leave the juiciest details of the Putin visit until I see you, except to say he'll have an interesting guest with him at the Dorchester – Josef Belov.'

Dillon was stunned. 'How can that be?' and then he saw it. 'Max Zubin's going to do Belov again in London?'

'Something like that. We'll talk again.'

Dillon thought about it, then put the boat on automatic pilot and went below to tell Ferguson the extraordinary news.

*   *   *

In Moscow at the Kremlin, Max Zubin, bundled out of bed at Station Gorky, ordered to be dressed and ready in an hour, then flown at what had seemed like express speed, now stood in front of Volkov's desk.

'You have a wonderful opportunity to serve your country. Your finest hour. You will visit Paris as part of the President's entourage, travel to London to perform the same service at the Dorchester Hotel, and then return to Moscow.'

'But what is the service I perform, Comrade?'

'Just your role as Josef Belov. There will even be appearances on television. I'm sure you'll do very well.'

'Yes, but in the theatre we're expected to know our lines.'

'That's really very good. There's a press release here. Have a quick look.' Zubin scanned it and handed it back. 'I see.'

'So now you know what it's about if anyone talks to you, but we'll keep conversation to a minimum. Just remember you are Josef Belov.'

'Except to my captors.'

'Don't be silly. Those who guard you at Station Gorky call you Belov because that's who they think you are. Of course, your controller listening to your phone calls knows.'

'Can I see my mother while I'm here?'

'If you introduce yourself as a friend. After all, you couldn't possibly be her son, if you follow me. You were bearded – that's who Mikhail, her chauffeur, knew.'

Zubin shook his head. 'So my driver, Ivan Kurlovsky, thinks I'm the real Belov?'

'Of course.'

'I'm just like the King in *The Prisoner of Zenda*.'

'What on earth are you talking about?'

'I'm sorry, I got confused. May I go?'

'Right now.'

Zubin got out fast, and was escorted to his limousine. He gave Ivan, the driver, his mother's address and sat back, brooding. When they reached the destination, Zubin put on his sternest voice.

'You will wait here. I am visiting a friend. One hour and then we go to the hotel.'

It was his mother who answered the door, and her face lit up. 'How handsome you look,' and she drew him in.

'Where's Sonia?'

'Very ill. She's gone to stay with her sister. Come and sit down. Why didn't you let me know you were coming?'

'I didn't know myself. Things are moving very fast.'

She gave him a vodka and sat beside him, holding his hand. 'So tell me about it.'

'My performance, Mama?' He swallowed the vodka. 'The greatest of my life.' He handed her his glass. 'Give me another.'

Sitting in Roper's computer room at Holland Park, they were all there. Ferguson said, 'Any trouble with the girl?'

'Not particularly. She thinks she's being held illegally, of course.'

'Tough luck. After some of the stunts she's pulled, she's lucky not to be in a cell. Now let's get down to it. What's going on?'

'Before I start, can I ask you if the Prime Minister knows about the play-acting over Belov?'

'Yes, President Cazalet discussed it with him. It's one of those things where they prefer not to know officially, if you follow me, but I keep him informed. Anyway, what's it all about?'

'Putin has a meeting in Paris with the EU, then he visits London, spends a night at the Dorchester – trade delegation stuff – then dinner with the Prime Minister.'

'Go on.'

'Lurking among his staff will be one Josef Belov.'

'What's the purpose of his presence?'

'To be seen, to have him on television close to Putin, with any luck close to the Prime Minister. He won't have a lot to say, if anything. They'll keep tight control.'

'Any interviews?'

'No, but there will be a press release.'

'What about?'

'The Belov Protocol.'

'And what in the hell is that?'

'Well, excuse me if it sounds like a lecture, but here goes. Some years ago the old Soviet government were going through economic crisis after crisis, always short of the almighty dollar, so they started selling off government utilities at knockdown prices, oilfields, gas, the wealth of Siberia. The oligarchs came along, men like the robber barons in the old days in the USA, men like Belov. He started with a billion and the word is he got it from Saddam. In oil alone, his wealth can only be measured in billions.'

'Yes, I know that,' Ferguson said.

'Then when the Rashid empire was up for grabs, he took over.'

'So where is this getting us?' Dillon asked.

'To the United Nations Common Policy Division. Belov International has become so enormous, its tentacles reach every developing country in the world. It's truly global. Can you imagine the effect all that could have if it was controlled by a single government?'

'The Russian Federation?' Ferguson asked.

'Many Russian politicians think it was a mistake to allow the State's assets to pass into private ownership in the first place. Times have changed, Putin is a hard man, the Russians like strength. Things are getting more like the Cold War every day. Now is the time for a truly magnificent gesture from a Russian hero, Josef Belov. He'll sign an item called the Belov Protocol, transferring all of Belov International into the hands of the government of the Russian Federation.'

'Just a minute,' Harry said. 'If this United Nations outfit were worried about Belov International putting things out of balance, being too powerful, they aren't going to be too happy about Russia taking over.'

'Neither will the United States, nor the UK, nor Europe,' Ferguson put in.

Harry said, 'When I was young under the Labour government after the war, we used to nationalize things, didn't we? Well, this would be something similar. Putting things back into government control.'

'And an incredible boost in power and prestige for Russia,' Ferguson said.

Dillon nodded. 'All performed in front of cameras, Max Zubin standing in for Belov.'

'I hope he's practised how to do Belov's signature,' Harry said.

'Oh, that will be taken care of, no problem,' Roper said.

'And the beautiful thing from their point of view is that we can't stand up and say, "That isn't Josef Belov,"' Ferguson said, '"Because we blew him up."'

'So there it is.' Roper shook his head. 'A wonderful confidence trick. I don't know about Putin, but Volkov must be laughing up his sleeve.'

'And there's nothing we can do about it?' Billy asked.

'I'm not so sure.' Dillon turned to Ferguson. 'Tomorrow night at the Dorchester, the Russian Embassy'll have a reception. Putin will be there, the Prime Minister, and Josef Belov.'

'What are you suggesting?'

'I think we should go. Billy and I got into Igor Levin's room when he was there. I don't see why I couldn't manage the same thing where Max Zubin is concerned.'

'To what purpose?'

'I haven't the slightest idea, but he might have things to say, some personal suggestions.'

'You know, I think you could be right.' Ferguson nodded. 'We'll go. You, me and Billy.'

'Excellent.' Dillon turned to Roper. 'You've often boasted in the past that if it's out there in cyberspace, you can find it.'

'So what do you want me to do?'

'Go through the entire story from the beginning, access all Russian sources, check out who's going to be at the Dorchester function, what kind of security the Putin delegation will have. Something might be there, lurking in the woodwork. Everything in life has a flaw.'

'Well, if there's one to this whole affair, I'll find it.'

12

And work at it Roper did. There wasn't an aspect of the entire affair that wasn't covered. All relevant traffic out and in at the Russian Embassy in London, traffic from the Kremlin, dealings with the IRA. It was never-ending.

Another interminable night, then, of sandwiches and whiskey and constant smoking, and Doyle, on the duty shift, bringing innumerable cups of tea.

At five o'clock Doyle pulled up the blinds. 'Dirty morning, raining away.' He turned, 'Look, sir, don't you think you're overdoing it a bit?'

'You always are when you're looking for the little things, Sergeant, so it pays to take care. I learned that lesson with my last bomb in Londonderry. It was just a

Mini car with a shopping bag on the rear seat, so I didn't
treat it seriously.'

'Bad luck, sir.'

'Sheer carelessness, so it pays to take care. Check everything.' At that precise moment he was proved right.

The intercept was one of many relevant to Station Gorky,
mainly messages to do with administration, work structure,
now and then commands from Volkov himself. Roper was
reviewing them, when he stopped, then frowned and reversed
the screen listings. The message which had caught his eye
referred to transportation for Belov's flight from Station
Gorky, but not to Moscow Airport. Some little distance from
it was the Belov Complex, which specialized in private planes,
executive jets and the like, even courier aircraft from foreign
countries, making their regular pilgrimages in and out with
Embassy material.

The particular message made the point that Colonel Josef
Belov's chauffeur, one Ivan Kurbsky, would meet the plane
and transfer the Colonel straight to the Kremlin before Belov
moved on to the Excelsior Hotel to his usual suite.

It hadn't struck Roper before, the reference to Belov's old
KGB rank, and he went back to the beginning of the traffic
from Moscow to Station Gorky. No reference to Max Zubin.
Well, of course there wouldn't be. The whole emphasis was
on Belov, even in the most trivial matters.

Perhaps he was tired, or slightly out of his mind by that
stage, but a wild idea had formed in his head. Crazy, obvious

and simple. What if *everyone* dealing with Max Zubin at Station Gorky actually believed he was Josef Belov?

He turned to Doyle. 'See if the Major's stirring, Sergeant, and ask her if she'd fancy some early breakfast with me, and I'd like you to help me out with her,' and he explained.

'Certainly, sir.'

Roper poured a whiskey to pull himself together. The implications were obvious. 'Right, old son, don't mess up,' he murmured.

'You look terrible,' Greta told him.

'I've looked terrible for some years now.'

She was genuinely sorry and shook her head. 'But your diet seems to consist solely of Irish whiskey.'

'That's Dillon for you.'

'I expect so. And too many cigarettes.'

'They help calm me down. I get neurological symptoms. Can't sleep.'

'And you only eat sandwiches. I haven't seen you tackle a decent meal.'

'Well, you will now. I've ordered a full English breakfast. I thought you'd like to join me. Start with the tea, Sergeant,' he said to Doyle. 'Oh, and pass the morning papers.'

'Coming up, sir.'

Doyle picked up *The Times* and the *Daily Mail* from a side table and passed them over. Both of them featured

Putin's visit, also the press release announcing details of the Belov Protocol.

'My God,' she said, as she looked at the *Mail*.

'My God, indeed.' Roper poured another whiskey. 'This is purely medicinal, I assure you, but a toast to Russian bare-faced cheek.'

She read the piece quickly and looked up. 'Why do you say that?'

'Oh, come on, you'll never get away with it.'

'That's what you think. Ashimov passed Max Zubin off in Paris the other year with no trouble. Not only does Zubin really look like Belov, he's a damn good actor. Ashimov told me he handled it really well. It fooled everybody. French Intelligence, the CIA, the Brits.'

Doyle had come in with a trolley and laid a table by the fire. She carried on talking.

'If it worked then, it will work now.'

He wheeled his chair to the table and started on the bacon and eggs. 'Come on, eat up, it'll get cold.'

She took his advice. 'Say, this is good. But you must understand, Roper, we Russians are used to the cold.'

'Well, you didn't do too well in the Cold War.'

He was pushing her now, and she flared. 'We did all right. Gave you your share of bloody noses, you and the Americans both. And some you don't even know about.'

Doyle brought a bottle across and two glasses. 'I'm sorry, Major Novikova. Major Roper told me a vodka usually starts a Russian breakfast. I forgot.'

'It certainly does, he's right there.' He poured, she took it down in one go. 'Another, Sergeant.' She was on her mettle. 'I've invented a new breakfast for you English. Vodka and bacon and eggs.'

'Actually, I'm Irish, Major,' he smiled. 'What they call Black Irish.'

'God, I can never understand this. Why do you Irish always fight for the English? You should hate them.'

'Not really, Major.' He slipped another vodka in her empty glass. 'I mean, they're a bit like your mother-in-law. An inconvenience when she calls.'

She fell about laughing and finished the third vodka. 'Your mother-in-law? I like that. Do you like it?' she asked Roper.

He pushed his plate away. 'If you do, but enough of this chat. I'm telling you, this Belov Protocol will never work.'

'Why not?'

'Too many people know what happened to the real Belov, know about Zubin, I mean, everybody who worked with him at Station Gorky.'

She exploded, almost in fury. 'Are you stupid or something? Don't you understand? To everyone at Station Gorky, Max Zubin *is* Josef Belov.'

There was a moment's stillness and Roper said, 'Is that really true?'

'But of course. Only a handful of us know the truth – Ashimov, me, General Volkov, and through him, the President.'

'And we do.'

'Because Dillon pressed a button and killed Belov.'

'So when you present Zubin at Station Gorky . . .'

'He's got to be Belov.' She shook her head. 'Surely you

can see that? Even his chauffeur in Moscow thinks he's Belov. People accept. And what can you do?' She held her glass up to Doyle. He refilled it obediently.

'Is Ferguson going to stand up at the Dorchester and say: "Excuse me, this isn't Josef Belov, we assassinated him with American connivance?"' She took the vodka down. 'I think not.'

'An amazing situation,' Roper said. 'When you think of it, he could be Josef Belov for the rest of his life.'

'I don't understand.' She was befuddled with too much vodka now.

'It's just an interesting point. You know, the appearance of things and people believing in it.' He smiled. 'Anyway, I've got work to do. Take Major Novikova back to her quarters, Sergeant.'

She got up, staggered a little, and leaned on the table. 'What was all this about? What were you after?'

'I'd go back to bed if I were you, Greta, have another sleep.'

She staggered slightly and Doyle caught her. 'Steady now, Miss, just come along with me.'

Roper lit a cigarette and thought about it, then turned back to the computers. The last message on his screen was the one about transportation facilities to Belov Complex, where his chauffeur, Ivan Kurbsky, would meet the plane and convey him to the Kremlin before the Excelsior Hotel. That would be for Volkov to give him a final briefing.

He sat there brooding, thinking of every aspect, and it all began to come together. He thought about it some more and phoned Ferguson and found him still at home at Cavendish Place.

'I need to see you.'

'Why?'

'How would you like to make the Belov Protocol into a total balls-up? How would you like to leave the Russians with nothing but egg on their faces?'

'Tell me more.'

Which Roper proceeded to do.

When he was finished, Ferguson said, 'Totally mad and also quite brilliant. It could be absurdly simple.'

'The old Swiss watch syndrome. If it all worked.'

'All right, what do you want?'

'A meeting with you at the soonest with me, Dillon, Billy, Squadron Leader Lacey and Parry.'

'Is there anything I should know before we meet?'

'Yes, I've got a few requests.' He went through them. 'There are a number of things I can sort out via my computers. I'll take care of those aspects. Can we meet in, say, two hours?'

'Absolutely. Holland Park?'

'I think so. It's useful if we need to refer back to computer information.'

'Of course. There is one thing I've got to say.'

'And what's that?'

'Max Zubin – it would all depend on his willingness to play ball.'

'Well, we'll see about that.'

Roper switched off and went back to his screens.

*   *   *

At Holland Park, Roper was doing the briefing. 'This whole thing hinges on some sort of contact being made at the Dorchester with Max Zubin. It seems obvious to me that he'll return to Moscow still playing his role for the sake of his mother. That means the day after tomorrow he'll be seen on the world stage signing the Belov Protocol. The only way to prevent that would be to get Zubin out of Moscow with his mother.'

'And how do we do that?' Billy asked.

Roper turned to Lacey. 'You know the Belov Complex in Moscow?'

'Of course. We've been there a few times. It's close to the main airport, handles private traffic, executive aircraft and courier planes. We've done it for the Embassy run a few times.'

'So if the great Josef Belov turned up there with his mother and had a walk around, how do you think he'd be treated?'

'With fear and great respect. I know Russia.'

'And if they ended up on your courier plane and you got out of there fast, how long would it take you to leave Russian airspace?'

'If I was given the Citation X, half an hour at the most. Since the demise of Concorde it's arguably the fastest commercial plane in the world.'

'So you'd be out of it, in effect, probably before they'd even had a chance to scramble another aircraft to see what you were up to?'

'With any kind of luck, yes.'

'If you volunteer for this, you'd be in uniform, RAF

roundels on the plane and so on, everything to confuse the issue.'

'That's good, sir, and by the way, we do volunteer.'

'My God,' Billy said. 'It could work. It's so bleeding simple.'

'Which only leaves us with the problem of getting Max Zubin to agree,' Roper said.

'I'd say you've already worked that out.' Dillon smiled.

'There's plenty of security at the hotel, both Russian and British. You, Billy, have your identification, so that's all right. The fact that you speak Russian, Sean, could be useful. You could growl your head off at any unfortunate room service waiter as much as you want and carry your copy of the Putin warrant just in case, to confuse any Russian security people.'

'But meeting Zubin will be difficult.'

'Not at all. He's been given one of those magnificent Park Suites on the fifth floor, as befits his status as Josef Belov. There is a small bedroom with separate bathroom next to it, double doors in between, which are kept locked unless it's booked, to provide a second bedroom for the suite.'

'And this one isn't?'

'Well, it was, but I cancelled and then fiddled the computer to make it look as if it's still occupied. I recall when you got into Levin's room, you had a house key like staff use.'

'Still do.'

'With regards to Levin, he's with the Russian Embassy party and Boris Luhzkov. I suppose they know we won't lift Levin.'

'What would be the point?' Ferguson said. 'And they can't lay a finger on us. I'm going and you two can join me,' he said to Dillon and Billy. He turned to Lacey. 'You'd better get on with arranging the courier flight out of Farley. You have full authority.'

'Certainly, sir.'

They all got up, and Roper said, 'I was thinking, Dillon. Take an extra Codex Four. If this idea works and Zubin agrees, it will give him a link with you.'

'Good thinking.'

'Well, let's get on with it. The game's afoot,' Ferguson said.

At the Russian Embassy, Boris Luhzkov was in his office when Igor Levin went in. 'I got your message. What's up?'

'Nothing, just a thousand and one things to do.'

'You worry too much.' Levin lit a cigarette and sat on the window seat.

Luhzkov said, 'It's all right for you, the big war hero, used to running around at the Kremlin.'

'Luhzkov, what can I do for you?'

'Volkov insists on your presence tonight so you can make yourself useful.'

'I'm not exactly *persona grata* to our British friends these days. You're sure Charles Ferguson won't try to have me picked up once I'm on the street?'

'Look, Igor, I don't know what you've been mixed up in and I don't want to know. You work for Volkov, carry the Putin warrant, that's enough for me. One thing I do know. You've got diplomatic immunity. If the Brits want you for anything, all they can do is send you home. Now go along to the Dorchester and check how our security people are getting on.'

'On the instant, boss.'

'Always the clown, Igor.' Luhzkov shook his head. 'Greta Novikova is still gainfully employed, I trust?'

'I wouldn't ask, Boris, I really wouldn't.'

When Ferguson was admitted to Number Ten Downing Street, a waiting aide took him upstairs past the pictures of every past Prime Minister and along the corridor.

'Five minutes only, General. He's due at Northolt to greet Putin, but he did want a word with you.'

He opened the door, Ferguson went in and there was the Prime Minister behind his desk. 'Sit down, General.'

'Thank you, Prime Minister.'

'I just want to reassure myself about certain, shall we say, unfortunate aspects of present events. Things are in order at the Dorchester, I take it?'

'I believe so, but I'm visiting personally after our meeting.'

'Let me be plain, General Ferguson. I know I find it prudent on many occasions where matters of intelligence are concerned to look the other way, but aspects of my meeting today, this Belov Protocol? It can't be allowed to happen.'

'It won't, Prime Minister. Everything will be resolved within the next two days to your satisfaction.' He smiled. 'Or you can have my resignation.'

'Oh, I wouldn't want that, so I'll just have to take your word for it. Now I must go. Northolt awaits.'

The door behind was eased open as if by magic and Ferguson was eased out.

When the Daimler picked him up, Dillon and Billy were in the back and Ferguson climbed in. The Daimler pulled away and Dillon said, 'Where to?'

'The Dorchester. I want to check security.'

'Did the PM have much to say?'

'In five minutes? Hardly. Of course, he did tell me the Belov Protocol can't be allowed to happen and I told him it would be resolved to his satisfaction over the next two days.'

'Charles, your confidence is breathtaking.'

'You've got it wrong, Dillon. It's a sign of my total faith in your ability to achieve miracles.'

Igor Levin made contact with his security colleagues at the hotel. The President, of course, was in the most exclusive suite at the very top of the hotel, members of his entourage on lower floors, Belov on floor five in a Park Suite. Everything seemed in order, so he went down to the Piano Bar and ordered a vodka in crushed ice, the special way they did it, the Dorchester way, got a couple of newspapers and went and sat by the piano and worked his way through them.

Someone brushed past him to the piano. He didn't look

up, engrossed in what *The Times* was saying about Putin and Belov. The pianist started to play a song popular with soldiers during the war in Chechnya. Levin remembered it well, they all did, those young soldiers. 'Moscow Nights'.

He looked up, and Sean Dillon, seated at the piano, said, 'We just wanted to make you feel at home, Igor, my old son, me and Billy here.'

Billy was standing by the piano, arms crossed. 'That was quite a gig you played in Khufra, Captain. It was you who knocked off Tomac, we presume?'

'He annoyed me.'

'A right bastard. Screwed up our floatplane. We went in nose first for the deep six.'

Levin stopped smiling. 'That was nothing to do with me.' He hesitated. 'And Greta was with you in that plane?'

Dillon said, 'I held her hand all the way up from the bottom.'

Levin smiled again. 'How romantic. She's well, I trust?'

'In excellent accommodation. Oh, here comes the boss.'

Ferguson came down the steps from the bar. 'My dear chap, we keep missing each other. Tried to catch up again at Drumore Place yesterday, but you weren't at home.'

'And neither was Ashimov. Dublin, I understand.' Dillon shook his head. 'Liam Bell did a runner, but we depleted the ranks of the IRA.'

'You must be feeling pleased.' Levin stood up.

Ferguson said, 'Don't go. Join us in a drink.'

Levin smiled. 'Now that would really be too much. I'm sure I'll see enough of you tonight.'

He went out. Ferguson said, 'Pity, I rather liked him. Still, we can have something while we're here,' and he waved to Guiliano.

In the ballroom later that night, all London was there. Politicians by the score, big business, the media, anybody who was anybody and lots of men in black suits, ever watchful as waiters passed through the crowd with trays loaded with champagne, vodka, canapés.

'They stand out a mile, don't they?' Billy said to Dillon as they stood by a temporary bar.

'Who do you mean?'

'The security men. It's the black suits.'

Ferguson was away, glad-handing a few people. Dillon said, 'Just because Ferguson made us wear black tie for tonight, don't let it go to your head. There's Igor Levin over there. Keep him in view and let him keep you in view. I'm going up now to try and play Roper's trump card.' He eased out of the crowd by the rear lift, pushed open a side door and ran up the stairs to the fifth floor. The room adjacent to Max Zubin's suite was just around a bend in the corridor opposite. He produced his pass key and entered.

It was small, comfortably furnished, the door giving access to the living room of Zubin's locked suite. Dillon slipped in an earpiece and listened. There was a sound of movement, but no voices.

He took off his coat, removed a small suitcase from the wardrobe and pulled out a white waiter's coat, which he put on. On the sideboard tray, champagne stood ready in an ice bucket with two glasses. He took a deep breath, picked the tray up and went out. Just a few yards down the corridor was all it took. He paused at the door, then pressed the bell.

It opened surprisingly quickly and there stood Zubin in shirt sleeves adjusting his black tie.

'Champagne, sir?' Dillon asked.

'I don't think I ordered that,' Zubin said.

'It's on the house, sir, Dorchester champagne.'

'OK, bring it in, but don't open it.'

He turned away into the living room and Dillon put the tray on the table. 'I'd better open it just in case somebody comes,' he said in fluent and rapid Russian.

Strangely, Zubin didn't look alarmed, but there was an instant frown. 'What in the hell is this?'

'Nobody here is what they seem. My name is Sean Dillon and I work for British Intelligence. You're Max Zubin pretending to be Josef Belov, and not liking it very much. However, they have your mother in Moscow, so you have to play ball, you have to go back to her.'

Zubin adjusted his tie and reached for his jacket. 'If any of this were true, what could I do about it?'

'Go back tomorrow, you'd have to do that, then we'd bring you out, you and your mother.'

'You could do that?'

'Yes. I'll explain after dinner.'

'I'm not doing dinner. From what I know, I'll be back up here at around nine to nine thirty.'

'I've got the room next door. We'll talk later. If you're on your own, knock on the door.' He'd finished uncorking and pouring a glass. 'You're taking this remarkably well.'

Zubin took the glass. 'I was a paratrooper in Chechnya. You sound like the real thing. Unless they're employing raving lunatics here who start off with an Irish accent and move into fluent Russian.'

The door bell sounded.

'Shower stall,' Dillon whispered. 'I know these suites.'

He moved into the small hall bathroom, left the door partly open and stepped into the shower.

Outside, Zubin opened the door, 'Ah, Levin, there you are. Are they ready for me?'

He was obviously in his Belov role, voice measured. 'No need to take that tone with me,' Levin said. 'Now, remember the cameras. Be nice and forbidding, so people will feel it better not to speak to you.'

'I could frighten them to death. I can do an excellent Hamlet's father. He was a ghost, you know.'

'Come on, it's show time.'

The door closed, Dillon waited, then went out and returned next door.

Round the corridor at the far end of the corridor, Levin and Zubin waited for the lift. 'You're feeling good?' Levin said.

'Of course, I always do on an opening night,' and the lift doors parted and he and Levin joined four other people.

Inside himself, Zubin felt only tremendous excitement.

Could it be true, could he really confound all of them, bring the whole house of cards tottering down? Well, as far as he was concerned, it wouldn't be from want of trying.

When Dillon returned, Ferguson had joined Billy. 'You look excited,' he said. 'How did it go?'

'Couldn't have been better.' He told them what had happened. 'The important thing is he isn't doing the dinner. That gives me a great chance of accessing him from the room next door later and really laying it on the line.'

'The Putin plane is leaving at eleven from Northolt. The Citation X perhaps an hour later. The courier flight will be logged in and out again, all perfectly legitimate.' He handed Dillon an envelope. 'Times and so forth, the whole schedule. Discuss it with him, then destroy it.'

'Of course.'

There was a sudden disturbance at the far end of the room, a great deal of clapping as Putin moved through the crowd, the Prime Minister taking another section.

'He's there,' Dillon said, 'moving close to the President, Levin behind him.'

There was Zubin, pausing while the TV cameras did their work and press cameras flashed, turning closer to the President so they were tied together, as it were. The President nodded to him and moved on and Zubin walked into the crowd, Levin behind him, pausing to greet people who spoke to him. Finally, he accepted a glass of champagne and stood by the wall, as if holding court, a number of guests obviously hanging on to his every word, and Levin was checking his watch.

'I bet that isn't in the script,' Ferguson said.

'He's an actor,' Dillon said. 'Can't resist making the most of his role. I was one myself.'

'Yes, we do know about that,' Ferguson said. 'The one person who appears to be missing is Volkov.'

'Not any longer,' Dillon said, as Volkov moved through the crowd, taking two glasses of champagne from a passing waiter and pausing beside Putin and handing him one of the glasses. He murmured something to Putin and they turned and looked across at Ferguson, Dillon and Billy. And then Putin did a strange thing. He raised his glass towards them and Ferguson raised his.

'Old adversaries from the Cold War, a long time ago,' he said.

A voice echoed over the speaker. 'Ladies and gentlemen, dinner is served.'

Volkov moved across to Zubin and Levin and spoke to them and Levin nodded, touched Zubin on the arm and they made for the door. Those going on to the dinner flooded out. Quite a number, who obviously were not, stood around finishing their drinks.

Ferguson said, 'I'll get off home and leave you to it. Good luck upstairs and let me know instantly how it's gone.'

He walked away and Dillon said, 'Let's get on with it, Billy. We'll take the stairs.'

*   *   *

They made it to the room with no trouble, went in quietly and Dillon tried the earpiece again and put his head to the door. There was a murmur of voices.

'Levin must still be with him,' Dillon said, as he checked his watch. 'Just after nine. We'll have to wait.'

'For as long as it takes.'

Billy lay on the bed, head pillowed on his hands. Dillon sat on the dressing table chair. At half past nine, he checked and still heard voices. Not long after, there was the sound of laughter and then silence and then there were two distinct knocks on the door.

Zubin stood there, undoing his black tie. 'Ah, Mr Dillon. Who's your friend?'

'Salter,' Billy said. 'I look after him when he can't look after himself.'

'Sorry I'm late, as it were,' Zubin said. 'My security man was talking over old times. We were paratroopers together in Chechnya. Not exactly cheek to cheek. I was a captain in those days, he was a lieutenant. Big hero.'

'We know him well,' Billy said.

'How well?'

'Traded shots,' Dillon told him. 'Are we coming in?'

'Of course. Levin's OK in a strange way. He can't take things seriously. He's an actor.'

'Where have I heard that before?' Billy said. 'Your new friend here went to RADA.'

Zubin positively glowed. 'My goodness, I am impressed.'

'Well, don't be,' Dillon told him. 'I was waylaid by the IRA and took to the Theatre of the Street, and a bloody awful role it was. Now let's get serious. Do you feel like going for it?'

'By God, I do. I've been trapped, forced into another man's skin, my moves monitored, my life. I'm a puppet. Volkov pulls my strings, I jump. I'm fifty years of age. Do you think I want to spend the rest of my life this way?'

'I shouldn't imagine so.'

'But I've got no choice. In Paris the other year, I couldn't make a break for it because of my mother. I can't try and drop out of things here in London because of my mother. They use her, I know that, but Volkov also knows I would never let her down. You talked earlier of my return to Moscow and you bringing both of us out. Can this be possible?'

'It could be, but how would your mother feel about it?'

Zubin poured a little champagne. 'For both our sakes and to get us out of this situation, she would come.'

'Excellent. Read this.' Dillon gave him Ferguson's letter and poured himself a glass of champagne as well.

Zubin finished and handed him the letter back. 'Yes, I understand.'

'You're sure?'

'One of my strengths is my ability to retain lines.'

'Right. I'll just go over it again with you. You return to Moscow on Putin's plane tomorrow. Is Levin going with you?'

'No, he stays here. I'm in Volkov's hands. I'm put up at my usual hotel, the Excelsior, and the day after tomorrow I sign the Belov Protocol at the Kremlin.'

'No, you don't. That's why our timing is so crucial. You leave in Putin's plane, and the Royal Air Force courier plane, the Citation X, follows an hour, perhaps two, later. It lands with legitimate documents for the British Embassy, receives legitimate documents for the return journey which is logged out of Belov Complex at seven-thirty, Russian time. You know Belov Complex?'

'Of course. I landed there from Station Gorky.'

'The timing has been chosen because it's dark. We'll make a quick getaway, and with the extraordinary speed of this plane we should be out of Russian airspace in thirty minutes.'

'You say "we"?'

'Yes. Two pilots, RAF naturally. Billy here will wear the uniform of an RAF Sergeant as Steward. I will wear the uniform of a GRU Captain, one Igor Levin, complete with paratrooper wings, medals, the lot. You won't be the only one acting.'

'And you'd do this, you'd take this chance? My God, if it went wrong you'd be shot or sent to the Gulag.'

'True, but the simplicity of the whole thing is in its favour. I'll ask you one more time. Will your mother do it? She'll be walking out of her apartment with nothing. All the mementoes of a remarkable life gone.'

'She'll do it for me and I'll do it for her.'

'Good. There's something not mentioned in Ferguson's letter.'

'What's that?'

'Once in London there's your future to think of. Our computer expert has been able to access Belov International bank deposits in London, using your authority. You are, after all, Josef Belov.'

'How much?' Zubin asked.

'Twenty million didn't seem unreasonable. I mean, property prices have gone up in the city.'

Zubin smiled. 'I think you could say that will be perfectly satisfactory.'

Billy took two things from his pocket, a Colt .25 and a Codex Four. 'The gun is for obvious emergencies and is silenced. The mobile was specially manufactured for our purposes. It doesn't look like much, but it can go anywhere, do anything, it's waterproof and the battery lasts a year. It's programmed. You press the red button and you're through to a guy named Roper. He'll contact us on your behalf. There are one or two extras in the briefcase, just in case.'

'It is simple.' Zubin shook his head. 'If everything works, it really would be very simple.'

'At all times, remember you *are* Josef Belov. In a way, Volkov's created a Frankenstein's monster. Only a few important people know your real identity. To everyone else, you're the great man.'

'I suppose that's right.'

'Ferguson was telling me that during the Second World War SOE had someone very like you who impersonated Field-Marshal Erwin Rommel on a mission to Jersey in the German-occupied Channel Islands. It was said that what helped him most was discovering that everyone who met him believed he *was* Rommel, but more importantly, he himself discovered that to be Rommel was to be all-powerful.

People automatically obeyed him. You might be surprised how effective that could be.'

'I'll try to remember it.'

'You've been seen on British television already tonight. During the next few hours, it'll be the same for the USA, Europe and the Russian Federation. When you get off the plane in Moscow, you'll be a star on the level of the President. Everyone will recognize you.'

Zubin took a deep breath and pulled himself together. 'A short run, if we're lucky.'

'And a quick transfer to the West End,' Billy said.

'Yes, I can see that. I can also see that you gentlemen are putting yourselves in harm's way by accompanying me on this affair.'

'Well, that's the name of the game.' Billy shook hands.

Zubin said, 'You're not an actor, too, Mr Salter?'

'No, I'm a gangster,' Billy told him.

'Good God,' Zubin said.

Dillon said, 'Goodbye, Mr Zubin. We will see you in Moscow tomorrow night.'

'You sound certain.'

'I am. I'll tell your mother why when I'm on that plane with her, leaving Moscow.' He turned. 'Come on, Billy.'

They went out. He locked the connecting doors. 'The bedclothes,' he said.

Billy rumpled them and the pillows. 'Just in case a maid looks in,' Dillon said, and opened the door. The corridor was silent. 'Come on,' he whispered and they went down the back stairs beside the lift. They stood on the steps in Park

Lane, sheltering from hard, driving rain for a few moments and tried to flag down a taxi.

There were still a few people around from the function, limousines drawing up to collect passengers and, of all people, Igor Levin emerged and stood on the steps, taking out a box of cigarettes, and saw them.

'Still here, you two?' He selected a cigarette and offered them. 'Russian.'

'I could see you were a gentleman.' Dillon pinched the cardboard expertly and accepted the light offered. He inhaled. 'Excellent.'

Levin said, 'Only the best.'

'Back to Moscow for you, old son?'

'How could I leave you two on the loose?' A black Mercedes turned in, he opened the main door, sat beside the driver and was driven away.

'Now there's a happy man,' Billy said, and at that moment, in response to his raised hand, a taxi swerved in.

Afterwards they sat with Ferguson by the fire at his apartment in Cavendish Place and discussed the evening. Ferguson was particularly interested in the incident with Levin.

'Why do you think they're keeping him on here?' Dillon asked.

'It suits Volkov. He's smart, clever, ruthless. Doesn't fit the mould of your usual agent.'

'I reckon it's more than that,' Billy said. 'He's getting at you, General. It's like reminding you that there's nothing you can do about Levin.'

'You could well be right, young Billy. I'll outplay him on that one, of course.'

'How?'

'By you two bringing Max Zubin and his mother out of Russia.' He stood up. 'I'll see you off at Farley tomorrow. You'd better move on. You'll need a good night's sleep.'

Outside, another taxi. As it swerved in, Billy said, 'We'll drop you at your place first.'

'No, you won't,' Dillon said. 'You haven't told Harry about this caper, have you?' he asked.

'No,' Billy said. 'He'd blow his top. I mean, we've done enough in the past, bad things, hard things, but this? One false move in Moscow, Dillon, and it's curtains. They'll swallow us whole.'

They got in the back of the taxi. Dillon said, 'You're right. It could go as smoothly as silk . . .'

'Or we might end up in deep shit.'

'Well, if you're worried,' Dillon said, 'maybe it doesn't need the two of us.'

'Oh, no, you go, I go. I won't have it any other way.'

It was late, but there were still a few people in the saloon bar of the Dark Man. Harry was seated in his usual spot in the corner booth, Baxter and Hall hanging around.

Dillon said, 'Other end of the bar, you two. Billy needs to talk to Harry. It's family.' They looked surprised, but went. 'OK, tell him.' Dillon went to the bar and ordered a large Bushmills.

He drank it down and ordered another, then went back to the booth. Harry looked pale and angry.

'This is bleeding enough. It's insane.'

'No, it's important, Harry, it's of world importance. I just thought you should know.' He patted Billy on the shoulder and swallowed his Bushmills. 'See you at Farley at eleven o'clock, Billy.'

He gave Harry a look, turned and went out. At the door, he stood in the porch buttoning his coat against the rain. Harry came up behind him, Joe Baxter at his shoulder.

'Did you want a word?'

'We'll leave at ten-thirty tomorrow.'

'You said eleven.'

'Yes, well, we all make mistakes. He's a good kid.'

'So you're a sentimentalist at heart.' Harry shook his hand. 'Take him home, Joe,' and he went back inside.

Moscow

13

In the Putin plane things weren't organized the way Air Force One was for the American President. On that famous plane there was a certain relaxation, a constant coming and going of staff. Even the members of the press on board could circulate to a degree.

No, conditions on the Russian President's plane were stricter, more regimented. On the other hand, Zubin didn't find himself sitting at the back with the rabble, as they were known in Russian political circles. After all, he was Josef Belov, which secured him three vacant seats and, following whispered instructions, he sat in the third one next to a window and blanked off from people.

Rising up out of London, he wasn't as excited as he'd been

the previous evening, but calm and serious, considering the situation. There had been no security check at RAF Northolt, but it had been obvious that there wouldn't be, not for VIPs, so the Colt .25 they'd given him and the Codex Four mobile were at the bottom of his briefcase. He'd also discovered a couple of pairs of plastic handcuffs, a street map of central Moscow, his route from the Excelsior to his mother's apartment clearly marked and onwards to the Belov Complex, a spray can of CS gas and some night glasses.

It was mad, the whole idea that it could be got away with, but the other future was too awful to contemplate. He was staring into space thinking about it, when someone sat beside him. He turned and found it was Volkov.

'Yes, General,' he said. 'How can I be of service?'

'Oh, you already have.' Volkov was in a jovial mood and took two vodkas from a passing waiter and gave Zubin one.

'A fine performance. The President is very pleased with you, and tomorrow at the Kremlin will be your biggest performance ever. Signing the Belov Protocol in front of the world's cameras. The President will decorate you. Hero of the Soviet Union.'

'Ah, I thought we'd done away with that?'

'Well, something similar.'

'May I see my mother?' Zubin held his breath and hoped, but Volkov was in high good humour.

'You may order your chauffeur to take you to your mother's apartment on the way to the Excelsior when we get in, but fifteen minutes only, Zubin, at least for now.' He waved for two more vodkas and passed one over.

'Everything's worked out perfectly. You've been splashed all over Russian television in the company of the President and the British Prime Minister in London. It's made you quite a star, and news of the Belov Protocol with ordinary people has done even more. It's made you a hero.' He smiled jovially and tossed down his vodka. 'A great triumph for us all.'

He got up and walked away and Zubin sat there, trying to take it all in, then leaned back in his seat and wondered what Dillon was up to.

Dillon arrived at Farley the following morning, rain driving in. He parked the Mini Cooper, got out, a raincoat over his shoulders, and ran across to the operations room under the control tower, the rain heavy. The Citation X stood a few yards away, its RAF roundels proud, and as Dillon went up the steps Squadron Leader Lacey emerged from behind some bushes wearing a flying jacket, standard uniform underneath, medals clear, his Air Force Cross well on display.

'You look good,' Dillon said.

'You know how it is, Sean. It's special, this one, so it seems fitting we do it right. Parry's got things moving along. We'll be out of here fast.'

'You're pushing it, aren't you?'

'There are headwinds across Europe, and a front from Siberia westwards later today – you know how it is. Billy's waiting inside.'

'He's what?'

'Apparently there was some confusion over the time.'

Dillon walked into the operations room and found Harry and Ferguson having coffee.

'You're a little tardy this morning,' Ferguson said.

Dillon shook his head at Harry. 'Where is he?'

'Back room, changing. You really think he'd have gone for that? Go on, get on with it. I can't wait to see you dressed as a Russian.'

Billy was adjusting his tie and pulled on his sergeant's tunic. 'Hey, I've got campaign medals – Ireland, the first Gulf War.'

'How would you know?'

Dillon's uniform hung by a locker, quite spectacular. 'Levin must be quite a guy,' Billy said. 'He's got more medals than me and his uniform is prettier.'

'If you say so.' Dillon started to change and pulled on his jackboots.

Billy said, 'Oh, I do. And another thing. Don't try to pull a stunt like that again. It's a good thing Harry has an old-fashioned sense of family honour.'

'Your choice.'

Dillon tightened his tie, pulled on the tunic and buttoned it. He fastened his belt with the holstered pistol, then adjusted his cap. When he checked in the mirror, a rather sinister-looking man stared out at him, a figure of grim authority.

'Dillon, that's you,' Billy said. 'That is very definitely you. Now let's move it.'

They went out and found Lacey back with Harry and Ferguson. 'Very smart,' he said. 'The Russians do like their uniforms, don't they?'

'What about me?' Billy asked.

'Good turn-out, Sergeant, a credit to the Squadron. The Quartermaster's bag is on board, the Embassy boxes. Could we go, please?'

There was a slight pause, then Harry said, 'Just get on with it.'

Ferguson said, 'Keep the faith.'

Billy led the way up the Airstair door, Dillon followed, Lacey after him, turning to close the door, then moving to the cockpit to join Parry as the engines throbbed. Billy and Dillon belted in on either side of the aisle.

Dilly said, 'Are you all right, then?'

'What in the hell do you think?' Billy leaned back, closed his eyes and the plane surged forward.

At Moscow in late afternoon verging into early evening, the Putin plane landed at the airport with the usual pomp and ceremony associated with the homecoming of the President after his appearance on the world stage.

He went down the steps, met the usual functionaries and generals, rather more of those these days, or so it appeared, and moved to his limousine. Lesser mortals had disembarked and stood waiting, among them Max Zubin.

Zubin was conscious of a strange air of fatalism. He was here, this was it; what would be, would be. Always the actor, always playing a part. And then it struck him, a sudden thought, and he smiled and murmured to himself.

'Hey, in Chechnya they cast you as a paratrooper, Max,

no stand-ins. That was a charnel house and you were a hell
of a good paratrooper. They gave you a medal, you, Max
Zubin, Yiddish boy, actor, pianist, comedian. If you could do
that, you can do this.'

He began to walk, the briefcase Billy Salter had given him
in his hand. He followed the crowd through, and a strange
thing started to happen when he entered the terminal.
Various officials, scanning the crowd, jumped to attention
when they saw him, and started clapping.

'It's Belov,' someone cried, and as he went forward people
turned and smiled and there was shouting and applause and
then, moving into the VIP tunnel, he reached the end and
there was his chauffeur, Ivan Kurbsky.

'I've got your suitcase, Max,' he said and led the way.

Max. In one shocking moment, everything was different.

Zubin tried a recovery, put on his best Belov voice. 'What
on earth are you talking about, Kurbsky?'

'Oh, come off it, Zubin. I'm ex-KGB. General Volkov
always felt you needed a proper minder. He appointed me
himself.'

'Mikhail, my mother's driver, does he know, too?'

'That prick? No way. You're all mine, Max.'

'But why are you telling me now?'

'Because, frankly, seeing you there on television with the
President, the Prime Minister, all those toffs, it just doesn't
feel right. You getting all that attention and me getting
nothing at all. I figured it was time to remind you who you
are.'

'As if I could,' Zubin said.

'And as soon as you've signed that protocol of theirs tomorrow, you know what's going to happen to you? It's back to Station Gorky for you, that's what – you *and* your mother.'

'Both of us? You're sure about that?'

'I wouldn't bet against me, Zubin.' They reached the limousine, he put the suitcase in the boot and opened the rear door. 'So in you get, big man. Enjoy your brief moment of fame.'

Volkov had promised him fifteen minutes with his mother, and there was nothing Kurbsky could do about that. When Zubin rang the doorbell, his mother answered quickly. Her face lit up and she pulled him inside. 'I saw you on television, with the President and the British Prime Minister. What a performance!'

She embraced him, he pushed her away gently and said urgently, 'Shut up, Mama, I only have a few minutes. I've just discovered that Kurbsky is ex-KGB, working for the government. I've also discovered that after signing this wretched protocol tomorrow I'm being shunted back to Siberia, and you with me.'

She was shocked, 'Siberia! For God's sake, no.'

'How would you like to leave with me tonight and fly to London to a new life?'

'What are you talking about?'

He told her quickly.

'So,' he said, 'the RAF plane is booked out at seven-thirty.

I'll be back at seven. You must be ready. You can take nothing, only the clothes you're wearing. If you won't do this, then neither will I. We'll go to Siberia together.'

'Like hell we will.' She flung her arms around his neck. 'London. God, it would be the most marvellous thing in the world to spend my final years there and know you were safe.'

'I'll see you at seven then.' He kissed her and there was a knock on the door. He opened it, found Kurbsky there, turned and kissed her hand. 'Goodnight, Mama.'

'God bless you, and good luck tomorrow.'

She closed the door and Zubin turned to Kurbsky, who was smiling cynically. 'Right on time.'

'Only doing my job. Let's get you to the Excelsior and tuck you in for the night. And don't forget, I'll be in a room down the hall.'

At the Excelsior, it was a reprise of the airport. Kurbsky parked in a lay-by at the front and carried Zubin's suitcase in. The two doormen applauded, inside the two porters on reception clapped. The duty manager appeared to shake Zubin's hand vigorously.

'Mr Belov – wonderful, unbelievable. Let me get you your key. May I show you to your suite?'

'That won't be necessary.' Zubin took the key. 'Kurbsky can see to the suitcase,' and he walked to the lift.

As they went up, Kurbsky said, 'It's all gone to your head, hasn't it?'

'If you say so.'

'They'll knock that out of you when you get back to Siberia.' What he didn't add was that after a proper interval a convenient accident would be arranged for both of them, Max and Mama. Kurbsky opened the door. 'In you go. You be a good boy.'

'If I'm not, it wouldn't look good for you, would it?' Zubin said. 'Imagine everyone there at the Kremlin, Putin and Volkov, waiting for the signing, but no Belov.' He smiled. 'They'd hang you up by your balls.'

Kurbsky's face contorted with rage. 'Get in there, you bastard.' He pushed Zubin inside and threw his bag through. He slammed the door and locked it, then went down the hall to his room and found a bottle of vodka.

At the Belov Complex, the Citation X landed at five-thirty and taxied to its designated parking spot. Formalities were minimal, no security involved, diplomatic immunity absolute. They rolled to a halt, and Lacey came back.

'This is how it works. There will be an Embassy limousine in the small VIP car park round the corner. They'll be called shortly, drive out and pick up stuff we've brought from the UK and hand over stuff we're taking back. They're our people, so there'll be no problems.'

'What about refuelling?' Dillon asked.

'They'll have a tanker out here in the next half hour.'

'We still haven't heard from Zubin.'

'I'll go and sign in, leave Parry with you.' He looked out

at the runway, snow banked to each side. 'Good, it's starting to snow again, not too bad, just enough to confuse things.' He handed Dillon a raincoat. 'I'd wear this if you want to venture out and then dump it if you want to play your friend, Levin.'

He turned and opened the Airstair door, and Dillon's Codex Four rang.

Zubin, in his suite, had a couple of stiff vodkas to pep him up, then opened the briefcase, selected the Colt .25, which he put in his pocket, and then the other items. The handcuffs he laid on his coffee table with the canister of CS gas. There was also a roll of some sort of sticky tape. He took out the Codex Four and pressed the red button.

At Holland Park, Roper jumped to attention for he'd just had a call from Dillon saying no contact had been made, and that was worrying. He hadn't needed to call Ferguson, for he and Harry were in the canteen and staying the night.

'Is that Roper?'

'Yes. What's wrong, Max?'

'My cover has been broken. My chauffeur, Kurbsky, turns out to be ex-KGB and a Federal Agent.'

'Is there nothing you can do?'

'Oh, yes. I'm not going to let that bastard spoil my greatest performance. I'm calling him to my room and then I'm going to tackle him. I just wanted you to know. If I'm successful

I'll call you back in fifteen minutes. If I'm not, it's good-night Vienna.'

He switched off, and Roper told Doyle, 'Get the General at once. Tell him there's been contact.'

In his room, the vodka flowing while he watched a porn movie, Kurbsky was furious at being disturbed by the room phone.

'Who is it?'

'Me, you pig.' Zubin was doing a very good drunk. 'I just wanted to let you know what a piece of shit you are, Ivan. I mean, there's shit and shit, but you really are something special.'

'You bastard,' Kurbsky cried. 'I'll show you. You need a lesson, you piece of Jewish –'

He was cut off, slammed down his phone, rushed down the hall, got Zubin's key out and opened the door. But a hand grabbed him by the shirt front, pulling him in. Zubin gave him the CS spray full in the face, kicked him expertly under the kneecap, yanked him forward and head-butted him like a pro. Kurbsky went down, moaning. Zubin turned him over, affixed one pair of the plastic handcuffs to his wrists, the other to his ankles. He turned him on his back.

'I could kill you, but I won't. Do you know why? Because when Volkov finds I'm gone, it's you who he'll send to Siberia, for the rest of your life. If you're lucky.'

He tore off a piece of sticky tape and applied it to Kurbsky's mouth, then phoned Roper and got an instant reply.

'Are you OK?' Roper demanded.

'Yes, I've taken care of him. I'm leaving now for my mother. I'll let you know when I've got her. I'm out of here.'

He went through Kurbsky's pockets, found the car keys, put the Colt in one jacket pocket, the Codex Four in the other, grabbed his raincoat and left.

Roper, who'd put everything on conference call so Ferguson and Harry could hear, said, 'There he goes.'

'God help him,' Ferguson said.

At the front entrance cabs were delivering people constantly, the doorman busy. Zubin, dodging around, reached the limousine, unlocked the door and climbed in. Snow was falling now, rather pretty in the light of the streetlamps, and traffic not too busy. He reached his mother's apartment block in fifteen minutes, left the car close to the main entrance and went upstairs. She answered the door at once, dressed in boots, a fur hat and coat, and embraced him.

'Thank God. I've been waiting.'

'No Mikhail?'

'I'm never bothered at night, he goes home. I mean, where would I have to go?'

'Well, you have somewhere now. Let's go.'

She indicated a suitcase. 'Could you carry it for me?'

'Mama, I said bring nothing.'

'They're photos from the top of the piano. I've spent the time taking them out of their frames. My whole life is in those photos, Max. I even have one with Stalin, God rot him.'

'All right, we can get you new frames in London.' He picked up the suitcase, pulled her out and slammed the door. 'Let's get out of here.' As they went down the stairs, he called Roper. 'I have my mother, we're on our way.'

At Holland Park, Roper immediately relayed the call to Dillon, who called to Lacey, 'They're coming.'

The snow was falling quite heavily now. Lacey pulled the raincoat over his shoulders, concealing his uniform, put his cap underneath, went down the steps and crossed towards the reception area. Behind him, a small tanker drove up to start the process of refuelling the Citation X. Dillon dodged in a doorway, took out the cap, adjusted it, then opened the raincoat so it simply dropped from his shoulders, revealing his GRU uniform. He went to the glass doors at the entrance to reception. Lacey was at the desk, doing paperwork with a young man in a dark green uniform and fur hat.

Dillon stood watching, looking quite striking in his uniform, lit a cigarette and turned to see what was obviously the Embassy limousine come round the corner and park by the Airstair door. A chauffeur got out, bringing what looked like mail sacks with him, and Billy appeared in the door with similar sacks and an exchange took place. The limousine drove away.

In Zubin's suite at the Excelsior, Kurbsky had managed to wriggle across to the door with great difficulty. The CS gas hadn't done him any good and the tape on his mouth was half-choking him, but lying on his back, he started kicking his bound feet at the door and, after a while, it had an effect. A room service waiter appeared and found him.

Belov drove up to the gate entrance of the VIP lot at the Belov Complex and turned in. The guard on duty came out of the hut.

'Papers.'

'On the windshield, man, can't you see? This is a Belov International limousine and I'm Josef Belov.'

'I still need to see your papers, even if you are Mr Big.'

Zubin took out the silenced Colt and shot the guard between the eyes. He jumped out, dragged the man into the hut out of sight, got back into the limousine and drove around to the side of reception. The Citation X with its RAF roundels was plain to see.

'Come on, Mama, take your last walk on Russian soil.'

They started forward, her hand on his arm while he carried the suitcase, but as they passed reception a voice called, 'Where are you going?'

He turned and found a young man in a green uniform and fur hat standing on the steps.

'I'm Josef Belov,' he bellowed. 'Surely you recognize me?'

The young man peered at him. 'Good God, yes. I saw you on television, but where are you going?'

Dillon moved out of the shadows, resplendent in that chilling GRU uniform. 'Young man, this is an official matter. Come with me and I'll explain. I'm Captain Levin.'

The youth was totally intimidated. 'Of course, sir.'

From the plane, Billy called, 'Come on, Dil— uh, Igor.'

Dillon nodded to Zubin, 'Carry on, Mr Belov,' and he turned and took the youth inside, guiding him into an office at the back of the reception desk, where he promptly took out his pistol and stunned him with a violent blow.

The engines had fired up in the Citation X, Zubin and his mother inside, Billy standing in the entrance. Dillon ran for the steps and scrambled up, and the door closed. There was chatter from the cockpit, and they moved forward through the falling snow, the runway lights gleaming.

'Just like bleeding Christmas,' Billy said, and turned to Zubin and Bella. 'Belt up, we're on our way.'

Dillon looked at his watch. 'Seven-thirty, dead on time. That's the RAF for you.'

They climbed quickly to 40,000 feet. Kurbsky's frantic phone message to Volkov made no impact for quite some time for, after all, no one knew exactly what was going on. The youth at reception was unconscious for twenty minutes, and it was only with his report on Belov's presence, and the discovery of the body of the gate guard, that Volkov made any sense of it at all.

By then, of course, it was far too late, as Lacey had predicted. The extreme speed of the Citation X had taken them out of Russian airspace in thirty minutes and they were well on their way.

*   *   *

At Holland Park, Roper had listened to Dillon and now turned to Ferguson and Harry. 'They've actually done it.'

Ferguson said, 'You're certain they're out of harm's way?'

'They're just over German airspace now and winging into French.'

'You going to call the Prime Minister?' Harry asked.

'No, I think I'll leave the champagne until they land at Farley Field.' Ferguson shook his head. 'Who in the hell would have believed it?'

'I tell you what,' Harry said. 'Vladimir Putin isn't going to be pleased. Where does this leave his bleeding Belov Protocol?'

And to that, of course, there was no answer.

In the plane, they all sat back, and Billy opened the ice box and found a bottle of champagne. 'Somebody had faith,' he said and got it open.

Drinking, Bella Zubin said, 'It's like an impossible dream.'

'Thanks to Dillon here and Mr Salter,' her son said.

'So what do you think they'll do?' Dillon asked.

'About the protocol? I don't know. But I can tell you one thing. Putin's about to give a royal reaming to that bastard Volkov.'

'And Volkov will get straight on the phone to Drumore Place and put the boot into Boris Ashimov, and that, Billy, I'd like to see.'

He turned to Bella. 'When I was seventeen I was a student at the Royal Academy of Dramatic Art. You were appearing at the Old Vic in *The Three Sisters* with Olivier. You came to RADA and lectured. You said Chekhov should always be played on a London stage. I've never forgotten you.'

'My god, an actor,' Bella said.

'All my life . . .' and Dillon kissed her on the cheek.

LONDON

14

At the White House, Blake Johnson listened to Ferguson almost in disbelief. 'My God, I can't believe you've managed to pull it off, Charles.'

'No, not me, Blake. Credit Roper, Dillon and Billy, and two superb RAF pilots willing to put themselves on the line. I'll get back to you as things develop.'

Blake almost burst into the Oval Office and found Jake Cazalet up to his eyes in documents as ever.

'What the hell is this, Blake?' Cazalet sat back, his reading glasses perched on the end of his nose.

Blake told him – and Cazalet couldn't stop laughing. 'God, I can only imagine the look on Putin's face! Go on, Blake, this is a special occasion, there's Scotch in the cabinet. I'll toast you.'

*   *   *

At Farley Field, the Citation X coasted in as early light filtered through the dawn sky. Ferguson and Harry stood watching as it landed and taxied up and stopped. The Airstair door opened, Parry got out and turned and gave his hand to Bella Zubin. She came down the steps, Billy followed with her suitcase, then came Max and Dillon and the pilots.

Ferguson went to meet them. 'Mrs Zubin, I can't tell you what this means. I'm General Ferguson.'

'I can't tell you what it means to *me* to be here after all these years, and my son with me. I still can't believe it's true. All thanks to these wonderful men. Heroes, all of them.'

'Yes, I'd agree there. I have a safehouse at Holland Park. We'll take you there to settle in, then we'll decide where you'd like to go. There's a limousine here for you.'

His driver came forward and picked up her suitcase. She said, 'That's all I brought out of Russia, General, the images of a full life. Other than that, just the clothes I'm standing up in.'

'Well, we'll soon put that right.'

She got into the limousine, and Max Zubin followed her. 'We'll see you later,' Dillon said.

They moved away and Harry hugged Billy. 'Jesus, you got away with it.'

'It was like a dream, really,' Billy said. 'Lots of snow and Dillon poncing around dressed in the Russian equivalent of an SS uniform. That bleeding plane, it's so fast, you're there and then you're here. It's weird.'

Ferguson turned to Lacey and Parry. 'Since the Russians can never admit this happened, I'm sure courier service planes will continue to operate as normal. On the other hand, I'd suggest you gentlemen avoid the duty in the future. In view of the extreme hazard you engaged in, however, the consequences if you'd been apprehended, I intend to have you both awarded a bar to your Air Force Cross.'

'I don't know what to say, sir,' Lacey said.

'He's right.' Dillon smiled. 'It would have been the Gulag for you two.'

'And what about you, Billy?' Lacey demanded.

'Personally, all I want is to get down to the Dark Man and get the chef on to a great English breakfast. If you'd phone him, Harry, I'd be obliged, and if the rest of you have any bleeding sense you'll join me, including the pride of the RAF. Come on, Dillon,' and he led the way to Harry's Range Rover.

While the plane had still been in the air, Volkov had been at the Belov Complex, viewing the guard before they put his corpse in a body bag. 'No burial, instant cremation,' he ordered the GRU captain in charge.

Snow drifting, he went up to the reception area of the Belov Complex and found the receptionist in his green uniform being treated by paramedics. He took the avuncular approach.

'You've done well. This must have been a terrible shock for you.'

'I can't understand it. It was Mr Belov himself, with some

old lady. He said, "I'm Josef Belov. Surely you recognize me?"'

'And then what happened?'

'Someone called out in English. It was from the plane. He said, "Come on, Igor." No – wait. He started to say something else. Dil— something.'

Volkov's heart chilled. 'And what happened next?'

'A GRU captain appeared. He said it was a matter of state and that his name was Captain Levin. He told Mr Belov to get on the plane, and then he took me into the office and knocked me out.'

Dear God, Dillon. Volkov patted him reassuringly on the shoulder. 'You've done well,' he repeated, turned, walked away and beckoned to the GRU captain.

'Make sure he's on the penal battalion plane for Station Gorky tomorrow. Destroy his records. He ceases to exist.'

'At your orders, General.'

Volkov went back through the snow to his limousine. 'Dillon,' he murmured. 'You cunning bastard.' And yet he felt a certain admiration. 'To follow us so closely, to do it so quickly. Who in the hell would have thought of it?' There was an almost reluctant smile on his face. '"I'm Captain Levin,"' he murmured. 'You dog, Dillon.'

He lit a Russian cigarette, leaned back and said to his driver, 'The Kremlin.'

There was nothing certain in this life, except that the President would not be pleased.

*   *   *

He sat in his office for quite some time until the secret door opened and the President stalked in. 'We're going to look like fools!'

'Mr President, we can always say he's ill, so the ceremony has to be postponed. Maybe he's had cancer all along. That would explain his generosity to the State. And then after an appropriate amount of time ... maybe he'll die. Willing it all to the State, of course. We can still do this.'

Putin stood lost in thought. 'Maybe. For your sake, I hope so, Volkov.' He glowered at the general, then stalked back out, the secret door closing behind him.

Volkov sat there, still feeling uneasy. Perhaps more could be done here. There were loose ends. He lifted his coded phone, checked on his list of numbers and called Ashimov.

At Drumore Place, Ashimov was seated by the fire with Liam Bell, enjoying a drink, and he jumped to attention.

'I've got bad news for you, Ashimov.'

He told him all about it, and emphasized, 'You're in deep shit as well. We've been outfoxed by Ferguson and Dillon over and over again. This business in Algiers, the loss of Major Novikova, all those botched attempts in London, in Drumore, and now this débâcle in Moscow. And the final insolence – Dillon masquerading as Levin. The President is mad as hell.'

Ashimov was choking. 'What can I say, General?'

'I think you'd better come home, Major. We'll discuss your future when I see you.'

He switched off, smiling, but Ashimov wasn't smiling at his end. A return home and a discussion of his future could mean anything from a bullet in the head to a one-way trip to some Gulag. On the other hand, if he could recover the situation, dispose of Max Zubin and his mother, for example, perhaps even Dillon . . . The rage boiled up in him. Always Dillon.

He poured a large vodka and slopped it down. Liam Bell said, 'What's your problem?'

And Ashimov poured it all out.

At the same time, Volkov phoned Levin, who had moved back to the Dorchester and the delights of the Piano Bar. He was at a corner table indulging in iced vodka and Beluga caviare, like a true Russian, but as Volkov spoke Levin was all attention.

Afterwards he said, 'You've got to give it to him. It was a stroke of genius, the whole caper.'

'You don't need to exaggerate. I wish he worked for me. I've spoken to Ashimov, pointed out his blame in the matter, and suggested he return home. He knows what that means, so I suspect he'll try to come up with some scheme to eradicate the Zubins in London. Something to make him look good to me. He'll probably try to recruit the Irishman, Liam Bell.'

'He'll certainly try to recruit me,' Levin said.

'Exactly. I'm not sure I can rely on you, but do what you can.'

* * *

When Ashimov was finished, Liam Bell shook his head. 'You're in more than a tight corner, my friend. Go back home and God knows what Volkov will have done to you.'

'Where else can I go?' Ashimov said, 'But if I can go back with some sort of victory, knock off Zubin, his mother, even Dillon . . .'

There was a madness about him now, Liam Bell saw that. He shrugged. 'How in the hell could you achieve that?'

'Igor Levin is still in place at the London Embassy. If he'll join me, he'll have all the GRU Intelligence sources we need to find what Ferguson's done with Zubin and his mother.'

'I suppose that's possible.'

'You could help. You've still got London contacts.'

'Oh, no,' Bell said. 'I've had enough on this one.'

'I've got a fortune in the contingency fund in the safe in my study. I'll call in a company Falcon, we land at Archbury. A couple of days should do it. I'll give you twenty-five thousand pounds in advance, another twenty-five when we get back.'

And, as usual, greed won the day. 'Two days?' Bell said. 'And I want the fifty in advance.'

'All right.' Ashmimov didn't even argue.

'Well, phone Igor Levin, set it up and let's see the colour of your money.'

After Volkov's call, Levin had been waiting to hear from Drumore Place, had been wondering how to handle Ashimov when he was contacted. Ashimov reached him in his suite at the Dorchester.

Ashimov said, 'We've had problems in Moscow.'

Levin had decided on the direct approach. 'I know all about the whole bloody mess.'

'God, if I could get my hands on Dillon,' Ashimov said.

'Well, you can't, old stick. So Volkov's told you to come home, is that it?'

'Yes!'

'We all know what that means.'

'I'm coming over,' Ashimov said, and his desperation was plain. 'If we could find where they have Zubin and his mother, I could deal with them.'

'Get them back to Russia, you mean? I think it's too late for that.'

'They can end up in the Thames as far as I'm concerned,' Ashimov exploded. 'Just find out where they are. Dammit, you've got all the resources of the GRU – find out! I'll be flying into Archbury.'

'Alone?'

'No, Bell has agreed to accompany me.'

'Out of loyalty or for money?'

'Money, of course.'

'Always the best way. I'll see what I can do.'

He sat there, thinking about it. There had been a disturbing edge of madness about Ashimov, but maybe there always had been. Still, he had a certain duty in this matter, so he found his coat, called for his Mercedes and drove to the Russian Embassy in Kensington.

*   *   *

In his office, Luhzkov sat and listened as Levin made certain demands.

'But this is really asking too much, Igor. You ask for full cooperation from us at every level. How can I agree to it when I don't even know what is so urgent that you request this?'

Levin produced his mobile, made a call and said, 'It's good to speak to you, General. I'm having problems with Colonel Luhzkov at the London Embassy. He questions the importance of my mission.' He listened, then passed the phone across. 'General Volkov would appreciate a word.'

Volkov said, 'You've got a good record, Luhzkov, a fine officer. I'm amazed at your attitude in this matter. I'm sure Levin misheard. Ask him to speak to me again.'

Luhzkov did, already trembling. Levin listened, then said, 'Of course, General.'

He took the Putin warrant from his pocket and laid it before the Colonel. Luhzkov read it, remembering when Levin had first shown it to him in the pub, and Volkov said, 'Would you dispute an order from your President, Colonel?'

'Of course not, General. Anything I can do, anything.'

'This is a matter of the highest state security, Colonel. Captain Levin acts not only with my total authority, as head of the GRU, but under direct order from the President himself.'

'I understand, General.' Luhzkov was in deep water and he realized it.

'In this matter, Captain Levin has total control. I've already spoken to the Ambassador. Until the present emergency is solved, Captain Levin is in charge and will be offered every assistance.'

'Anything I can do, you may rely on me, General.'

He handed the phone to Levin, his face very pale. Levin said, 'Look, General, I don't know what you expect all this to achieve, but I'll do what Ashimov wants. You do realize he's a madman, don't you?'

'Yes.'

'And I'm not.'

'Actually, that's what I'm relying on.'

Volkov switched off and Levin put the mobile in his pocket. 'The first thing you do, Luhzkov, is speak to Ferguson, and ask for any news he has of the whereabouts of Major Greta Novikova. You will tell him you have information that she's being held at Holland Park. As a diplomatic attaché at our Embassy she is entitled to diplomatic immunity and the right to be returned to Russia.'

'Can this be true?'

'For God's sake, Boris, get real. The days of shepherd's pie and beer at the pub are long gone. Do it!'

'As you say.'

'I do say. You also make it clear to all GRU personnel in the Embassy that I'm in charge. Anything I want, I get. Men, equipment, whatever.'

'Of course.'

'As long as we know where we are.' Levin smiled. 'I'd better go and get on with it.'

He arranged a command centre at the Embassy, with Sergeant Chomsky in charge of communications. A team of six men followed, with full use of anything needed in the vehicle pool. Suzuki motorcycles figured largely, there was a telecom van in the garage, and another rather artistic van, emblazoned with signs claiming to belong to a courier service.

Levin assembled Chomsky and the men. 'Line up.' They did and he allowed each man to read the Putin warrant. 'Any questions?' he asked. No one said a word. 'This is a matter of extreme importance, so nobody questions, nobody argues. If you do, I'll have you sent to a very unpleasant place. Chomsky?'

'At your orders, Captain.'

'Sergeant Chomsky and I survived Afghanistan and Chechnya. London is far preferable, so we've no intention of fucking up here, have we, sergeant?'

'Absolutely not, sir.'

'Good. I'll issue a list of my requirements. Anything you want, you get.' He smiled. 'Except women. Women are your responsibility.'

He walked away from the motor pool. The men laughed nervously. One of them said, 'Where'd he get an accent like that? And that suit! What is he, some kind of ponce?'

Chomsky gave him a long look. 'I wouldn't advise you letting him hear you say that. He'd kill you and smile while he's doing it. Now let's get to work.'

The safehouse at Holland Park was an obvious target. A few yards up the road, Chomsky had a telecom van parked, a manhole cover up, a man in a yellow jacket and helmet working. He was backed up by a motorcyclist in a side street.

In Cavendish Place outside Ferguson's apartment, a gardener was working in the central area of the square.

Levin debated about Dillon's cottage in Stable Mews, but decided against it. More and more, he felt an affinity with Dillon.

He said to Chomsky, 'Not Dillon. Anything in the slightest way out of the ordinary near his place, and he'd smell it like a hound dog. I would.'

Chomsky, a law student who'd only joined the army as a conscript, had fed on Afghanistan and Chechnya and found he liked it. He had immersed himself in the files of the whole affair.

'I don't think they'd put them up in a hotel, sir, so Holland Park makes sense, probably as a temporary measure.'

'And what comes after?'

'God knows. Some sort of house elsewhere. If the Captain will allow me?' He opened a file. 'I took the liberty of accessing these gangsters, the Salters. They make the Moscow Mafia look like rubbish. Millionaires many times over.'

'You're too smart for your own good, Chomsky. I'd forgotten you spent two years training for the law before the army.'

'They own houses and developments all over London, sir. I don't mean rubbish. First-class stuff in some of the most exclusive squares.'

'So what are you saying?'

'Everything stems from Hangman's Wharf, sir. The Dark Man. I've been and looked. Boats of every kind tie up at the wharf, some people live in them, others work on them. I found one for rent almost opposite the pub. I'll put Popov in it. His English is excellent. He can spend his time painting the damn boat or whatever. He'll have a Suzuki. Who knows what might come out of the Dark Man.'

'Excellent,' Levin told him. 'They all seem enthusiastic.'

'It's a little different from that, sir.' Chomsky was almost apologetic. 'They like it here, they like life in London. They don't want to screw up and get sent home.'

'Dear God, what's the world coming to? OK, straight to work. I need to know where the Zubins are being held as soon as possible.'

At Holland Park, Max Zubin and his mother were handed over to Sergeant Doyle. 'Temporary accommodation, I promise you,' said Ferguson.

After they'd gone upstairs, he went in to Roper. 'God, I feel knocked out. I can't believe it worked.'

'Thanks to Dillon and Billy Salter.' Roper lit a cigarette. 'Dillon's had a death wish for years. I worry that young Billy's inherited it. Where are they?'

'Dark Man for breakfast.'

'And why aren't we?'

'Damn you, you're right,' and Ferguson called to Doyle. 'Get the People Carrier out, Sergeant. Hangman's Wharf for breakfast.'

Ashimov, in the kitchen having breakfast with Bell, answered Levin's call.

'I've got a phony motorcycle policeman parked at Holland Park. A big van emerged, carrying Ferguson and Roper. My man followed, and guess what? The Dark Man at Wapping. I'd say it's certain Zubin and his mother were taken to Holland Park.'

'So what now?'

Levin went through the arrangements he had made. 'I think we've covered most options.'

'I think so, too. I've ordered the plane. Bell and I will come over later this morning. We're staying in some hotel he knows near the Embassy in Kensington. The Tangier. Small and unpretentious.'

Levin could have said that large and ostentatious was the best way to conceal anything, but let it go.

'I'll expect to hear from you.'

'I can't wait.'

Sitting after breakfast over coffee, Ferguson said, 'The question is, what do we do with them?'

'What's wrong with Holland Park?' Billy said.

'Too constrained, I'd like them established somewhere more comfortable.'

'What you want is quiet obscurity for a few weeks until Zubin grows a beard again,' Dillon said.

'Something like that.'

'The money's there,' Ferguson said. 'Plenty to buy a nice place.'

'Yes, but finding what you want takes time,' Billy said. 'I

like old Bella, she's a great lady. She deserves the best.' He frowned. 'Just a minute, I've got an idea, Harry. We've got a list of properties a yard long in Mayfair, the West End.'

'Billy, sometimes you get it right,' Harry said. 'We'll come up with something suitable, I'm sure.'

At eleven o'clock on Russian television, with an atmosphere of some solemnity and gloom, it was announced that Josef Belov had collapsed and been rushed to hospital. There was a suspicion of a recurrence of stomach cancer. There had been concern about his health for some time. There was a definite hint that he had made some sort of personal sacrifice as regards the future of Belov International. There was a significant absence of political figures to comment, but footage of Max Zubin at the Dorchester in London with Putin and the British Prime Minister was run and re-run.

The announcement was picked up by the BBC, where at Holland Park Zubin and his mother saw it. So did Greta Novikova, who immediately demanded Roper. She found him in the computer room.

'What the hell happened?' she asked.

'Well, as usual, Dillon happened, and a few friends.'

Afterwards, she sat there, shaking her head. 'Ashimov will be in serious trouble, Roper. You must understand, he'll be called home, and I wouldn't like to think of the price he'll have to pay. He'll be blamed for everything.'

'That's the problem.'

'So, the Zubins are here?'

'On the floor above you.' He glanced at his watch. 'They'll be down for lunch soon. Do you want to join in? After all, you met them in Moscow.'

She got up. 'Why not?' She walked to the door, Doyle following, and hesitated. 'I love my country, Roper. Does that make sense?'

'If you go back, you'll disappear from sight forever. Stalin may have died a long time ago, but nothing changes, Greta.'

She went out slowly, Doyle following.

Ashimov flew over from Ballykelly, rising up through heavy rain. He found the vodka and sat there drinking. 'Bloody country, it rains nearly every day. I'll be glad to get out of it.'

'To Russia? Lousy weather, I should have thought, at this time of the year. Don't you ever get tired of it?' asked Bell.

'Of what?'

'Oh, our line of work. Years of putting yourself on the line, dodgy passports like today, lies.'

Ashimov swallowed more vodka. 'I loved it, worked my way up from being a private soldier. They'd have made me a colonel for sure this year. I was still officially GRU, though I was responsible for all Belov's security. You know the good work I did with the KGB in the old days working for the Irish cause.'

'I can't deny that.'

'And then Ferguson and Dillon came on the scene, always Dillon. This business with Zubin has ruined my life.'

'And you think knocking off Zubin and his mother will put you back in Volkov's good books?'

'I'd be even better if it could be Ferguson and Dillon. I'd like to see them both rot in hell.'

In spite of being obviously drunk, he had another, and Bell, on the other side of the aisle, picked up a newspaper and pretended to read it, already regretting his involvement. But times were hard. It wasn't the old days any longer with a pistol in your pocket and a song in your heart for the glorious cause. Fifty thousand pounds. He'd just have to put up with this madman. After all, it was only two days.

Chomsky hadn't told Levin the exact truth about Popov, his man in the boat at Hangman's Wharf, for like Levin himself Popov's mother had been English. She had died of cancer while Popov served in Chechnya. The truth was she'd had a younger sister living in Islington, so Popov's posting to the London Embassy had presented him with an aunt and a ready-made extended family. His English was not only excellent, as Chomsky had said, it was perfect, which proved more than useful on his assignment at Hangman's Wharf, for nobody doubted he was English.

He ventured into the pub, had meat-and-potato pie, beer, even recognized Harry Salter and Billy from the photos he'd been shown. Outside working on the boat at the wharf, he'd noticed them walking down to the warehouse development and going in. He'd taken a walk that way, read the notice-board outside extolling the virtues of Salter Developments.

There was a small exhibition in the foyer, plans on display, leaflets declaring how special the apartments were and, most special of all, the penthouse. At that end of the wharf, the development continued, rising straight up from the Thames, a row of balconies sixty feet high, and what had originally been some sort of cargo gates.

A man in a security uniform wandered out of the entrance. He smiled, 'Impressive, isn't it?'

'You can say that again.'

'Do you live round here?'

'Only on a temporary basis. I'm doing one of the boats up along the wharf there. Just a paint job really. Charley Black.'

He held his hand out, the man shook it.

'Tony Small. I've not been here long myself.'

'Might see you in the pub later.'

'Could be.'

Levin's boys followed various vehicles out of Holland Park, sometimes cross-matching Ferguson from Cavendish Place or the other way round, Dillon in his Mini Cooper, the Salters, particular Billy, visiting a number of times, and occasionally the trail leading to the Ministry of Defence.

There was a breakthrough when Billy, in his uncle's Aston, left Holland Park with the Zubins. The man in the telecom manhole alerted his colleague on a security firm Suzuki, who followed them all over Mayfair and the West End, visiting twelve properties, eventually returning to Holland Park.

'House-hunting, Captain,' the false security man told him. 'Sometimes there was a For Rent or a For Sale board.'

'And sometimes not?'

'Yes, sir.'

'The estate agent's boards, what was the name?'

'Salter Enterprises.'

'And afterwards they returned to Holland Park?'

'No, sir, they stopped at Hangman's Wharf. There's a Salter warehouse development there. They went in and had a look. Came out an hour later. It's close to the Dark Man.'

'Did they go in the pub?'

'No. Billy Salter took them straight back to Holland Park.'

'Interesting,' Levin said to Chomsky. 'Contact Popov and tell him to find out what he can about this development on the wharf.'

Popov worked away at painting his boat by the wharf, and in the later part of the afternoon saw the security man, Tony Small, emerge from the development and walk along to the Dark Man. Popov left his work and went across to the pub. It had just started to rain.

Small was seated in a corner booth, eating a Cornish pasty, a beer at his elbow and reading the *Evening Standard*. Popov got a beer and turned and smiled.

'Hello, again.'

Small looked up. 'Oh, it's you. How's it going?'

'Just started to rain. Won't help the painting. Can I join you?'

'Why not?'

Popov sat on the other side of the table. 'I was really impressed with that place where you work. Somebody told me that this Salter company owns this pub.'

'They own more than that, mate. Harry Salter and his nephew, Billy, own just about everything you can see from here along the riverbank.'

'Is that so?'

'Millions in development. Restaurants, gambling, you name it, they're into it. It's strictly legal, but it wasn't always like that. King of the river, Harry. I should know, I spent five years with the river police. Nobody messed with Harry Salter.'

'I can't believe it.'

'I can't believe you're working here in Wapping and don't realize who he is.'

'No, I'm from Sussex,' Popov said. 'Had a estate agency in Chichester. I got a nice offer to take me over from a national company. Good money, so I took it.' Sticking with the truth, he went on, 'My old aunt lives in Islington. I'm staying with her and I'm doing the boat up for a friend of hers while I consider my options.'

'Oh, I see.' Small finished his beer, and waved to the bar. 'Two more.' He then went on to fill Popov with details of the wicked past of the Salters.

'My God,' Popov said when he'd finished. 'And now he's finished a place like your development. Must be making a fortune.'

'He will be when he's sold them. It's all being talked up in the trade. He's going to do that for a month, then kind of explode on the market. They're all nice, the apartments, but I tell you what – you should see the penthouse. It's fantastic. Great views of the Thames all the way down.'

'God, I'd love to see that,' Popov said. 'I mean, having been in the business.' He finished his beer. 'Fancy a Scotch?'

'Well, that's very nice of you. How can I refuse?'

By the time he'd accepted two large ones, mellowed by alcohol, he said, 'I should be getting back. Tell you what, come and have a look.'

Which Popov did, and saw everything. The two private lifts at the front, two more at the rear, the glorious penthouse spread across the top of the building, beautifully furnished, the old cargo gates jutting out over the river like terraces. It was all very impressive.

'This is wonderful,' he said.

'It's going to cost somebody a packet.'

'I thought I saw someone going in earlier,' Popov said.

'Yes, you did. Billy Salter was showing a couple round, a middle-aged guy and an old lady. She was ecstatic about it. He's invited them round for drinks at six-thirty.'

'It'll be dark then,' Popov said.

'Not too dark for champagne and caviare. He's having it brought round from the pub.'

'God, the rich know how to live.' Popov shook his head.

'Thanks, Tony. I'd better get back and see if the weather allows me to continue working.'

He hurried back to the boat, eager to get his mobile out and tell Chomsky everything.

Levin, sitting with Chomsky, said, 'So the Salters have invited the Zubins round to this penthouse. Why?'

'To discuss moving them in for a while?'

'Exactly. So, who else would be invited? Put your lawyer's mind to that.'

'Ferguson and Dillon. That's probably it.'

'They might have their minders.'

'I don't think so. It's only a hundred yards from the pub, and Harry, the gangster, might like to play the gracious host. I'd say he'll have the goodies delivered beforehand, everything laid out nicely, low lights, soft music.'

'He could also have a couple of hoods prowling around, armed to the teeth.'

'So I could be wrong.' His mobile went. It was Ashimov. 'We're at the Tangier.'

'You've told the Falcon to wait at Archbury?'

'Yes, but why?'

'My dear Boris, if there's one thing I've learned in this life, it's never to leave anything to chance. You never know when you're going to need to get out of somewhere in a hurry.'

'Never mind that. What's happening?'

'I'll call you back.'

Levin lit a Russian cigarette and offered one to Chomsky, who said, 'You're having second thoughts.' It was a statement, not a question.

Levin said, 'He's an oaf, that one. He's also a murderous bastard.'

'And Max Zubin was a paratrooper in Chechnya, and so were you.'

'True. I'm also an officer of the GRU who's supposed to obey orders and serve his country.'

'As a lawyer, I could argue that what you're obeying are General Volkov's orders, which might not be what actually is right for your country.'

'Yes, I take your point. We could argue this one until the crack of doom. Book a Mercedes, draw me two AK47s from the gun room and put them in the boot. I'll deal with Ashimov.'

He was angry, felt pushed, but there it was, so he phoned Ashimov and said, 'There you are. I know where they'll be at six-thirty. I'll take you there. Look for me,' and he switched off and said to Chomsky, 'There are some wonderful English passports in GRU files. If I were you, I'd fill one in.'

At Holland Park, Ferguson was talking to Roper when Dillon walked in. 'Good, I'm glad you could make it,' Ferguson said. 'Harry's putting himself out. Caviare, champagne. I can't persuade this one to join us.'

'I've hardly had a wink of sleep in three days,' Roper said. 'I'm winding down. If you want an extra guest, take Greta

Novikova. She'd actually met them in Moscow, had breakfast with them this morning. They like her.'

'An interesting idea,' Ferguson said, and turned to Doyle.
'Tell the major we're taking her out, sergeant, for some champagne and caviare.'

Doyle said, 'I would say she won't be able to resist, sir,'
and he went out.

Roper poured a Scotch. 'I hope you're carrying, Sean.'

'Always do. Why?'

'Because I still have the feeling this is not over yet.'

'To be frank, I've been thinking that, too.'

Dillon slipped a hand under the back of his jacket and
touched the butt of the Walther in the back of his waistband.

Greta appeared fifteen minutes later in a black suit and a
duster coat. 'What's this?' she asked Ferguson. 'Are you
trying to soften me up?'

'Not at all. It's a social occasion, my dear, to take you out
of yourself. We won't be needing you, sergeant, so let's be
off,' and he took her out through the door, his hand under
her elbow.

At the Hotel Tangier, Levin called Ashimov's suite, told him
he was in the bar, got himself a vodka and sat in the corner.
It was early evening, so no one was in the bar itself, two or
three people in the lounge area. After a while, Ashimov and
Bell arrived.

Ashimov was tanked up, eyes glittering. 'What's going
on?'

'Keep your voice down,' Levin said. 'Unless you want half the hotel to know our business.'

'How dare you speak to me like that? I'm your commanding officer.'

'I act under direct orders from General Volkov. That's the only reason I'm assisting in this matter at all. I'll take you where you want to go, but before we do I'll explain, as far as I know, the situation we'll find there.'

'What the hell is this?' Ashimov demanded loudly.

Levin got up and said to Bell, 'I'm going out to my Mercedes and I'm going to drive away. If you move fast, you can join me, but not unless this idiot here keeps his mouth shut.'

He walked out, got behind the wheel of the Mercedes and Bell and Ashimov scrambled in behind. 'There are two AK47s in the back of the car,' Levin said. 'We'll be where we're going in half an hour. Now keep quiet while I explain what I know of the situation. I'm letting you know now, I can't guarantee who'll be there other than the Zubins.'

Ashimov was burning. 'I'll have you court-martialled for this.'

Levin pulled in at the kerb, leaned back and drove his elbow into Ashimov's mouth. 'Any more, and I'll kick you out. Now make your mind up.'

Ashimov put a handkerchief to his bloodied mouth, Bell leaned over and patted Levin on the shoulder. 'Just take us there and let's get this thing over with.'

'Then persuade your friend.'

*　　*　　*

At Hangman's Wharf, Levin parked by the development, got out and opened the rear compartment. Bell and Ashimov joined him. 'There are your weapons.' He turned and waved, and Popov, on the deck of the boat, ran forward through the gathering darkness.

'Yes, Captain.'

'They're upstairs, are they?' Levin looked up at the lights in the penthouse.

'There was food and booze delivered earlier, when the Salters arrived.'

'No minders?'

'None. A short while ago a Daimler appeared. The Zubins, Ferguson and Dillon and Major Novikova.'

'Greta? Really? How interesting. Well . . . you've done a good job. Now get out of here. Tell Chomsky I've said he can do the same for you. He'll know what I mean.'

Popov cleared off rapidly. Bell said, 'Now what?'

'Well, I'll go and sort the security guard out. Once that's done I'll call you.'

He walked in the foyer, lighting a cigarette, and found Tony Small watering potted plants beside a huge fish tank. He turned and smiled. 'Can I help you, sir?'

'Not really, old chap.' Levin pulled a silenced Walther from his raincoat pocket and struck him across the side of the head. Small went down like a stone. Levin grasped him by the collar, dragged him behind the reception desk, opened the office door behind and deposited him inside. Then he locked the door. He turned and whistled, and Ashimov and Bell hastened to join him.

'Over here.' He led the way to the lifts and pressed the right button. 'All the way to the sixth floor and there's your party, Major.'

The open-plan kitchen of the penthouse was ideal for the kind of entertaining Harry had in mind. There was caviare, prawns, salads, Dom Perignon champagne. Greta, having been warmly received by Bella, busied herself offering caviare on toast while Billy saw to the champagne.

'It's perfect,' he said to Ferguson. 'They'll be way up over the world here. I mean, look at the views.' He pulled one shutter after another to one side and stepped out on the hardwood terrace and leaned on the rail. 'It's fantastic.' Lights sparkled on a passing boat in the gathering darkness below.

'It certainly is,' Ferguson said and went back inside. 'Bella, Max. Do you think you could put up with staying here for a while?'

'My dear General, who couldn't?' Bella said.

'First-rate security,' Harry said, as Billy went round topping up the champagne. 'Or it will be when we're up and running properly. You'll have no worries here. Drink up, folks. To a job well done – to friendship.'

They all joined in the toast, glasses raised, crystal lights illuminating the magnificent vista of the huge penthouse, the shutters opening to the terraces outside, lights from the river below. And at the far end of the entrance corridor the lift came smoothly to a halt and Igor Levin led the way out, followed by Ashimov and Bell.

Ashimov, his AK held at the ready, brushed Levin to the side roughly. 'Where are they? Let me get at them.'

He half ran along the corridor, Levin went after him, a Walther in his hand, and pursued by Bell. There was immediate shock in the party group, but Ashimov fired into the ceiling.

'Hold it – everybody! Just do as you're told. Hands on heads!'

Levin moved to one side and stood with his back to one of the entrances to the terrace outside. The men hesitated, then did as they were told.

Greta glanced at Levin. 'Igor, what a surprise.'

'Not as much as you being here, you traitress bitch. I should shoot you myself,' Ashimov said.

He held the AK on his hip, covering them. Bell was doing the same, while Levin's right hand was at his side, holding the Walther.

Ferguson said, 'You've got it wrong. Major Novikova is my prisoner. She is not here of her own free will.'

Ashimov stepped forward at once and smacked the butt of his AK into the side of Ferguson's neck. The General went down with a groan, falling against Harry, who tried to catch him, leaning over, and Ashimov gave him the same as Ferguson in the back of the neck.

Max Zubin held his mother close. Billy and Dillon stood there, hands behind the neck, Greta between them, trembling a little.

Ashimov said, 'So, shaking with fear, are you?'

She shook her head. '*You* should. You're a disgrace to your uniform.'

'You disgrace my country by your very existence, you animal.'

He struck her backhanded across the face, sending her staggering into Dillon, who caught her. Ashimov said, 'A traitor to her country, Captain Levin.' There was a strange formality to the way he spoke. 'You may have the honour of executing her.'

There was a stunned silence. Bella said, 'You take me back to the Gulag. Many people like you in charge there. No better than Nazis.'

'Shut up, old woman, your turn will come.' He looked at Levin. 'I gave you an order. Shoot Major Novikova.'

There was a pause while everyone waited. Levin had raised the Walther slightly, but now he said, 'Sorry I can't oblige, but I don't think I want to do that.'

His hand came up fast, but not fast enough, as Ashimov fired two rounds slamming into Levin's chest, sending him out on the terrace to go backwards over the hardwood rail and down into the river below.

Dillon pushed Greta to one side, his hand went under his jacket at the rear, the Walther came up smoothly, and he shot Ashimov in the forehead twice. Billy, on one knee, had reached for the Colt .25 in his ankle holster and caught Bell with a heart shot. The Irishman went backwards, involuntarily firing at the ceiling for a moment.

Greta ran out to the terrace rail and peered down into the dark. 'My God, Igor.'

Dillon put an arm around her. 'It's a tidal river, the Thames. What goes in goes out one way or the other. At the end, he just couldn't do it. We all have choices.'

Behind them they heard Ferguson on the phone. 'Ferguson here. I've got two disposals for you. Most immediate.' He gave the address.

Greta said, 'What does he mean, disposal?'

'We have access to a private crematorium in North London. The corpse goes in for thirty minutes. What's left is six pounds of grey ash.'

'And Ferguson can do that?'

'Ferguson can do anything.'

Harry said, 'I feel well used. The bastard could certainly dish it out.' He poured champagne down and swallowed it. 'Come on everybody. Another drink, then we'll see you home.'

Ferguson said to Bella and Zubin, 'I think you'll find this is the end of the affair.'

'A short run,' Bella said. 'And thank God for it.'

The lift returned and Billy got out. 'I found the security guard, Tony Small, in the back of reception. No serious damage, just a sore head. I told him it was a mob thing. Five hundred quid will keep him happy.'

'We'll get you good people back home,' Ferguson said. 'I'll leave you and Billy to handle the disposal people, Harry.'

'We'll be in touch, General.'

Some time earlier, Levin had drifted out of the Thames close to a ladder that took him up to the wharf. Rounds blocked by a bulletproof vest often knocked the recipient unconscious, but not in Levin's case. The ice-cold waters of the

Thames had taken care of that. He reached in his shirt, pulled out Ashimov's two rounds, then hurried to where he had left the Mercedes, got in and drove away.

Half an hour later, at the Dorchester, where he had arrived soaked to the skin, he showered, changed clothes and packed. He had various phone numbers from GRU records and one of them was the Holland Park safehouse. He phoned and a man answered.

'Who is this?'

'Would that be Major Roper?'

'And who would you be?'

'Igor Levin. Are you aware of what happened at the penthouse?'

'Of course. I was told Ashimov blew you away.'

'Over a railing and a rather steep fall into the Thames. Tell Dillon there's nothing like a titanium vest. I survived, got back to the Dorchester where my condition probably surprised the doorman, but being the best hotel in London they were able to cope. Just tell me. What happened after Ashimov shot me?'

Roper told him in a few short sentences. 'It's all taken care of. Ashimov and the ex-Chief of Staff of the IRA are, as we speak, being turned into six pounds each of grey ash. The Zubins have survived, so have Ferguson and Harry, though a little damaged.'

'I was surprised to see Greta there.'

'Only as a guest.'

'Give Dillon and Billy my respects.'

'What are you going to do?'

'I've got diplomatic immunity. You can't touch me.'

'And you would be advised to stay out of Russia.'

'Yes, but I have an English passport through my mother, and an Irish one through one of my grandmothers. Not to mention lots of money, Roper. I think I'll lie low in Dublin for a while. What the hell, you sound like a nice guy, so I'll give you my mobile number. If Dillon wants me, I'll make it easy.'

'Cheeky bastard,' but Roper took it.

'Take care, though for a man in a wheelchair you do well. Tell Greta not to be stupid.'

The line went dead.

Roper sat there, smiling, and then reached for the whisky bottle and found it empty. He pushed his chair to the drinks cabinet, found a bottle of Scotch and opened it. He poured a glass and held it high.

'Well, here's to you. Good luck.'

A moment later, Ferguson came in with Greta, Dillon and the Zubins.

'You look pleased with yourself,' Ferguson said.

'So I should.' Roper poured another Scotch. 'I've just been talking to a ghost. You know, someone who's returned from the dead.'

And it was Dillon, with that extraordinary sixth sense, who said, 'Igor Levin.'

'He was wearing a bulletproof vest, just like you favour, Sean. Head first into the Thames.'

'Thank God,' Bella Zubin said. 'He was always a lovely boy, wasn't he, Max?'

'Well, that's one way of describing him,' her son told her.

Greta was unable to stop smiling. 'He's himself alone, that one.'

'And he said, "Tell Greta not to be stupid."'

She stopped smiling and shrugged. Ferguson said, 'He's right, except that diplomatic immunity would send him home.'

'He is half English.'

'Volkov would crucify him.'

'I'm not so sure. He'll go from Archbury, there's a Falcon there. I've checked. Are you going to stop him?'

'Irish citizen. What would be the point?' He turned to Dillon. 'What do you think?'

'Well, we not only know where he is, he's left his mobile number.'

'Exactly,' Ferguson smiled. 'Damn his eyes, I like the bastard. Who knows what the future holds?'

Igor Levin waited on the High Street beside Kensington Palace Gardens. It was raining heavily, the Russian Embassy up there. The end of something in a way.

The phone rang and Volkov said, 'God, what a bloody mess. I don't blame you. Ashimov's insane, I should have realized that years ago. I've heard you've decided to flee to Dublin. That's the smart move, but there's part of you that's still a sentimentalist. Taking Chomsky and Popov with you, I understand.'

'Yes, they're very good. But then so were Ferguson's people.'

'Dillon – I wish he were available. Brutal, resourceful. And that language thing he has. Very useful.'

'And the Zubins?'

'Forget them. Ferguson will always have them guarded. Putin'll just have to get hold of Belov International another way. He's angrier than I've ever seen him, so we're all just lying low. Heads are going to roll, so I'm going to make damn sure one of them isn't mine.' He sighed. 'Take care, Igor.' And he switched off.

A moment or so later, Chomsky and Popov said goodbye to the Embassy of the Russian Federation, came down Kensington Palace Gardens, each with a couple of suitcases. They loaded up the Mercedes and Levin got out to help. They were as excited as schoolboys.

Levin said, 'You drive, Chomsky, and you sit with him, Popov. I'll spread myself in the back. Your passports are all in order, I trust.'

'Ah, yes, Captain,' Chomsky said. 'I thought we might as well go the whole hog and take two each from the files, English and Irish.'

'They're excellent, sir,' Popov said. 'Stamps on all the pages. We've been to places I haven't been, if you follow me.'

'Oh, I do,' Levin said. 'Put Archbury into the road-finder, Chomsky, and follow the instructions.'

'Will there be the chance of trouble, sir?'

'I doubt it. But let's not take any chances – let's move.'

He took out his Russian cigarettes, selected one, pinched the tube and lit it. Then he produced a couple of miniature bottles of vodka from his pocket, which he'd taken from the bar in his room at the Dorchester. There was a shelf in the Mercedes, water in plastic bottles and plastic tumblers. He filled one of them with the contents of the two vodka miniatures.

It had been a long day, a hard day, but here he was, against all the odds. He drank some of the vodka. Volkov had been extraordinarily well informed about his plans, and Levin, looking at the two young men in front, wondered which one it was, Chomsky or Popov. It had to be one of them, the information had been too fresh.

Not that it mattered. That was for another time. He examined the rest of his vodka and considered toasting Greta Novikova, but what would have been the point? He swallowed it down and sat back.

15

The following morning it was March weather, rain driving in across the Thames at Hangman's Wharf. Dillon sat at the corner booth in the Dark Man with Harry and Billy and they all ate breakfast.

Harry went through the food with gusto in spite of the brace around his neck. 'God,' he said, 'that was good.'

'How are you feeling?' Dillon asked.

'Well, that Ashimov bastard is finally dead, so I'm feeling good. I like the Zubins, so I'm feeling good about that, too. What about you?'

'You know what they say. Just another day at the office.'

'You think Ferguson was right to let Levin off the hook?'

'Why not? He can pull him in when it suits him.'

'What do you think, Billy?' Harry asked.

'That he could just as easily be pulled in by his own people.' Billy shrugged. 'It's like the Cold War's starting all over again.'

Dillon's mobile rang. He answered and found Roper at the other end. 'Listen, Sean, I've had Ferguson on. He's got a job for you.'

'What kind of a job?'

'Involving Novikova.'

'Fire away.' Roper did. Afterwards, Dillon said, 'Harry, can I borrow the Bentley?'

'No, you can't, it's still being repaired. You can have the Aston Martin, though. What's the gig?'

'Ferguson's releasing Novikova. He wants her delivered to the Russian Embassy.'

'Well, that's a turn-up,' Harry said.

Dillon turned to Billy. 'You can drive.'

'Suits me.'

Dillon looked out as rain pelted the windows. 'Never rains but it pours. See you later, Harry,' and he made for the door.

Driving down Wapping High Street, Billy said, 'What's the old man up to?'

'Being Ferguson' – Dillon lit a cigarette – 'the game, Billy, the game. Don't you ever get tired of it?'

'Not really. I was a two-bit gangster. OK, I worked for my uncle, and had plenty of money to throw away, but then there was that first time we got involved with you – you, that old bastard Ferguson, Hannah . . .' He swerved slightly, braking a little. 'Sorry, Dillon, I can't believe I said that.'

And Dillon said, 'Said what? You mentioned an old and loving friend. Always in our hearts, Billy.'

They turned into the Holland Park safehouse. 'I'm with you, Dillon, you know that. Whatever it takes, whatever turns up.'

'Oh, to be young,' said Dillon gloomily. 'Come on, let's go and get Greta.'

At his screens, Roper seemed cheerful enough. 'I've had our sources in Dublin confirm the arrival of the Belov Falcon. Chomsky and Popov are Englishmen with funny names, according to their passports.'

'Well, that's been going on a few hundred years,' Dillon told him.

'And Levin is Jewish enough to have been around since Oliver Cromwell,' said Roper. 'What are they up to?'

'God knows. We'll hear soon enough.'

'You think so?'

'I've been at this game for years. I know so,' said Dillon, smiling.

'What about madam?'

At that moment Doyle walked in, carrying her suitcase, and Greta followed, wearing the black trouser suit and duster coat.

'So what's all this?'

'Ferguson wants us to drop you at the Russian Embassy,' Dillon told her.

'I see.'

'He seems to think you don't see things his way.'

'I don't.'

'Well, there you are then.'

'I'd remind you,' Roper put in, 'that the last time Igor Levin spoke to me, he said to tell Greta not to be stupid. I'd say he's an expert at not being stupid.'

'An expert on what suits Igor Levin.'

Dillon said, 'All right, we're wasting time here. Take her suitcase to the Aston Martin, Doyle. We'll join you.'

Roper said, 'Last chance, Greta, or *are* you really going to be stupid?'

'To hell with it – to hell with all of you.' She walked out like a ship under sail.

Driving through the London streets, Dillon sitting beside Billy, she leaned back, looking from side to side, her face serious. Dillon didn't say a word and Billy seemed to take his cue from him.

The rain hammered down on lots of traffic, London traffic, and she appeared restless, ill at ease. They were hemmed in by cars for a while.

She said, 'Christ, look at it. Do people have to live like this?'

Billy said, 'It was snowing in Moscow when I was there the other night. It was a bloody sight colder than this.'

'But not as cold as it would be in Siberia,' Dillon said.

The Aston moved down the High Street and turned into

Kensington Palace Gardens and was moving towards the Embassy when she suddenly slammed a hand down on Billy's left shoulder.

'No!' she said.

He braked. 'No what?'

'I don't want to go in there. Take me to Ferguson.'

'Cavendish Place, Billy,' Dillon said wearily. 'You'll find she's expected.'

At Cavendish Place, Billy pulled in at the kerb and turned off the engine. He opened the door for her and retrieved her suitcase. Dillon got out, reached for an umbrella and put it up against the rain.

'Goodbye, Major,' he said.

'You bastard, Dillon.'

She turned and walked through the rain, mounted the steps to Ferguson's place and pressed the bell. Dillon caught a glimpse of Kim, Ferguson's Gurkha manservant, who stood to one side to let her pass and accepted the suitcase handed to him by Billy.

As the rain suddenly increased, Dillon closed the umbrella, got back in the Aston and Billy slid behind the wheel.

'What do you think?' he asked.

'About her having a change of heart? Not much. How about you?'

'Not for a minute – not for a bleeding minute.' Billy turned on the engine. 'But then, neither will Ferguson.' He smiled and drove away.